continued . . .

MIDNIGHT RUNNER

"The fun comes from the wisecracking band of dangerous but bighearted secret soldiers Higgins wheels out to save the world—and his galloping Hollywood-ready pace." —*People*

EDGE OF DANGER

"This is Higgins near the top of his game . . . another winner." —*Publishers Weekly*

DAY OF RECKONING

"The action is sleek and intensely absorbing." —*Publishers Weekly*

THE WHITE HOUSE CONNECTION

"*The White House Connection* has one heckuva heroine . . . [who] begins a one-woman assassination spree that will keep you turning the pages." —Larry King, *USA Today*

THE PRESIDENT'S DAUGHTER

"A tight story with plenty of action." —*Chattanooga Free Press*

NIGHT JUDGEMENT AT SINOS

"This is one you won't put down." —*The New York Times*

DRINK WITH THE DEVIL

"A most intoxicating thriller." —The Associated Press

YEAR OF THE TIGER

"Higgins spins as mean a tale as Ludlum, Forsyth, or any of them." —*Philadelphia Daily News*

TITLES BY JACK HIGGINS

THE WOLF
AT THE DOOR

JACK HIGGINS

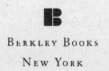

BERKLEY BOOKS
NEW YORK

THE BERKLEY PUBLISHING GROUP
Published by the Penguin Group
Penguin Group (USA) Inc.
375 Hudson Street, New York, New York 10014, USA
Penguin Group (Canada), 90 Eglinton Avenue East, Suite 700, Toronto, Ontario M4P 2Y3, Canada
(a division of Pearson Penguin Canada Inc.)
Penguin Books Ltd., 80 Strand, London WC2R 0RL, England
Penguin Group Ireland, 25 St. Stephen's Green, Dublin 2, Ireland (a division of Penguin Books Ltd.)
Penguin Group (Australia), 250 Camberwell Road, Camberwell, Victoria 3124, Australia
(a division of Pearson Australia Group Pty. Ltd.)
Penguin Books India Pvt. Ltd., 11 Community Centre, Panchsheel Park, New Delhi—110 017, India
Penguin Group (NZ), 67 Apollo Drive, Rosedale, North Shore 0632, New Zealand
(a division of Pearson New Zealand Ltd.)
Penguin Books (South Africa) (Pty.) Ltd., 24 Sturdee Avenue, Rosebank, Johannesburg 2196,
South Africa

Penguin Books Ltd., Registered Offices: 80 Strand, London WC2R 0RL, England

This is a work of fiction. Names, characters, places, and incidents either are the product of the author's
imagination or are used fictitiously, and any resemblance to actual persons, living or dead, business
establishments, events, or locales is entirely coincidental. The publisher does not have any control over
and does not assume any responsibility for author or third-party websites or their content.

THE WOLF AT THE DOOR

A Berkley Book / published by arrangement with HarperCollins Publishers Ltd.

PRINTING HISTORY
G. P. Putnam's Sons hardcover edition / January 2010
Berkley premium edition / February 2011

Copyright © 2010 by Harry Patterson.
Cover photograph of explosion copyright © by Mike Wiacek.
Cover design and photo illustration copyright © 2010 by Rob Wood/Wood Ronsaville Harlin, Inc.

ISBN: 978-0-425-23931-5

BERKLEY®
Berkley Books are published by The Berkley Publishing Group,
a division of Penguin Group (USA) Inc.,
375 Hudson Street, New York, New York 10014.
BERKLEY® is a registered trademark of Penguin Group (USA) Inc.
The "B" design is a trademark of Penguin Group (USA) Inc.

PRINTED IN THE UNITED STATES OF AMERICA

10   9   8   7   6   5   4   3   2   1

To Linda Van

with my sincere thanks . . .

The Wolf at the door is your greatest
Danger and not only in Winter.

—RUSSIAN PROVERB

1

At fifty-eight, his black hair flecked with gray, Blake Johnson still had a kind of rugged charm, the air of a man capable of looking after himself. He certainly didn't look old enough to have served in the Marines in Vietnam, though he had, with considerable honor and the medals to prove it. Johnson was personal security adviser to the President, and had been so for more years than he cared to remember. Presidents came and Presidents went, but he went on forever, or so it seemed, Blake thought ruefully, as he stood in the wheelhouse of a sport fisherman named *Lively Jane*, on the late afternoon it all began. He peered through the window at Long Island, a light rain blowing against the glass. It was almost six. He'd have to hurry.

He had a beach house in Quogue, supposedly for holidays, which hardly ever came, and this time looked to be no different. Vladimir Putin, Prime Minister of the Russian Federation, was speaking at the United Nations in New York, and the President wanted him to attend and report in, not only on the speech but on the general attitude of the Russian delegation.

The British Prime Minister wasn't coming either, but, interestingly, he'd sent his personal troubleshooter, Harry Miller, to the speech, presumably to do the same thing Blake was doing. With him was Sean Dillon, once a feared enforcer with the Provisional IRA, now a security adviser himself, and a friend to Blake in good times and bad.

Dillon & Miller. Blake smiled. Dillon would have said it sounded like a cabaret act. He throttled back and coasted in between the boats, so that the *Lively Jane* nudged against the pier.

A man was on the pier in a yellow oilskin coat, the hood pulled up against the rain, which was driving down now. Blake emerged from the wheelhouse and picked up the line to throw it.

"Can you give me a hand? Catch the line and tie her up, and I'll switch off."

"I don't think so. I'll be needing that engine to drop you into the Sound," the man in the hood said.

His hand came out of his right pocket holding a Beretta, and Blake, his senses sharpened by years of hard living, was already hurling himself over the rail, aware of the muffled sound of the silenced weapon fired twice and a burning sensation in his right shoulder, and then he was diving down into twenty feet of murky water.

He swam under the boat, his back scraping the keel, and surfaced on the other side, as she drifted, the engine still throbbing. He saw the man at the stern, leaning over the rail and emptying the Beretta into the water, then ejecting the magazine and taking another from his pocket.

Blake heaved himself over and scrambled into the wheelhouse. There was a flap under the instrument panel and it opened at his touch. Held by two clips inside was a short-barreled Smith & Wesson .38, and he was holding it as he turned.

The man in the hood was frantically shoving the magazine up the butt of the Beretta. Blake said, "Don't be stupid. It's over."

Not that it did any good. "Fug you!" the man said, and his hand came up, and Blake shot him between the eyes, knocking him back into the water.

It was very quiet, out of season, nobody around. Even the little café on the pier was closed, so he did the only thing he could, he switched off the engine, went along the deck, and managed to loop a line to one of the pier rings, then went below.

His shoulder was hurting now, hurting bad. He sat down in the kitchen area and scrambled out his special mobile and called in. The familiar voice answered, the President's favorite Secret Service man.

"Clancy Smith."

"It's Blake, Clancy. I just came in to the pier on the *Lively Jane*, and a guy was waiting with a Beretta."

"For God's sake, Blake, what happened?"

"I've taken a bullet in the shoulder, but I put him over the rail." He was light-headed now. "Hell, Clancy, there's nobody here. Closed down for the season."

"Just hang in there, I'll have the police there in no time. Hold on, Blake, hold on. I'll call you back."

Blake reached into a cupboard, pulled the cork on a bottle of very old brandy, and swallowed deeply. "Hold on," he muttered. "That's what the man said." He took another gulp from the bottle, fainted, and slid to the floor.

At the same time in London, it was an hour before midnight at the Garrick Club, where a dinner for twenty ministers from various Commonwealth countries was drawing to a close. General Charles Ferguson, for his sins, had been asked to deliver a speech on the economic consequences of terrorism in the modern age, and he couldn't wait to leave.

The affair had been expected to finish at ten, but it was now eleven, thanks to a certain amount of squabbling during the question-and-answer sessions, and naturally, and to his great annoyance, Ferguson had been involved. He'd had to call his driver on three separate occasions until, at last, the whole sorry business came to an end. He made his escape as fast as possible, found a string of limousines waiting and his not among them. His beloved Daimler had suffered damage and was being refurbished, and the Cabinet Office had provided an Amara and a driver named Pool, who now came forward anxiously.

"And what's this?" Ferguson demanded ominously.

"We kept getting moved on by security. I'm two streets away, in Venable Row." He had a cockney accent, but with a slight whine to it that Ferguson didn't like.

"For God's sake, man, just lead the way. I want to get home to bed."

Pool scuttled away. Ferguson sighed. Poor sod. It wasn't his fault when you thought of it, but what a bloody evening. As Pool reached the end of the street, a limousine came around the corner and ran through a large puddle, splashing the driver severely. It kept on going, and he shouted after it.

"Holy Mother of God, you've soaked me, you bastards." His voice was quite different, more Irish than anything else, and he turned to Ferguson and called hurriedly, "Sorry, sir," and disappeared around the corner.

"What in the hell is going on?" Ferguson asked softly, and turned into Venable Row. There was some construction going on there, a cleared area and a fence around it with an opening for an entrance, along with a couple of diggers and a work truck. It was dark in there, just a little light in the glare of a streetlight. The silver Amara was parked some yards inside, and Pool was standing beside it.

"Here we are, sir."

Ferguson moved closer, and, as he approached, Pool turned and started to run away, and the Amara blew up, the explosion echoing between the buildings on either side and setting off their fire alarms.

Ferguson was hurled backwards by the blast, lay there

for a moment, then stood up, aware that he was in one piece but that the Amara was burning furiously. The explosion had come from the trunk, and Pool had been closer to the rear of the car. Ferguson lurched towards him, dropped to his knees, and turned Pool over. There was a great deal of blood, and his face was gashed.

Pool's eyes opened. Ferguson said, "Steady, old son, you'll be fine. Help coming."

Pool's voice was very weak. "I messed up. All my fault."

"Nonsense," Ferguson said. "The only person to blame is the bastard who put that bomb in my car."

Not that Pool heard him, for he'd already stopped breathing, and Ferguson knelt there, a feeling of total desolation passing through him, aware of the sirens of the police and the emergency services approaching, holding a hand already turning cold.

"Not your fault, old son," he said softly. "Not your fault at all." As he got to his feet, the first police car roared into the street.

In New York, Harry Miller and Sean Dillon were enjoying a drink in the wood-paneled Oak Bar of the Plaza Hotel, where they were sharing a suite.

"I like this place," Dillon said. "The Edwardian splendor of it. They say it was Mark Twain's home away from home. I had a drink in this very bar on my first trip to New York." The small Irishman was wearing slacks of black velvet corduroy and a black Armani shirt that seemed to complement the hair, so fair it was almost white. He looked calm and relaxed, with the half smile of a man who couldn't take the world seriously.

"The IRA must have been generous with their expenses. I presume you were after some wretched informer on the run from Belfast?"

"As a matter of fact, I was," Dillon said, still smiling. "Another one?"

"Why not, but then you'd better get changed. You are, after all, representing the British Government at the UN. I think I'll stretch my legs while you do."

Miller was dressed formally in a navy blue suit, a blue trench coat on the seat beside him. He was a little under six feet, with saturnine gray eyes, dark brown hair, and a scar bisecting his left cheek.

"God bless Your Honor for reminding me, the simple Irish boy I am. What do you think Putin's up to?"

"God knows," Miller said. "If he thought his presence at the UN was going to force the President and the Prime Minister to attend as well, he's been sadly misinformed."

The waiter provided two more Bushmills whiskeys and departed. Dillon said gloomily, "Sometimes I wonder what the UN is for anymore. Not enough muscle, I suppose."

"Well, it has eighteen acres of land alongside the East River, and its own police force, fire department, and post office," Miller said. "I suppose they'll have to be content with that." He swallowed his whiskey, stood up, and pulled on his trench coat. "I'm going across the street for a stroll in Central Park. The Embassy car will be here in an hour."

"Better take care. That place can be tricky."

"That was then, this is now, Sean. These days, New York is safer than London."

"If you say so, Major." Dillon toasted him. "See you later."

Miller accepted the offer of an umbrella from the doorman, crossed to Central Park, and entered. There were few people around in the fading light of late afternoon just before the early evening darkness.

He realized suddenly that he was alone, except for voices somewhere in the distance, a dog barking hollowly, and then the footfalls of someone running up behind him. He glanced over his shoulder. A man in a dark green tracksuit, wearing gloves and a knitted cap, came up fast and swerved to one side. He said hello and kept on going, turning through the trees at the end of the path. A moment later, he reappeared, paused to look at Miller, then walked forward.

Miller dropped his umbrella as if by accident and, under cover of picking it up, reached down and found the Colt .25 in the ankle holder. He straightened up, raised the umbrella again, and turned to go.

The man called, "Hey, you, we've got business to discuss."

He ran forward, then slowed, his right hand sliding into a pocket of his tracksuit.

"And what would that be?" Miller asked.

"Wallet, cards, mobile phone. In any order you please." He was up close now, his right hand still in his pocket.

Miller took two quick steps so that the two of them were good and close, then held the silenced Colt almost touching the man's left knee and fired. The man cried out, lurching back as Miller pushed him towards a park bench at the side of the park.

"Oh, Jesus," the man cried, and Miller reached in the tracksuit pocket and found a silenced pistol, which he tossed into the bushes.

"Wallet, cards, mobile phone, wasn't that what you said?"

The man had grasped his knee with both hands, blood pumping through. "What have you done to me? They didn't say it would be like this."

"I've crippled you, you bastard," Miller said. "Hollow-point cartridges. Now, speak up, or I'll give it to you in the other knee as well. Who's 'they'?"

"I don't know. I'm a free lance. People contact me, I provide a service."

"You mean you're a professional hit man?"

"That's it. I got a call. I don't know who it was. There was a package, I don't know who from. A photo of you staying at the Plaza, with instructions, and two thousand dollars in hundreds."

"And you don't know who the client was? That's hard to believe. Why would they trust you?"

"You mean trust me with the money? That's the way it works. Take the money and run, and I'd be the target next time. Now, for the love of God, man, help me."

"Where's the money?"

"In the bank."

"Well, there you go," Miller said. "I'll keep your wallet and cards and leave you your mobile. Call an ambulance and say you've been mugged. No point in trying to involve me. For what you tried to pull, you'd get twenty years in Ossining, or maybe you've already done time there? Maybe you're a three-time loser."

"Just fuck off," the man said.

"Yes, I thought you'd say that." Miller turned and walked rapidly away, leaving the man to make his call.

In the two-bedroom suite they were sharing at the Plaza, Dillon was standing at his bathroom mirror adjusting a tie as black as his shirt. His jacket, like his slacks, was black corduroy, and he reached for it and pulled it on.

"Will I do?" he asked as Miller walked in the door.

"In that outfit, Putin is going to think the undertaker's come for him."

"Away with you. You hardly ever see old Vladimir wearing anything but a black suit. It's his personal statement."

"The hard man, you mean? Never mind that now. We need to talk."

"What about?"

Miller put his right foot on the edge of the bathtub, eased up the leg of his slacks, and removed the ankle holder.

"What the hell is that for?" Dillon said. "I'd like to remind you it's the United Nations we're going to. You wouldn't have got inside the door wearing that."

"True, but I never intended to try. On the other hand, a walk in Central Park is quite another matter, it seems, so it's a good thing I was carrying."

As always with Dillon, it was as if a shadow passed across his face that in the briefest of moments changed his entire personality.

"Tell me."

Miller did, brief and succinct, because of the soldier in him, and, when he was finished, he took out the wallet he'd taken from his assailant and offered it.

"A folded computer photo of me, no credit cards, a Social Security card, plus a driver's license in the name of Frank Barry, with an address in Brooklyn. I doubt any of it is genuine, but there you are. I need a shower and a fresh shirt, and we're short on time."

He cleared off to his own bedroom, and Dillon took the items from the wallet and unfolded the computer photo. It showed Miller walking on a relatively crowded pavement, one half of a truck in view and, behind it, the side of a London cab. Now, where had that come from? A long way from Central Park.

Dillon went to the sideboard and poured himself a whiskey, thinking of Frank Barry, the hit man. Poor bastard, he hadn't known what he was up against. Miller was hardly your usual politician. He'd served in the British Army during some of the worst years of the Irish Troubles, for some of that time an apparent deskman in the Intelligence Corps. But Dillon knew the truth. Miller had long ago decided that summary justice was the only way to fight terrorism. Since the death of his wife, the victim of a terrorist attack aimed at Miller himself, he had grown even more ruthless.

Dillon folded the computer photo and tried to slide it back into the wallet. It refused to go because there was something there. He fiddled about and managed to pull out a card that was rather ornate, gold around the edges, with a sentiment inscribed in curling type. *Holy Mary, Mother of God, pray for us sinners, now and at the hour of our death, we who are ourselves alone.*

Miller came in, ready to go. "What have you got there?"

"Something you missed in the wallet." The card was creased and obviously old, and Dillon held it to his nose. "Candles, incense, and the holy water."

"What in hell do you mean?" Miller held out his hand, and examined the card.

"So Barry is a Catholic, so what?"

"Such cards are very rare. They go back in history to Michael Collins, the Easter Rising. The card begs the Virgin to pray for 'we who are ourselves alone.' The Irish for 'ourselves alone' is *Sinn Fein*."

Miller stared at the card, frowning. "And you think that's significant?"

"Maybe not, but Barry is an Irish name, and you told me that after you shot him he said, 'They didn't say it would be like this.'"

"That's true, but he claimed he didn't know who'd hired him, even when I threatened to put one through his other knee."

Dillon shrugged. "Maybe he lied in spite of the pain." He took the card from Miller's fingers and replaced it in the wallet.

Miller said, "Are you saying there could be a smell of IRA here?"

Dillon smiled. "I suppose anything is possible in the worst of all possible worlds. You were right not to kill him, though. He'll stick like glue to the story of being the victim of a mugging. He wouldn't want the police to think anything else."

"And the IRA connection?"

"If there was one, it's done them no good at all." He put the wallet in his inside pocket. "An intriguing present for Roper when we get back to London. Now can we get moving? Putin awaits us."

At the UN that evening, there was no sign of Blake Johnson, which surprised Dillon because Blake had said he'd be there, but maybe he'd decided he just had better things to do. Vladimir Putin said nothing that he had not said before. The usual warning that if the U.S. went ahead with a missile defense system, the Russians would have to deploy in kind, and implying that the Russian invasion of Georgia was a warning shot. Delving deep into history, he warned the U.S. about overconfidence in its military might. "Rome may have destroyed Carthage, but eventually it was destroyed by barbarians."

"That's a good one," Miller murmured.

"I know," Dillon said. "Though I don't know if equating Russia with the barbarians is really a good idea for him."

Putin then moved on to Britain, turning to look at the British Ambassador to the UN as if addressing him personally. Britain was guilty of granting asylum to some who had been traitors to the Russian people. London had become a launching pad to fight Russia. In the end, it seemed impossible to have normal relations anymore. And on and on.

Many people sitting there obviously agreed with him, and there was applause. The British Ambassador answered robustly, pointing out that the British Security Service had identified Russia as a menace to national safety, the third-most-serious threat facing the country, after Al Qaeda terrorism and Iranian nuclear proliferation.

At the champagne reception afterwards, Miller said, "The trouble is, Vladimir Putin is dangerously capable. Afghanistan, Iraq, Chechnya, not to mention his career with the KGB."

"I agree." Dillon nodded. "But, in a way, the most significant thing about him is that he's a patriot. He believes what he says. That's what makes him the most dangerous of all." He nodded towards the Russian delegation, who were hanging on Putin's every word as he spoke to a Hamas representative. "Anyone of special interest over there?"

"Actually, there is," Miller said. "The scholarly looking man with the rather weary face and auburn hair."

"Gray suit, about fifty?"

"Colonel Josef Lermov, new Head of Station for the GRU at the London Embassy. At least, that's the whisper Ferguson's heard. He only told me yesterday and pulled out Lermov's photo."

"I see," Dillon said. "So they've given up on finding his predecessor, dear old Boris Luzhkov?"

"It seems so."

"It's hardly likely they would have succeeded, considering he went into the Thames with a bullet between the eyes. Ferguson had the disposal team fish him out the same day," Dillon told him.

"Ashes to ashes?" Miller said.

"If he couldn't take the consequences, he shouldn't have joined. Lermov is coming this way."

Lermov was. Even his smile seemed weary. "Major Miller, I believe? Josef Lermov." He turned to Dillon and held out his hand. "So nice to meet you, Mr. Dillon."

"How flattering to be recognized," Dillon told him.

"Oh, your reputation precedes you."

Miller smiled. "How's Luzhkov? Still on holiday?"

Lermov gave no sign of being fazed. "I understand he is in Moscow being considered for a new post as we speak."

"What a shame," Dillon said. "He loved London. He must regret leaving after all those years."

"Time to move on," Lermov told him.

"And his number two man, Major Yuri Bounine? Was it time for him to move on?" A loaded question from Miller if ever there was one, considering that said Yuri Bounine, having defected, was being held by Ferguson in a secure location in London.

Lermov said patiently, "He is on special assignment, that is all I can say. I can only speak for my own situation in London and not for Moscow. You spent enough time serving in British Army intelligence to know what I mean."

"Oh, I do." Miller beckoned to a waiter. "Now join us in a glass of champagne, Josef? We could celebrate your London appointment."

"Most kind of you." A brief smile flickered, as if he was amused at Miller's familiarity.

Dillon said, "It isn't vodka, but it will do to take along." He raised his glass. "To Vladimir Putin. That was quite a speech."

"You think so?" Lermov said.

"A bit of a genius, if you look at it," Dillon said.

Miller smiled. "Definitely a man to keep your eye on."

Lermov said, "Your friend, Blake Johnson, I expected him to be here, too. I wonder what's happened to him? Ah, well, I suppose he's moved on also." He smiled that odd smile and walked away.

At Mercy Hospital on the Upper East Side, the man known as Frank Barry lay in a room on the fifth floor, where he had been prepped to get the bullet out of his knee. His eyes were closed, and he was hooked up to everything in sight, the only sounds electronic beepings. A young intern entered, dressed for the operating room, a nurse behind him. He raised the sheet over Barry's left knee and shuddered.

"Christ, that's as bad as I've seen. This guy's going to be crippled." Barry didn't move. "He's been thoroughly prepped, I take it."

"The anesthetist on this one is Dr. Hale. The guy was in such agony, he was begging for mercy. Mind you, I caught him making a phone call earlier in spite of the pain, so I confiscated it. It's on the side there. He said his name is Frank Barry and he lives in the Village. Mugged in Central Park."

"Just when I thought it was safe to go there," Hale said. "The police have been notified?"

"Nobody's turned up yet, but they've been told he's going into the OR, so I suppose they think they can take their time."

"Okay," the intern said. "Twenty minutes." He went out, and the nurse followed him.

It was quiet in the corridor. The man who emerged from the elevator at the far end wore green scrubs, a skullcap, and a surgical mask. He took his time, checking the names on doors almost casually, found what he was looking for, and went in.

Barry was out, there was no doubt about that, as the man produced a hypo from his pocket, ready charged, exposed the needle, and injected its contents in Barry's left arm. The man stood there, looking down for a moment, noticed Barry's mobile phone on the bedside table, picked it up, and turned to dump the hypo in the wastebasket. The door suddenly opened, and the nurse came in.

She was immediately alarmed. "Who are you? What are you doing?"

He dropped the hypo in the bin and punched her brutally, knocking her to the floor. He went out, hurried along the corridor, and, as an alarm sounded behind him, didn't bother with the elevator but took the stairs, plunging down fast, finally reaching the basement parking garage. A few moments later, he was driving out.

Upstairs, of course, it was pandemonium on the fifth floor with the discovery of the unconscious nurse, but it would be some time before she would be able to explain what had happened. The only certainty was that the man known as Frank Barry was dead.

It was just before midnight in London when Major Giles Roper, of the bomb-scarred face, sitting at his computer at the Holland Park safe house, got the phone call from Ferguson.

"Little late for you, General."

"Never mind that. Some bugger just tried to blow me up after I'd been to that do at the Garrick."

Roper turned his wheelchair to the drinks table, poured a large scotch, and said, "Tell me."

Which Ferguson did, the whole affair, including the death of Pool. "I'm at Rosedene now," he said, naming the very private hospital he had created for his people in London, a place of absolute total privacy and security, headed by the finest general surgeon in London. "Bellamy's insisting on checking me thoroughly. I was knocked over by the blast."

"You've been lucky," Roper said ruefully. "And I'm the expert."

"But not Pool."

"From what you've told me, there's a story with him that bears investigation."

"You could be right. He wasn't my usual man, and the Cabinet Office uses hired-car companies when it's under pressure. I've told the antiterrorism people at Scotland Yard to play it down as much as possible. Fault in the car, petrol explosion, that kind of thing. Don't want the press leaping in and implying Muslim bombs."

"Maybe it was."

"Well, we don't want another public panic. Bellamy's had Pool's body brought here, and George Langley will do the postmortem. I'll stay till he's done."

After hanging up, Roper sat there thinking about it, and Tony Doyle, the military police sergeant on night duty, came in. "Still at it, Major? What am I going to do with you?"

"That was General Ferguson. He was going to his car when it blew up. The driver's dead."

"My God," Doyle said softly. "Takes you back to Ireland in the Troubles. Like someone's walked over my grave." He shivered. "Can I get you anything?"

"Sustenance, Tony, that's what I need. Get me a bacon sandwich. I'd better get in touch with Miller and Dillon in New York."

"Christ, they'll go berserk, those two."

He went out. Roper poured another whiskey, then phoned Miller on his Codex.

2

Miller and Dillon were walking back to their limousine outside the UN, discussing where to go for dinner, when Miller took the call. He listened, his face grim, then said, "Tell Dillon."

He handed his Codex over, and Dillon listened, his face darkening. "You're sure the old sod's okay?"

"So it would appear. Not the driver, though. Something fishy there, I think."

"Then you'd better investigate."

"What are you going to do?"

"I don't know, Harry's in charge. I'm just his minder."

"As if he needs one."

"Certainly not on this trip. He went for a walk in Central Park, and some bastard had a go."

"Mugged him, you mean?"

"Not sure. There could have been a bit more to it than that."

"Tell me about it."

Which Dillon did, and afterwards Roper said, "Very strange, especially the prayer card. You've got a point, Sean, I'll check it online. Okay, talk things over and let me know what you decide."

Dillon handed the Codex back. "What do you want to do?"

"Let's go back to the hotel and talk."

But just as soon as they got back to the Plaza and reached the suite, the room telephone sounded. It was Clancy Smith.

"I heard you were in town."

"Good to hear from you," Dillon said, and put the phone on speaker.

"Not this time, Sean. I believe you and Major Miller were expecting to see Blake?"

"We certainly were. He missed quite a speech."

"He's in a hospital on Long Island, suffering from a gunshot wound. I'm with him now, but he's just had surgery so he's not exactly in top shape. The police recovered the body of his assailant, a man named Jack Flynn."

"An Irish name," Dillon said, his voice grim.

"We've recovered his Social Security card and driver's license, and an American passport, and they look kosher to me. Place of birth: New York. We'll check to see if he's got a record, which I expect he has. Something's odd about all this. Blake rambled a lot to the receiving doctor and said the guy started to fire at him the moment he got on the boat. He seemed intent on killing him from the word go."

"I see." Dillon frowned. "Anything else? Anything about this Flynn character that would help with his background?"

"Not really," Clancy said. "Except for one thing. He appears to have been of a religious turn of mind. There was a sort of prayer card in his wallet."

Dillon said, "*'Holy Mary, Mother of God, pray for us sinners, now and at the hour of our death, we who are ourselves alone'?*"

"How in hell do you know that?" Clancy was truly shocked.

"The Irish for 'ourselves alone' is *Sinn Fein,* Clancy."

"Are you saying this has got something to do with the IRA?"

"Clancy, this is Miller," the Major interrupted. "Early evening before we left for the UN, I took a walk in Central Park. I was carrying a Colt .25 in an ankle holster, and good job I was."

"Okay," Clancy said. "Tell me the worst."

Miller did. "I could have killed this Barry guy, but I didn't. It seemed unlikely he'd want to make a police case out of it. It was only later, when Dillon was looking at the computer photo of me Barry had in his wallet, that he discovered the prayer card. It seemed like a curio, but, now that we have two of them, it gets more interesting."

"It sure does," Clancy said. "I'll make careful inquiries with the NYPD and find out where this Barry guy ended up, then move him so we can get some answers. I can assure you that you will be kept out of it, Major."

"Well, that eases my mind," Miller told him. "You seem on top of your game, Clancy."

"I'd better get moving. When are you returning to London?"

"Sooner than we'd expected," Miller said. "Because we've got more news for you. Just after eleven o'clock London time, General Ferguson was leaving a function to go home, and his car blew up."

Clancy was horrified. "What happened to him?"

"He was blown over by the blast as he walked towards the limousine. They've been checking him out at Rosedene, and he seems all right."

"Unfortunately, the driver was killed. I think he was closer to the car, and the bomb went off prematurely," Dillon said. "Ferguson's going to play the whole thing down as some sort of engine failure leading to the explosion. No talk of bombs."

"Well, that makes sense. I can see where he's going. But for this to happen to Charles Ferguson, on top of everything else tonight, is hardly a coincidence."

"Which is why I'm going to call our two pilots now. We're leaving instantly."

"Well, don't let me hold you, gentlemen. I'll stay in touch."

Perhaps an hour and a half later, their Gulfstream lifted out into the Atlantic, leaving the lights of New York behind, and rose to thirty thousand feet and headed east. Miller and Dillon sat on either side of the cabin in wide, comfortable seats, and Parry, one of the pilots, entered the cabin.

"If there's anything you want, it's in the kitchen area. You know where the drinks cabinet is, Sean."

"You're too kind," Dillon told him. "How long?"

"The weather in the mid-Atlantic isn't perfect, but, at the worst, I'd say we'll make Farley Field in six hours."

He went out, and Dillon's Codex sounded. It was Clancy. "Have I got news for you."

Dillon put his phone on speaker and leaned towards Miller.

"I traced Barry to Mercy Hospital, and get this. He was waiting to go into the operating room when some guy in scrubs turned up and stuck a hypodermic in him. A nurse discovered him, and he knocked her out and ran for it. Long gone, my friends."

"Whoever was behind Barry didn't trust him to keep his mouth shut," Dillon said. "But how did they find out where he was so quickly?"

"I've seen the nurse's statement. When he was in great pain and waiting to be prepped, she heard him call somebody on his mobile, very worked up, very agitated. He said, 'It's me, you bastard. I'm in Mercy Hospital with a bullet in my knee, and you'd better do something about it or else.' She said she took the phone from him and put it on the bedside table."

"Don't tell me," Dillon said. "It's gone."

"So no way of tracing who his employer was. No point in showing the nurse any faces. The guy was in green scrubs, a face mask, skullcap, the works. Oh, the police will go through the motions, but I'd say that's it. You're still out of it, Major, which is the main thing. Stay in touch. And if you make any sense out of the prayer card thing, let me know."

Dillon switched off his phone. Got up, went to the kitchen, found a half bottle of Krug champagne in the icebox, thumbed off the cork, took two glasses, and returned to his seat. He filled one glass and handed it to Miller, then filled the other.

"Are we celebrating something?" Miller asked.

"Not exactly. It's just that champagne always concentrates my mind wonderfully. Drink up, and we'll decide who's going to call Roper."

Roper listened with considerable calm, under the circumstances. But, then, as the man constantly at the center of the storm at the Holland Park safe house communications center, he had long since stopped being surprised at anything.

"So one prayer card is certainly interesting, and two, more than a coincidence."

"Exactly," Dillon said. "And three would be enemy action."

"George Langley's doing the postmortem now on

Pool, so Ferguson's still at Rosedene. I'll give him a call and ask him to have a look in Pool's wallet. I'll be back."

"There you go," Dillon said to Miller. "Mystery piles on mystery."

"We'll wait and see," Miller told him. "What about a little shut-eye?"

"On a plane? Never." Dillon rose and picked up the empty half bottle of Krug. "I'm sure there was another half bottle in the kitchen. I'll go and see."

At Rosedene, Maggie Duncan, the matron, a no-nonsense Scot, produced Pool's ravaged and bloodstained suit in the anteroom next to the operating room where Professor George Langley was performing the postmortem on the corpse of the unfortunate chauffeur. She wore latex gloves, as did Ferguson, and gingerly emptied the pockets and laid the contents on a towel spread on a table.

A half-empty pack of cigarettes, a plastic lighter, what looked like house keys on a ring, a comb, a car key with a plastic black-and-gold tab with a telephone number on it but no name.

"Do you want to examine the wallet, General?" she asked.

"No, just take out what you find."

She did. There was cash, forty-five pounds in banknotes, a driver's license, a national insurance card, a Premier credit card, and a cheaply printed business card that she found in one of the pockets and handed over.

Ferguson examined the business card. "'Henry Pool, Private Hire, 15 Green Street, Kilburn.'" He put it down on the towel, and, as he did, she extracted another card from the wallet.

"This is interesting," she said. *"Holy Mary, Mother of God, pray for us sinners, now and at the hour of our death, we who are ourselves alone.'"* Ferguson took it from her. "Is it important?" she asked.

"It certainly is, my dear." Ferguson put the card down, took out his Codex, and called Roper. "It's here," he said when the Major answered. "Also a business card: 'Henry Pool, Private Hire, 15 Green Street, Kilburn.' Check it out, and let Dillon and Miller know. And here's an interesting point that I just remembered. Pool had a slight cockney accent, but when I was following him along the pavement from the Garrick and a limousine drove past and splashed him, he got very angry and abused them. I remember what he said because his accent suddenly sounded a little Irish. He said, 'Holy Mother of God, you've soaked me, you bastards.' Then he turned to me as if embarrassed and said he was sorry—but with the cockney back again."

"Curiouser and curiouser, especially since his address is in Kilburn, the Irish quarter of our city since time immemorial. I'll see you soon."

Doyle brought Roper a mug of tea as the man in the wheelchair worked his keyboard. "Making progress, Major?"

"I think so. Look at this: Henry Pool, born in London

in 1946, mother Irish, Mary Kennedy. She came to England in the Second World War, worked as a cook, married a Londoner named Ernest Pool, who served in the
army, was wounded in April 'forty-five, and received a
medical discharge plus pension. They moved to 15 Green
Street, Kilburn."

"He must have got down to work sharpish, old Ernest,
for the baby to be produced in 1946."

"The bad news is, he died of a stroke two years later,"
Roper said. "The wound had been in the head."

"Poor sod," Tony said.

"The mother never remarried. According to her Social
Security records, she continued as a cook until her late
sixties. Died four years ago, aged eighty. Lung cancer."

"And Henry?"

"Worked as a driver of some sort, delivery vans, trucks,
was a black-cab driver for years, then started being referred to as 'a chauffeur.' Continued to live at the same
address through all the years."

"Wife . . . family?"

"No evidence of a marriage."

"It sounds like a bad play, if you ask me," Tony said.
"The old woman, widowed all those years, and the son—a
right cozy couple, just like Norman Bates and his mum
in the movie."

"Could be." Roper's fingers moved over the keys
again. "So he's been in the private-hire business for
twelve years. On the Ministry's approved list for the last
six. Owned a first-class Amara limousine, approved by the
Cabinet Office at Grade A level."

"Which explains somebody as important as the General getting him."

"And yet it just doesn't add up. How long have you been in the military police, Tony?"

"Seventeen years, you know that."

"Well, you don't need to be Sherlock Holmes . . . What's the most interesting thing here?"

"Yes, tell us, Sergeant." They both glanced around and found Ferguson leaning in the doorway.

"Aside from the cards, the nature of the targets," Doyle said. "Blake Johnson, Major Miller, and you, General—you've all worked together on some very rough cases in the past."

"I agree, which means, Major," Ferguson said to Roper, "we need to take a look at the various matters we've been involved in recently."

"As you say, General. I'm still intrigued by the religious element in the prayer cards, though, and the IRA element."

His fingers moved over the keys again. The borough of Kilburn appeared on the screen, drifted into an enlargement. "There we are, Green Street," Roper said. "And the nearest Roman Catholic church would appear to be Holy Name, only three streets away, the priest in charge, Monsignor James Murphy. I think we should pay him a visit. It might be rewarding."

"In what way?" said Ferguson.

"Pool would have been a parishioner at this Holy Name place. The priest might be able to tell us where he comes into it."

"All right, go talk to him, but you know what Catholic priests are like. Seal of the Confessional and all that stuff. He'll never tell you anything."

"True," Roper said, "but he might talk to a fellow Irishman."

"Dillon? Yes, as I recall, he lived in Kilburn for a while in his youth, didn't he? Have you spoken to him about what you just found out about Pool?"

"Not yet."

"Well, get on with it, for heaven's sake." Ferguson turned to Doyle. "Lead on to the kitchen, Sergeant. I need a pot of coffee, very hot and very strong."

"As you say, General."

They went out and Roper sat there thinking about it, then called Dillon, who answered at once. "Any progress to report?"

"I'm afraid you've got enemy action," Roper said. "Ferguson found a prayer card in the driver Pool's wallet."

Dillon reached over and shook Miller awake. "You'd better listen to this."

Miller came awake instantly and listened to the call on speaker. "Can you explain anything more? I mean, the driver and so on."

Roper went straight into Henry Pool, his background, the facts as known. When he was finished, Dillon said, "This notion you have about seeing the priest at Holy Name, I'll handle that. I agree it could be useful."

"On the other hand, Pool was only half Irish, through his mother."

"They're sometimes the worst. De Valera had a Spanish father and was born in New York, but his Irish mother was the making of him. We'll be seeing you round breakfast time. We'd better have words with Clancy Smith, I promised to call him back."

He switched off, and Miller said, "Sean, you were a top enforcer with the IRA and you never got your collar felt once. Do you really think this is some kind of IRA hit?"

"Not really. Most men of influence in the Provisional IRA are now serving in government and the community in one way or the other. Of course, there are splinter groups still in existence—that bunch called the Real IRA, and rumors that the Irish National Liberation Army still waits."

"INLA," Miller said. "The ones who probably killed Mountbatten and certainly assassinated Airey Neave coming out of the underground car park in the House of Commons."

"True," Dillon said. "And they were the great ones for using sleepers. Middle-class professional men, sometimes university educated, accountants, lawyers, even doctors. People think there's something new in the fact that Islamic terror is able to recruit from the professions, but the IRA was there long before them."

"Do you believe IRA sleepers still exist?" Miller asked.

"I guess we can't take the chance they don't. I'm going to call Clancy."

Clancy said, "This really raises the game," once they

reached him. "I'm sitting at Blake's bedside now. I'll let you talk to him, but don't talk too long. By the way, we've established that Flynn's American passport was a first-class forgery."

Blake said, "That you, Sean?"

"It sure is, old stick," Dillon said.

"Clancy filled me in about Miller and me and some sort of possible IRA link with these prayer cards."

"And we've now discovered the same card in Ferguson's driver's wallet, and I hear the guy who tried to waste you, Flynn, had a false American passport."

Blake laughed weakly. "I'll tell you something funny about him, Sean. When I had him covered and told him to give up, he didn't say 'Fuck you.' He said 'Fug you.' I only ever heard that when I was in Northern Ireland."

"Which shows you what gentlemen we are over there. Take care, old son, and sleep well." Dillon switched off, and turned to Miller. "You heard all that, so there we are."

Miller glanced at his watch. "Two hours to go. I'll try to get some sleep." He closed his eyes and turned his head against the pillow behind him, reaching to switch off the light.

Dillon simply sat there, staring into the shadows, the verse from the prayer card repeating endlessly in his brain, remembering a nineteen-year-old actor who had walked out of the Royal Academy of Dramatic Art to accept an offer to work with the National Theatre, and the night when the local priest in Kilburn called to break the news to him that his father, on a visit to Belfast, had been caught in a firefight between PIRA activists and British troops and killed.

"A casualty of war, Sean," Father James Murphy of the Holy Name church had said. "You must say your prayers, not only the Hail Mary, but this special one on the prayer card I give you now. It is a comfort for all victims of a great cause. *'Holy Mary, Mother of God, pray for us sinners, now and at the hour of our death, we who are ourselves alone.'*"

He tried closing his eyes, but it still went around and around in his brain, and he opened them again, filled with despair, just as he had felt it that day, desolation turning into rage, a need for revenge that had taken the nineteen-year-old on a violent path which had shaped his whole life, a path from which there could be no turning back. Yet, as always, he was saved by that dark streak of gallows humor in him.

"Jesus, Sean," he told himself softly. "What are you going to do, cut your throat? Well, you don't have a razor, so let's have a drink on it."

They landed at Farley just past six in the morning, bad winter weather, gray and rainy. Miller and Dillon went their separate ways, for Miller had a Mercedes provided by the Cabinet Office, his driver, Arthur Fox, waiting. Tony Doyle had driven down from Holland Park, under Roper's orders, in Dillon's own Mini Cooper.

"I'm going home, Sean, to see to my mail, knock out

a report on my impressions of Putin and the Russian delegation at the UN, then take it to Downing Street. The Prime Minister will want to see me personally, but he likes things on paper, he's very precise."

"Will you tell him of your exploits in Central Park?"

"I've no reason not to. It happened to me, Sean, I didn't happen to it, if you follow me. The way it's being handled, there is no story, not for the press anyway. The whole thing is an intelligence matter that needs to be solved. He'll understand. He's a moralist by nature but also very practical. He won't be pleased at what's happened, and he'll expect a result."

"Well, let's see how quickly we can give him one."

Dillon got in the Mini beside Tony Doyle, and they drove away. Miller got in the back of the Mercedes and discovered a bunch of mail.

"Good man, Arthur." He opened the first letter.

"Thought you'd like to get started, Major. Traffic's building up already. Could take us an hour to get to Dover Street."

"No problem. I can save a lot of time here due to your usual efficiency."

Dillon arrived at Holland Park just after seven. "I'm going to shower and change, and then I'm going to partake of Maggie Hall's Jamaican version of the great British breakfast."

"Hey, I could give you that," Doyle said, for he was of Jamaican stock, born in the East End of London.

Dillon went into the computer room, but there was no sign of Roper, and then Henderson, the other sergeant, entered wearing a tracksuit.

"Good to see you back, sir. Major Roper's in the wet room having a good soak. We're also hosting General Ferguson. He's in one of the second-floor suites, no sign of movement. If you'll excuse me, I'll get back to the Major."

"Fine, I'm going to my room. Tell him I'll join him for breakfast."

At Dover Street, Miller told Arthur to get a breakfast at the local café and come back in an hour. Once inside the house, he went straight upstairs to the spare bedroom, which was now his. It was a decent size for an eighteenth-century town house and had its own shower room. The magnificent master bedroom suite at the end of the landing, once shared with his wife, he had kept exactly as it was before her murder, but the door was locked and opened only once a week by the housekeeper, seeing to the room and keeping it fresh.

He stripped his clothes off, left them in the laundry basket, showered and shaved, pulled on a terry-cloth robe, and went down to the kitchen. He ate two bananas, drank a glass of cold milk from the refrigerator, went into his study, sat at his computer, and produced his report. Satisfied, he went upstairs and changed, ready for Arthur exactly on time as ordered.

He called in at Downing Street, showing his face at the Cabinet Office, where he was greeted with enthusiasm by Henry Frankel, a good friend who had smoothed the way for Miller in many ways in the terrible days following the death of his wife.

"You look well, Harry. How was Vladimir?"

"Worrying, Henry. To be honest, I think I find him rather impressive on occasion, and I'm not supposed to."

"Certainly not."

Miller handed him his report. "All there, but I expect the PM saw it on television."

"Not the same, sweetheart," said Henry, his gayness breaking through occasionally. "Who believes in TV anymore? You've got a genius for seeing things as they really are."

"Lermov was with Putin. I hear he's the new Head of Station in Kensington."

"I believe he's expected this weekend. I wonder what they've done with Boris Luzhkov?"

"God knows," Miller said. There were few things Henry Frankel didn't know about, but Boris Luzhkov ending up dead in the Thames was one of them.

"The boss is in, and he's expecting this, so I'll deliver it now. He said you're to wait, so help yourself. Coffee, all kinds of tea, juices. We've got a miracle machine now. Just press the right button."

Which Miller did and also glanced at the *Times*. Frankel was in and out several times, but it was thirty-five minutes before he came over to him and smiled.

"Everything on the go this morning, but he'll see you

now." Miller followed him. Frankel opened the door of the office and stood to one side.

"Come in, Harry." The PM was behind his desk. "Take a chair. First-class report."

"Thank you, Prime Minister. Putin didn't say anything he hasn't said before, but he does have this dangerous gift of sounding quite reasonable."

"As I know, to my cost, but I must tell you that I've had Charles Ferguson on the phone. A terrible business, this incident with his car and the death of the driver."

"I don't know what the General has told you, Prime Minister, but it now seems certain that the driver was party to the whole affair. It would seem likely that the device, whatever it was, exploded prematurely, unfortunately for him. General Ferguson is handling the matter as if it was an accident, not a bomb, so there should be no problem with the media."

"Yes, that's the last thing we need. Ferguson's also filled me in on the unfortunate business on Long Island, and on your own brush with death in Central Park." He sighed. "Trouble follows you everywhere I send you—Kosovo, Washington, Lebanon. You always end up shooting someone. You are the most irregular Member of Parliament I have ever known."

"Hardly my fault, Prime Minister, when you send me to places where people are liable to do a bit of shooting themselves."

"A valid point. All those years in the Intelligence Corps dealing with the wild men of Ulster made you spectacularly good at violent solutions. Your decision to leave the army on your father's death and put yourself up for his seat in Parliament has proved most fortuitous, although it would have been slightly more convenient if we'd both been members of the same political party."

"Well, you can't have everything," Miller said.

"I'm aware of that. No one in the Cabinet has any kind of military experience whatsoever, which is why I broke the rules and made you an under-secretary of state. You can be, on occasion, a thoroughly ruthless bastard, and there are times when that's something that's needed."

"But I am attached to you, Prime Minister, and that makes all the difference."

"Flattery gets you nowhere, Miller. I'm due in the House soon, so you've got fifteen minutes to explain this whole damn mess and what you and Ferguson intend to do about it."

Which Miller did, rapidly and fluently, covering everything. "That's it, I think."

"And quite enough. Prayer cards, killings, a bombing, and, to top all that, this suggestion of an IRA link. That can't be possible. I've enough on my plate with all these banks failing, plus the worst recession in years. I know there are a few crackpot organizations out there still demanding a United Ireland, but enough is enough. Sort it, Harry, sort it—and quickly."

He stood up, the door opened behind Miller as he rose, and Henry Frankel ushered him out.

"How do you know when people are leaving?" Dillon asked. "Are you a magician or something?"

"Absolutely, love. Take care." Miller went out, calling Arthur on his mobile.

"As soon as you like, and we'll make it Holland Park."

Dillon, after a shower and change, went to the canteen, where he discovered Roper, hair still damp, sitting in his wheelchair in a blue tracksuit, enjoying breakfast and immensely cheerful. Ferguson was sitting opposite, enjoying scrambled eggs.

"There you are, you devil, what went on in New York, then? You were supposed to be his minder. It's a miracle he was wearing that ankle holster."

"Which I knew nothing about."

Maggie Hall entered with scrambled eggs, and withdrew.

"Diplomatic immunity covered us when we landed in the Gulfstream, obviously, but he couldn't have worn it to the UN."

"Probably just a whim," Ferguson said. "There's no question of him going into Parliament with it, but I suspect he does in other places in London." He glanced at Dillon. "Do you agree?"

Dillon reached down to his right ankle and produced a Colt .25. "All the rage, these days. I wouldn't be without one."

Roper said, "A damn good job he was carrying when he took that walk in the park."

Dillon reached for toast and marmalade, and said cheerfully, "Oh, I suspect he'd have thought of something ghastly as an alternative. A man of infinite resource and guile, our Harry."

"You can say that again." He took a piece of Dillon's toast, and his Codex sounded. It was Billy Salter. "That you, Roper? I'm at the Dark Man. We've had a right old business down here. Some geezer tried a little arson in the early hours."

Roper waved a hand at the others, and turned his Codex on speaker. "Say again, Billy?"

"We'd all gone to bed early—Ruby, Harry, me, Joe Baxter, and Sam Hall," he continued, naming the Salters' minders. "Joe was still dressed and watching a late-night movie on television when he heard a noise from the bar. He knocked on Sam's door to alert him, then smelt petrol, so he moved into the bar, turned on the lights, and found this guy emptying a can of petrol all over the place, the till rifled, cash drawers open."

"Who was it?"

"How do I know? They're just fishing him out of the Thames. He was wearing a black tracksuit and ski mask, Joe said, and he looked like a terrorist from central casting. Joe had his Smith and Wesson with him. He wasn't keen on firing, in case the petrol ignited, so the guy threw the can at him and legged it. Sam had joined Joe by then, and they went after him."

"What happened?"

"The old Ford van at the end of the wharf? It always has a key in it, not worth stealing. I reckon he'd checked it out previously, because he ran straight for it, was in and driving off, but the wrong way. There was no place to turn, and he simply ran over the edge of the wharf in the dark."

"With him in it?"

"The police are here now. They'll have a recovery team get the truck later, but a police diver's been down, and he's found the guy. He's gone down again with another diver to try and get him. Harry's here, and he'd like a word."

The unmistakable cockney voice of Billy's uncle echoed around the canteen. Harry Salter, a gangster for most of his life and now a property millionaire, said, "Well, this is nice, Roper, we could all have been roasted in our beds. What the hell was the bugger playing at? There was a grand in the till. Wasn't that enough?"

It was Ferguson who said, "It's me, Harry, and Dillon's just back from New York with the strangest story you've heard in a long time." He turned to Roper. "You explain."

Which Roper did.

Standing on Cable Wharf in Wapping near his beloved pub, the Dark Man, Harry said, "Jesus Christ, Roper, this is incredible."

"But true, Harry. The guy who shot Blake, the one who attacked Miller, and then the General's rogue driver last night, all were in possession of the same prayer card."

"Tell me again what it says?"

Roper did. "The police will search your arsonist's body

when they get him up. Billy can use some muscle by flashing his MI5 card. See where it gets you, and call back."

Ferguson said, "An interesting one, gentlemen."

"What is?" Harry Miller entered at that moment.

"Well, it goes something like this . . ." Roper began.

At the end of Cable Wharf were three patrol cars and a medium-sized police truck, the sign on one side reading "Salvage & Recovery." There were two divers down there in scuba gear, four uniformed policemen, and an inspector who had turned up and gone to inspect the bar.

Harry and Billy were standing by watching with Baxter and Hall and Ruby Moon, who was wearing a reefer coat two sizes too large. The inspector emerged from the bar and approached.

"Nasty business, Mr. Salter. Stinks in there. You'll have to close for a while. Could have been very nasty if he'd dropped a match."

Harry had known him for years. "A real evil bastard, had to be, to do a thing like that. We could have all ended up cooked for breakfast."

"Sure you haven't been annoying anyone lately?"

"On my life, Parky, those days are long gone. I own most of the developments round here, and my nephew Billy's got an MI5 warrant card in his pocket."

"Yes, I heard they'd taken him on. I was impressed. I'd always understood they wouldn't accept anyone with a record."

"True, Parky, it was the folly of youth, where Billy was concerned, but all wiped clean now."

"You must have friends in high places these days, Billy."

"Oh, I do, Inspector," Billy said. "And here's my warrant to prove it." He offered it. "As you know, I'm involved in cases where the highest security and the welfare of the nation is involved—so I'd like to check the identity of the man who's being hauled up at this moment. It could explain the severity of his intentions."

"Are you saying you could have been his target?"

"It's possible," Billy said, and at that moment an ambulance rolled up, two paramedics emerged, opened the rear door, and pulled out a stretcher, which they took forward to where the four policemen were hauling up the drowned man in a sling.

Water poured from the man as they laid him down on the stretcher, and one of the paramedics removed the balaclava, revealing the unshaven face, handsome enough, eyes closed in death, dark hair with silver streaks in it.

"Good God, I know this one," Parky said. "He used to live round here when I was a young constable. Bagged him coming out of a booze shop he'd broken into on Wapping High Street. Costello, Fergus Costello. He went down the steps for two years. Petty criminal, when he got out. Irish bloke, drunk and disorderly, that kind of thing, always getting arrested."

"Can you remember what happened to him?" Billy asked.

"Not really, it's so long ago." They watched as a police officer went through the dead man's pockets, producing a bunch of skeleton keys, a folded flick-knife, and a .38 Smith & Wesson revolver, which they handed to Parky.

"He certainly meant business."

A passport came next, which turned out to be Irish. "See, I was right," Parky said, but frowned when he opened it. "John Docherty, and there's a Dublin address." He shook his head and handed the passport to Billy. "Even though he's dead, you can see from the photo it's the same man."

"You're right." Billy gave it to Harry. "Must be a forgery. Let's see what's in the wallet."

Parky went to his car, opened the wallet, and took out the wet contents—a driver's license, a Social Security card, and a credit card. "All in the name of John Docherty, and an address in Point Street, Kilburn."

"So he was living under a false name," Harry said.

Parky nodded. "You know, I remember now, it's all coming back. He used to get in a lot of trouble over the drink, and then there was a refuge opened, run by Catholics. They used to get visits from a priest, who had a big influence on the boozers there. I can't remember his name, but, as I recall, Costello stopped getting into trouble and started churchgoing, and then he cleared off."

The officer who had been searching the pockets said, "There's this, sir, tucked away."

He offered the damp card, and Parky examined it. "I've seen something like this before. It's a prayer card."

Billy took it from him and read it aloud. *"Holy Mary, Mother of God, pray for us sinners, now and at the hour of our death, we who are ourselves alone."*

Harry said, "But what the hell does it mean?"

Parky smiled. "I told you he'd turned to religion, didn't I, so I was right."

"You certainly were," Billy said. "I'll hang on to this and the passport. You can keep the rest."

3

They met in the computer room at Holland Park, all of them, Ferguson presiding, and Harry Salter was a very angry man indeed.

"I mean, what in the hell is going on?"

"It's simple, Harry," said Dillon. "You've been targeted, you and Billy, just like Blake Johnson, General Ferguson, and Major Miller. Maybe somebody thinks it's payback time."

"All very well," Harry pointed out. "But that bastard Costello or Docherty, or whatever he called himself, was prepared to torch the pub, just to get at Billy and me."

"Whoever these people are, they're highly organized and totally ruthless. The would-be assassin in Central Park, Frank Barry, called somebody and told them where he was. The instant response was an executioner."

"Exactly," Miller put in. "And one professional enough

to remember to snatch Barry's mobile before departing, so details of that call couldn't be traced."

"I've spoken to Clancy Smith, brought him up to speed, including the arson attack on the pub," Roper said. "His people have established that Flynn's passport was an extremely good forgery, as was his driver's license and Social Security card."

"So there's no way of checking if he had a police record?" Ferguson put in.

"Exactly," Roper carried on. "His address in Greenwich Village is a one-room apartment, sparsely furnished, basic belongings, not much more than clothes. An old lady on the same floor said he was polite and kept to himself. She'd no idea what he did for a living, and was surprised to hear he had an American passport, as she'd always thought he was Irish. She's a Catholic herself and often saw him at Mass at the local church."

Miller said, "Interesting that Costello-cum-Docherty has a forged Irish passport, too, and his religion had been the saving of him, according to Inspector Parkinson."

"A passport which claims he was born in Dublin, yet we know from his other identity documents that his address is in Point Street, Kilburn," Dillon said.

"And Henry Pool from Green Street, Kilburn," Ferguson said. "Too many connections here. This would appear to be a carefully mounted campaign."

"Another point worth remembering," Roper said. "I've processed the computer photo of Major Miller that was in Barry's wallet." His fingers worked the keys, and the photo came on screen. "Just a crowded street, but that's definitely the side of a London black cab at the edge of the pavement. The photo was definitely taken in London, I'd say."

"Careful preparation beforehand by someone who knew I was going to New York," Miller said.

"Yes, and remember that Blake was only visiting his place on Long Island because he was going to the UN." Roper shook his head. "It's scary stuff, when you think about it."

Salter said, "But nobody had a go at you, Dillon, when you were in New York. Why not?"

"Because I wasn't supposed to be there. It was only decided at the last moment that I should join Harry."

"Nobody has had a go at me either," Roper told him. "But that doesn't mean they're not going to."

"Exactly," Ferguson said. "Which raises the point again—what in the hell is this all about?"

"Let's face it," Billy said. "We've been up against a lot of very bad people in our day. Al Qaeda, a wide range of Islamic terrorists, Hamas, Hezbollah. We've been in Lebanon, Hazar, Bosnia, Kosovo. And you older guys talk about the Cold War. But the Cold War is back, it seems to me, so we can add in the Russians."

"Which adds up to a lot of enemies," Dillon put in. "Lermov, who'll be the new Head of Station for the GRU here, was at the UN reception with Putin, and we were talking to him. Baited him, really. Asked after Boris Luzhkov, and was told he was in Moscow being considered for a new post."

"Six pounds of gray ash, that bastard," Billy said.

"And when I asked after Yuri Bounine, he said he'd been given another assignment."

"He knew something," Miller said. "I'm sure of it."

"Well, if he knows that Bounine is guarding Alex Kurbsky at his aunt Svetlana's house in Belsize Park, we're in trouble," Ferguson told him.

They were all silent at the mention of the famous Russian writer whose defection had caused so much mayhem recently but of whom they'd all become unaccountably fond.

Dillon said, "We're going to have to do something, General. They could be in harm's way."

"I'm aware of that, Dillon," Ferguson snapped. "But you could widen the circle to include a lot of people who've been involved with us." He turned to Miller. "What about your sister, Major? She helped us out in that business involving the IRA in County Louth last year. She even shot one of them."

Miller's sister, Lady Monica Starling, an archaeologist and Cambridge don, had indeed proved her mettle—and, in the process, had become as close a friend to Dillon as a woman could.

Miller frowned and turned to Dillon. "He's got a point, Sean, we should speak to her."

Roper said, "If the rest of you can shut up for a moment, I'll get her on the line." He was answered at once. She sounded fraught, her voice echoing through the speakers.

"Who is this?"

"No need to bite my head off, darling," said Miller. "It's your big brother."

"It's so good to hear from you, Harry, I was going to call. I thought you and Sean were still in New York."

"What's happened? Where are you?"

"I'm at the hospital here in Cambridge."

"For God's sake, tell me, Monica."

"There was a faculty party at a hotel outside Cambridge last night. Dear old Professor George Dunkley was desperate to go. I volunteered to drive him there so he could enjoy his port and so on. Six miles out into the countryside, a bloody great truck started to follow us and just stayed on our tail. It didn't matter what I did, it wouldn't go away, and then, when we came to a wider section of the road, it came alongside and swerved into us."

"Are you okay?"

"Yes, but George has his left arm broken. We were hurled into a grass verge and crashed against a wall. I called the police on my mobile, and they were there in no time."

"And the truck?"

"Oh, he crashed farther on. They found the wreck, but the driver had cleared off. The police sergeant who's been dealing with me says the truck was stolen from somewhere in London. George is going to be in hospital for a while. A terrible thing at his age."

"And you are coming to Dover Street to stay at the house with me?"

"That's sweet of you, Harry, but I've got seminars, and there's my book."

"To hell with your seminars, and you can work on your book at Dover Street."

"Harry, what's happening?"

Dillon cut in. "Monica, my love, listen to the man. It's no coincidence what's happened to you. Bad things have been happening to all of us. We need you safe and among friends."

Her voice was quiet. "What's going on, Sean?"

"I'll explain when I pick you up," Miller said. "We should be there in round two hours. Go straight back to your rooms, pack, and don't go out again."

"If you say so, Harry."

The line cleared, and everyone was silent for a moment. Miller said, "Sorry, General, I must go."

"Of course you must, so get moving."

Miller went out fast, and Roper said, "Open warfare. They certainly mean business, whoever they are. Do you think there's an IRA touch to this?"

Dillon nodded. "Since the Peace Process, the IRA hands have fanned out, looking to make money," he said. "We've dealt with plenty of them in the past, desperate for work, who've offered their skills to various countries in the Russian Federation, worked with the PLO, Hamas, Hezbollah. Then there was Kosovo and Chechnya."

"Iraq," Roper said. "Plenty of money to be made there, one way or another, for the kind of men who were members of the Provisional IRA, with all their military skills."

"Which is exactly the kind of thing I was doing for years, until the General here made me an offer I couldn't refuse." Dillon shook his head. "That's what this all smells like to me—IRA for hire. I'll take myself off to Kilburn and see what I can find out."

"Would you care for some company?" Billy said.

"Why not? What about you, Harry?"

Salter got up. "You go with Dillon, Billy. I'll take your Alfa and get back to the Dark Man and see how Ruby's coping with the cleaning."

He went out, and Ferguson said, "On your way, then, you two, I'm going to have a word with Clancy at the White House, then I'll visit our Russian friends in Belsize Park." He turned to Roper. "Whenever you're ready, Major, call Clancy on his personal line."

Clancy answered at once, nine o'clock on a Washington morning. "General, how are things?"

"They've moved at some speed, but, before I fill you in, how is Blake?"

"What would you expect from an old Vietnam hand? He's being airlifted in a Medical Corps helicopter to a hospital in Washington this afternoon."

"Give him our best. Let me tell you what's happened now."

Which he did, and Clancy was horrified. "This is incredible. Whoever these people are, they certainly don't take prisoners. Everything that's already happened, and now the attempted arson attack on the Dark Man and the assault on Monica Starling, shows we're up against truly ruthless people. And I take your point about who could be next."

"Exactly. Alexander Kurbsky, his aunt Svetlana, and

their friend, Katya Zorin. Kurbsky's a marked man. He's still posing as a leukemia victim on chemotherapy, and the change in his physical appearance is remarkable, but if the Russians get wind of his location, that won't hold them for long."

Kurbsky had originally been sent in by the GRU to penetrate British intelligence, but once he'd found out how his bosses had duped him about his sister he'd had a change of heart. In particular, he'd saved Blake Johnson's ass when he'd been kidnapped in London, and then he and Bounine had saved the Vice President's life from a crazed Luzhkov.

"As I recall," said Clancy, "there was a Presidential promise of asylum in the U.S. if Kurbsky ever wanted it. I'm sure that would be honored, if you think it's a good idea."

"What would you suggest?"

"We have a list of facilities, but Heron Island off the Florida coast would be perfect. The Secret Service uses it only for the most special cases. A hundred percent security, the staff vetted in every possible way, decent climate, and the house I'm thinking of is spectacular."

"How soon could you arrange all this?"

"Twenty-four hours. I assume you'll handle your end. It may not be forever, General, but I can promise they'll be safe on Heron Island. With luck, we'll take care of the threat between us in a few weeks, and then we can think again."

"Thank you, old friend," Ferguson told him. "I'll be back to you."

Roper had, of course, heard everything. "Sounds good. Are you going up to see them now?"

"Yes, I think so. One less problem if they agree," and Ferguson went out.

His Daimler was back and, with it, Martin, his usual driver, and they drove to Belsize Park. Ferguson, going through everything that had happened, still had not found a solution when Martin parked in the mews beside Chamber Court at the side entrance of the high stone wall. Ferguson announced himself to the intercom, and the gate buzzed and swung open.

The garden was beautiful—rhododendron bushes, cypress trees, plane trees, more bushes surrounding a lovely curving lawn. As he advanced towards the conservatory, Bounine stepped out of the bushes, wearing overalls, holding a baseball bat menacingly in his hand.

"It's General Ferguson, you idiot." Kurbsky emerged from the trees, a sad, gaunt figure, with the skull and the haunted face of someone on chemotherapy, although, in his case, he took drugs to make him look that way.

"What's up?" Ferguson asked.

"We've had an intruder," Kurbsky said. "Yesterday, after supper, we were going to watch television with the ladies. I stepped out of the conservatory to have a smoke and thought I heard something over by the garage, so I went to investigate. Someone jumped me, a man in a bomber jacket and jeans. He was closer to the garage than me and made the security lights come on."

"What happened?"

"He pulled a flick-knife and sprung the blade, so I smacked him about a bit. He was on the ground after I took the knife, so I relieved him of his wallet, and I moved over to the garage security lights to inspect it. Bounine came out on the terrace and called, which distracted me. The guy scrambled up, ran like hell, and got over the wall."

"Were the ladies alarmed?"

"Obviously. The security alarms sound inside the house. But they were easily reassured. Russian women are tough as nails."

"The wallet, were the contents interesting?"

"Not particularly. Fifty-four pounds, a Social Security card, and a credit card, all in the name of Matthew Cochran."

"Did he live in Kilburn?"

"No. Close, though. Camden Town. Sixty Lower Church Street."

"And that's it? Nothing like: *'Holy Mary, Mother of God, pray for us sinners, now and at the hour of our death, we who are ourselves alone'*?"

"The prayer card," Bounine said to Kurbsky. "You forgot that."

Kurbsky frowned, and said, "Why, is it important?"

"It means you are all in great danger. Let's find the ladies, and I'll spell it out for you," and he led the way along to the terrace and the conservatory.

In the Victorian conservatory, crammed with plants, there was silence when Ferguson finished talking. Kurbsky had produced Cochran's wallet and taken out the prayer card, which lay on a small iron table beside it.

Svetlana Kelly, Kurbsky's aunt, sat in a wicker chair. Katya Zorin, Svetlana's partner, a handsome forty-year-old with cropped hair, who was an artist and theater scene designer, sat close to her, holding the older woman's right hand.

"These are terrible things you tell us, General. Such violence is too much to bear."

"But it must be faced, my dear. The prayer card was involved with all these attacks I've just discussed, except for the business involving Monica Starling. It's hardly a coincidence, and, when I come here, I find this." He picked up the prayer card and held it high. "I repeat, you are in great danger if you stay here, or stay in London for that matter. I think you should take the Americans' offer of sanctuary."

"To leave my home is a terrible prospect. All my beautiful things. The world is so untrustworthy these days." Svetlana was distressed.

Ferguson threw down the card. "You've heard the full story. Blake is in the hospital badly wounded, four of the cardholders are violently dead, the attempt to burn down Salter's pub could have killed everybody in it." He turned to Kurbsky. "Please, Alex, just go, and take them with you, and leave us to hunt down whoever is behind this."

Kurbsky bent down and kissed Svetlana on the head.

"He's right, *babushka*, my decision. We go, and we go tonight, is this not so, General?"

"You'll take the Gulfstream from Farley Field. Nobody will know you have gone."

She was weeping now, and Katya kissed her on the cheek. "All will be well, my love. Alexander is right. We must go."

Ferguson said, "I'll make a deal with you, Svetlana. It's important for Alex to go if there are strange and wicked people stirring, but you needn't worry about your paintings or your antiques. I'll arrange for a caretaker to live here and take care of them, all right? Now I must go."

Kurbsky walked to the gate with him. Ferguson opened it, and turned. "It really is the smart move until we get to the bottom of all this."

Kurbsky said, "I'm sure you're right. It's just that I've never been very good at running away."

"On this occasion, you must think of the women. I'll see you off from Farley. Roper will be in touch to confirm the timing."

As Martin got out of the Daimler, Ferguson said, "I'll sit beside you." Martin got the door open, it started to rain, and Ferguson scrambled inside. The big man slid behind the wheel and drove away.

"Thank God, that's sorted," Ferguson said.

"Things looking a bit better, General?" Martin inquired.

"Not really," Ferguson said. "Actually, the road ahead looks pretty bloody stony, but there it is." He leaned back, called Roper, and filled him in. "So the intruder at Belsize Park definitely makes their departure a top priority."

"I'll organize it at once. And that man Kurbsky tangled with—Matthew Cochran, wasn't it? Camden Town, Sixty Lower Church Street. We should check on him, too."

"You're right. See to it."

When Roper made the call, Dillon and Billy were in a bar on Camden High Street. Dillon had suggested a luncheon sandwich, but the truth was, he was thinking ahead, about what was waiting for him in Kilburn. Billy suspected that Dillon needed a drink and went along with the suggestion, though Billy never drank. He was a bit alarmed, though, when the Irishman downed his second large Bushmills. Then Roper called.

Dillon obviously couldn't put it on speaker in the pub, so he listened, then said, "Okay, we'll handle it. We're in Camden High Street now." He relayed to Billy what Roper had just told him. "We'll go and look this guy Cochran up. Do you know the address?"

"No, but the Sat Nav will," Billy said. "So let's move it."

They twisted and turned through a number of side streets, finally reaching one called Church. There was no number 60, and beyond the street was a vast site, obviously cleared for building. There was a convenience store on the corner called Patel's, freshly painted, incongruous against the old decaying houses.

"Wait for me," Dillon said, and got out of the Cooper.

The store was crammed with just about everything you would ever need, and the stocky Indian in traditional clothes was welcoming. "Can I help you, sir?"

"I was looking for an address—60 Lower Church Street."

"Ah, long gone. Many streets were knocked down last year, and Lower Church Street was one of them. They are to build flats."

"I was looking for a man named Matthew Cochran who used that address."

"But I remember number 60 well, it was a lodging house."

"Thanks very much." Dillon returned to the Cooper.

"No joy there. Lower Church Street was knocked down last year, and the address was just a lodging house. Let's move on."

Like many areas of London, Kilburn was changing, new apartment blocks here and there, but much of it was still what it had always been: streets of terrace houses dating from Victorian and Edwardian times, even rows of back-to-back houses. It was the favored Irish quarter of London—and always had been.

"It always reminds me of Northern Ireland, this place. We just passed a pub called the Green Tinker, so that's Catholic, and we're coming up to the Royal George, which has got to be Protestant. Just like Belfast, when you think about it," Billy said.

"Nothing's changed," Dillon told him. He thought back again, to his mother dying when he was born, his father raising him with the help of relatives, mainly from her family, until, in need of work, his father moved to London and took him with him. Dillon was twelve years old, and they did very well together right here in Kilburn. His father made decent money because he was a cabinet-maker, the highest kind of carpenter. He was never short of work. Dillon went to a top Catholic grammar school, which led him to a scholarship at RADA at sixteen, on-stage with the National Theatre at nineteen—and then came his father's death, and nothing was ever the same again.

Billy said, "Where did you live? Near here?"

"Lodge Lane, a Victorian back-to-back. He opened up the attic, my father did, put a bathroom in. A little palace by the time he had finished with it."

"Do you ever go back?"

"Nothing to go back to. The fella who tried to incinerate you, Costello/Docherty? His address was Point Street. We'll take a look."

"Will you still know your way?"

"Like the back of my hand, Billy, so just follow what I tell you."

Which Billy did, ending up in a street of terrace houses, doors opening to the pavement. There were cars of one kind or another parked here and there, but it was remarkably quiet.

"This is going back a few years," Billy said as they drew up.

The door of number 5 was interesting for two reasons. First, there was yellow scene-of-crime police tape across it, forbidding entrance. Second, a formal black mourning wreath hung from the door knocker.

"Interesting," Dillon said, and got out, and Billy followed. The curtain twitched at the window of the next house. "Let's have words. Knock them up." Billy did.

The door opened, and a young woman in jeans and a smock, holding a baby, appeared. "What is it?" she asked with what Dillon easily recognized as a Derry accent.

Billy flashed his MI5 warrant card. "Police. We're just checking that everything's okay."

"Your lot have been and gone hours ago. They explained that Docherty had been killed in a car accident. I don't know why they've sealed the door."

"To stop anyone getting in."

"He lived on his own, kept himself to himself."

"What, not even a girlfriend?"

"I never even saw him with a boyfriend, though he was of that persuasion if you ask me."

Dillon turned on his Belfast accent. "Is that a fact, girl dear? But one friend, surely, to leave that mourning wreath?"

She warmed to him at once. "Ah, that's Caitlin Daly, for you. A heart of gold, that woman, and goodness itself."

"Well, God bless her for that," Dillon told her. "A fine child you've got there."

"Why, thank you." She was beaming now.

They got in the Cooper, and Billy drove away. "You don't half turn it on when it suits you."

"Fifteen Green Street, now. Just follow my directions."

Billy did as he was told. "What's the point? We know Pool lived on his own. I thought you wanted to go and look up the local priest?"

"We'll get to that, so just do as I say," and Dillon gave him his directions.

The houses in Green Street were substantial: Edwardian and semi-detached, with a small garden in front and a narrow path around the side leading to a rear garden.

"This is better," Billy said. "No garages, though."

"People who lived here in 1900 had no need for garages."

Dillon opened a gate and walked up to the front door through the garden, followed by Billy. The door was exactly the same as the one in Point Street, with the police tape across it and the black mourning wreath hanging from the knocker.

"Caitlin Daly again, it would appear."

The door of the adjacent house was within touching distance over the hedge. It opened now, and a white-haired lady peered out. Dillon turned on the charm again, this time pulling out his own warrant card.

"Police," he told her. "Just checking that all is well."

The woman was very old, he could see that, and obviously distressed. "Such a tragedy. The police sergeant this morning told me he died in a terrible crash somewhere in central London. I can't understand it. I've driven with him, and he was so careful. A professional chauffeur."

"Yes, it's very sad," Dillon told her.

"I knew his mother, Mary, so well, a lovely Irish lady." She was rambling now. "Widowed for years, a nurse. It was a great blow to him when she died. Eighty-one, she was. From Cork."

Dillon said gently, "I know it well. Wasn't Michael Collins himself a Cork man?

"Who?" she said.

"I'm sorry, and me thinking you were Mrs. Caitlin Daly?" She looked bewildered. "The mourning wreath on the door."

"Oh, I'm not Caitlin, and I saw her leave it earlier. Her mother was a wonderful friend to me. Died last year from lung cancer. Only seventy-five. She was still living with Caitlin at the presbytery by the church. But Caitlin isn't married, never was. She's been housekeeper to Father Murphy for years. Used to teach at the Catholic school. Now she just looks after the presbytery and Father Murphy and two curates." She was very fey now. "Oh, dear, I've got it wrong again. He's Monsignor Murphy, now. A wonderful man."

Dillon gave her his best smile. "You've been very kind. God bless you."

They went back to the Cooper, and Billy said, as he settled behind the wheel, "Dillon, you'd talk the Devil into showing you the way out of hell. The information you got out of that old duck beggars belief."

"A gift, Billy," Dillon told him modestly. "You've got to be Irish to understand."

"Get stuffed," Billy told him.

"Sticks and stones," Dillon said. "But everything that befuddled old lady told me was useful information."

"I heard. Pool was wonderful, so was his mother, this Caitlin bird is beyond rubies, and, as for the good Monsignor Murphy, from the sound of it they got him from central casting." He turned left on Dillon's instructions. "Mind you, he must be good to get that kind of rank in a local church where he's their priest-in-charge."

"Turn right now," Dillon told him. "And what would you be knowing about it?"

"I've never talked much about my childhood, Dillon. My old man was a very violent man, killed in gang warfare when I was three. My mum was married to Harry's brother, and she was an exceptional lady who died of breast cancer when I was nineteen. I really went off the rails after that."

"Which is understandable."

"It was Harry who pulled me round, and you, you bastard, when you entered our lives. You introduced me to philosophy, remember, gave me a sense of myself."

"So where is this leading?" Dillon asked.

The Cooper turned another corner and pulled up outside their destination. "Church of the Holy Name," it said on the painted signboard beside the open gate, along with the times of Confession and Mass. The building had a Victorian-Gothic look to it, which made sense because it was only in the Victorian era that Roman Catholics by law were allowed to build churches again. Dillon saw a tower, a porch, a vast wooden door bound in iron in a failed attempt to achieve a medieval look.

They stayed in the car for a few moments. Billy said, "The thing is, my mother was a strict Roman Catholic. Not our Harry. He doesn't believe in anything he can't put his hand on, but she really put me onstage. When I was a kid, I was an acolyte. I tell you, Dillon, it meant everything to her when it was my turn to serve at Mass."

"I know," Dillon said. "Scarlet cassock, white cotta."

"Don't tell me you did that?"

"I'm afraid so, and, Billy, I've really got news for you. I did it in this very church we're about to enter. I was twelve when my father brought me from Northern Ireland to live with him in Kilburn. That means it was thirty-seven years ago when I first entered this church, and the priest in charge is the same man, James Murphy. As I recall, he was born in 1929, which would make him eighty."

"But why didn't you mention that to Ferguson and the others? What's going on? I knew something was, Dillon. Talk to me."

Dillon sat there for a moment longer, then took out his wallet and from one of the pockets produced a prayer card. It was old, creased, slightly curling at the golden edges. *Holy Mary, Mother of God, pray for us sinners, now and at the hour of our death, we who are ourselves alone.*

"Jesus, Dillon." Billy took it from him. "Where the hell did this come from?"

"It was Father James Murphy, as he was then, who first received the news of my father's death in that firefight in

Belfast, an incident that turned me into what I am, shaped my whole life. 'A casualty of war,' he told me, gave me the card, and begged me to pray." He smiled bleakly, took the card, and replaced it in the wallet. "So here we are. Let's go in, shall we? I see from the board someone's hearing confessions in there, although it may not be the great man himself."

He got out, and Billy joined him, his face pale. "I don't know what to say."

They entered and walked through the cemetery, which was also Victorian-Gothic and rather pleasant, marble effigies, winged angels, engraved headstones, and cypress trees to one side. "I used to like this when I was a boy, liked it more than I liked it inside the church in a way. It's what we all come to, when you think of it," Dillon said.

"For Christ's sake, cut it out," Billy said. "You're beginning to worry me."

He turned the ring on the great door, and Dillon followed him through. There was faint music playing, something subdued and soothing. The whole place was in a kind of half darkness, but was unexpectedly warm, no doubt because of central heating. The usual church smell, so familiar from childhood, filled his nostrils. Dillon dipped his fingers in the holy water font as he went past and crossed himself, and Billy, after hesitating, did the same.

The sanctuary lamp glowed through the gloom, and to the left there was a Mary Chapel, the Virgin and Child floating in a sea of candlelight. The place had obviously had money spent on it in the past. Victorian stained glass abounded, carvings that looked like medieval copies, and a Christ on the Cross which was extremely striking. The altar and choir stalls, too, were ornate and, it had to be admitted, beautifully carved.

A woman was down there wearing a green smock, arranging flowers by the altar. A strong face with a good mouth, handsome in a Jane Austen kind of way, the hair fair and well kept with no gray showing, although that was probably due more to the attentions of a good hairdresser than nature. She wore a white blouse and gray skirt under the smock, and half-heeled shoes. She held pruning scissors in one gloved hand, and she turned and glanced at them coolly for a moment, then returned to her flowers.

Dillon moved towards the confessional boxes on the far side. There were three of them, but the light was on in only one. Two middle-aged women were waiting, and Billy, sitting two pews behind them beside Dillon, leaned forward to decipher the name card in the slot on the priest's confessional door.

"You're all right, it says 'Monsignor James Murphy.'"

A man in a raincoat emerged from the box and walked away along the aisle, and one of the women went in. They sat there in silence, and she was out in not much more than five minutes. She sat down, and her friend went in. She was longer, more like fifteen minutes, then finally emerged, murmured to her friend, and they departed.

"Here I go," Dillon whispered to Billy, got up, opened the door of the confessional box, entered, and sat down.

"Please bless me, Father," he said to the man on the

other side of the grille, conscious of the strong, aquiline face in profile, the hair still long and silvery rather than gray.

Murphy said, "May our Lord Jesus bless you and help you to tell your sins."

"Oh, that would be impossible, for they are so many."

The head turned slightly towards him. "When did you last make a confession, my son?"

"So long ago, I can't remember."

"Are your sins so bad that you shrink from revealing them?"

"Not at all. I know the secrets of the confessional are inviolate, but acknowledging the deaths of so many at my hands in no way releases me from the burden of them."

Murphy seemed to straighten. "Ah, I think I see your problem. You are a soldier, or have been a soldier, as with so many men these days."

"That's true enough."

"Then you may certainly be absolved, but you must help by seeking comfort in prayer."

"Oh, I've tried that, Father, saying, 'Holy Mary, Mother of God, pray for us sinners, now and at the hour of our death, we who are ourselves alone.'"

There was a moment of silence, then Murphy turned full face, trying to peer through the grille. "Who are you?"

"God bless you, Father, but isn't that breaking the rules? Still, I'll let it go for once and put you out of your misery. Sean Dillon, as ever was. Thirty years since you last saw me. I was nineteen, and you were the man the police asked to break the news that my father was dead, killed accidently while on a trip to Belfast. You told me he was a casualty of war."

"Sean," Murphy's voice quavered. "I can't believe it. What can I say?"

"I think you said it all thirty years ago when you urged me to pray, particularly the special one on a prayer card you gave me, the prayer I've just quoted to you."

"Yes, I recollect now." The voice was unsteady. "A wonderful prayer to the Virgin Mary."

"I remember you saying it would be a comfort for all victims of a great cause. Which made sense, as the prayer is directed at we who are ourselves alone, and 'ourselves alone' in Irish is *Sinn Fein*. So it had a definite political twist to it, urging a nineteen-year-old boy whose father had ended up dead on a pavement in the Falls Road to get angry, clear off to Belfast, and join the Provos to fight for the Glorious Cause. Now, aren't you proud of me?"

The door to Dillon's half of the confessional box was yanked open, and the woman in the green smock was there, blazingly angry. "Come out of there," she shouted, and grabbed at him. Behind her, Billy moved in to pull her off.

"You got good and loud, Sean. Only her and me in the place, and we heard most of what you said."

She pulled away from Billy and glared at Dillon. "Get out of here before I call the police."

Billy produced his warrant card. "Don't waste your breath. MI5, and he's got one, too."

The other door opened, and Murphy came out, an imposing figure at six feet, with the silver hair, dressed in a full black cassock, an alb, violet stole draped over his shoulder.

"Leave it, Caitlin, this is Sean Dillon. As a boy of nineteen, I had to tell him his father was murdered by British soldiers in Ulster. He left for Belfast for his father's funeral and never returned. There were rumors that he had cast in his lot with the Provisional IRA. If so, I can't see that it in any way concerns me. As to the prayer card that I gave him as a comfort, it may be found on the Internet, if you look carefully, Sean, and has been available to all since Easter 1916. We have a Hope of Mary Hospice and Refuge where the card is readily available." He put a hand on Dillon's left shoulder. "You are deeply troubled, Sean, that is so obvious. Your dear father worked and did so much for the church in his spare time. The lectern in beechwood by the high altar was his work. If I can help you in any way, I am here."

"Not right now," Dillon said. "But before I go, the score for dead cardholders right now is four: Henry Pool, John Docherty, Frank Barry in New York, Jack Flynn on Long Island."

"What on earth are you talking about?" Murphy looked shocked.

"Don't listen to him, he's lost his wits entirely." Caitlin moved close to Dillon and slapped his face. "Get out."

"My, but you're the hard woman. Come on, Billy, let's go." Billy opened the great door, and Dillon turned, and Murphy and Caitlin were standing close, he with his head inclined while she whispered to him.

Dillon called, "If you know anybody named Cochran,

tell him we found his wallet, and the prayer card, too. God bless all here."

And Caitlin Daly snapped completely. "Get out, you bastard." Her voice echoed around the church, and Dillon followed Billy to the Cooper, and they drove away.

"Do you think there's anything doing?" Billy asked.

"Oh, yes," Dillon said. "However bizarre it sounds, I think there's something going on there."

"If that's so, don't you think you've given a lot away?"

"I intended to. Back to Holland Park, Billy," and he leaned back in his seat and closed his eyes, thinking about it.

At the sacristy, Caitlin Daly leaned against the door and fumbled in her shoulder bag, pushed aside a Belgian Leon .25 semi-automatic pistol, produced an encrypted mobile phone, and punched in a number. It was answered at once, a man's voice, the slightest tinge of a Yorkshire accent.

"Caitlin?"

"Just listen," she said. "We've got trouble." She quickly told him what had taken place. "What are we going to do?"

"How did Murphy take it?"

"How do you expect? He's too good for this bloody world. All he feels is pity for Dillon."

"Well, he would, wouldn't he? Leave it with me, I'll handle it somehow." The church was very quiet now when she returned, and Murphy knelt before the altar, his head bowed in prayer, and she sat in a front pew and waited. When he stood up and walked to her, she said, "You've been praying for Dillon, haven't you?"

"Of course. So sad, that business of his father's death in Belfast all those years ago. His life has so obviously been a hard and bitter one. What else can I do but pray for him?"

She stifled her anger with difficulty. "Sometimes, Monsignor, I think you're much too forgiving. But take my arm, and we'll go back to the presbytery for tea."

He did as he was told, and as they walked away he said, "Poor boy, he seems completely unhinged."

4

A little earlier, Miller and his sister had been on their way to Dover Street. Since becoming aware that her dearly loved brother was a man of dark secrets, Monica had also learned that anything he told her, however dangerous and extreme, was very probably true. For an academic like her, there was an undeniable thrill to it all, especially her involvement with Sean Dillon. When Miller picked her up at her rooms in Cambridge, she was already packed and waiting for him, and he filled her in on everything, as he knew it, right up to that moment.

Her reaction to the event in Central Park was highly practical. "Well, all I can say is, thank God you were carrying."

He grinned. "I see you've picked up the slang of our dark trade already."

"I don't have any option, not with you and Sean round. I've checked on George Dunkley, by the way, and he's doing fine. Thank God."

They were halfway to London when Roper called him and filled him in about Belsize Park and what was to happen.

"What about Sean?"

Roper said, "He went to see what he could dig up in Kilburn, took Billy with him."

"Is something wrong?" Monica asked him when he hung up.

"You could say that." He told her about the intruder at Belsize Park. "So this guy Cochran got away but lost his wallet, and they found another copy of that prayer card. We might as well call in at Holland Park instead of going straight to the house. They'll be finalizing the Gulfstream's departure from Farley this evening, and then there's Sean. God knows what he's getting up to in Kilburn, but, knowing him, it's bound to be interesting." He leaned over and said to Fox, "Change of plan, Arthur, as you've just heard."

"As you say, Major."

"Poor Svetlana," Monica said. "That beautiful house and all those lovely antiques and paintings. It's going to break her heart."

"I appreciate that, but it's not going to be forever, and she's got Katya to support her. And they'll be safe, that's the important thing. Whoever we're up against, they're pretty nasty."

"And Alexander?"

"Maybe in America he can get back to writing. Another *War and Peace* perhaps?"

"Which he's perfectly capable of producing," she said primly, and the Mercedes, approaching the Holland Park safe house, pulled up at the security gates and waited for them to open.

They found Roper in the computer room and Ferguson on his phone. He waved to them, then walked out, still talking.

Roper said, "He's been on and off the phone all afternoon. Half a dozen times with Clancy, but everything is set now. We pick them up at Belsize Park at seven. It'll take forty minutes to get to Farley Field, and they're all off by eight."

"Where are they heading?" Miller asked.

"Andrews Air Force Base, where they'll refuel, and then move on to another base in Florida, and then proceed by helicopter to the island."

Monica went and kissed him and ruffled his hair. "You look tired, love."

"I always do, these days, it's my new look. Sorry about Dunkley, there seem to be bad people out there. Are you okay?"

"A few bruises here and there. It could have been worse."

"I suppose so. At least with Kurbsky and the ladies out

of it, we'll have a level playing field, and we can just concentrate on discovering who these people are."

Maggie Hall appeared from the kitchen, face beaming.
"And how are you, Lady Monica? It's real nice to see you
again. Mr. Dillon will be smiling, I know that. Can I get
you some tea? I know you've been traveling."

Ferguson loomed up behind her. "We'll all have tea,
my dear, and some of those delicious chocolate biscuits
that you seem to have an inexhaustible supply of."

"You can have anything you want, General."

She departed, and Ferguson held Monica for a moment and kissed her cheek. "Sorry about having to drag
you away from Cambridge like this, but it's for your own
good, I'm afraid. Has it been made plain to you what
we're up against?"

"It's been made plain to me what's happened. The
behavior of the wretch who drove his truck into me was
proof enough of what we're up against."

"You're armed, I trust?" Ferguson asked.

She opened her shoulder bag and produced a Colt
.25. "As provided by Roper when I first signed up."

"Hollow-point cartridges at all times. We are really
going to war, my dear."

He turned to Roper. "Any sign of Dillon and Billy?"

"Not yet. I'll call them, if you like."

"No need," Ferguson said. "Here's the tea."

Maggie put her tray on the table and poured tea for
everyone and distributed biscuits, smiling and cheerful,
and made Ferguson, Roper, and Miller all laugh, too.

Monica thought how strange it was that these men she had come to know so well, including the brother she had never really known properly until now, these men who were so civilized and jolly, were all in the death business, had all killed people.

She felt slightly unreal for a moment, and Roper, with that ravaged face, glanced at her and stopped smiling. "Are you all right?"

"Yes, fine. I'll have a drink, if you don't mind. Long journey, and I'm tired."

She moved to the drinks cabinet, found a shot glass, opened a bottle of whiskey, filled the glass, and swallowed. It went straight to her head, releasing some lightness in her, and, as she turned, Dillon entered, along with Billy.

He had a paleness to him, the eyes dark, a look that she had never seen before. This man she had gotten to know well enough to love was suddenly a stranger, and she knew something must have happened.

He came and put a hand around her waist and kissed her lightly on the mouth. "It's good to see you, girl. I'd like to kill that bastard in the truck for what he did to you."

She ran her hand up and down his arm a couple of times. "It could have been worse, he could have succeeded. George is knocked about a bit, but he'll get over it." She looked at him searchingly. "You're angry, I think?"

"You could put it that way."

"Then tell us about it," Ferguson said.

"Billy and I went hunting, first of all in Camden in

search of Cochran. Turns out that address has been a brickfield since last year, waiting for a housing project. A helpful Indian storekeeper in the next street told me he remembered the address well because there used to be a lodging house there."

"I already checked on the computer," said Roper. "It only threw up two Matthew Cochrans, one a chemist at the School of Oriental Medicine and the other a head-master at a high school in Bayswater."

"So another false name," Ferguson said. "What else is new. What about Kilburn? Did you discover anything useful?"

"I think you could say that."

"For God's sake, Dillon," Billy exploded. "Get it off your chest." He turned to the others. "That priest you found, Roper, near Pool's address . . ."

Roper nodded. "Monsignor James Murphy."

"Dillon knew him. When he was nineteen and his dad was killed in Belfast, it was Murphy the police asked to break the news to him, which he did right there in Holy Name church, *and* he gave him one of the prayer cards."

There was a kind of stillness, and Monica took a step closer and reached for Dillon's hand. "Sean?"

Ferguson said, "Dillon, I don't think you've been completely straight with us on all this."

"That's nonsense. The card first reared its ugly head hidden in Frank Barry's wallet. I found it and showed it to Harry immediately. I also explained its significance, isn't that true, Harry?"

Miller nodded gravely. "Yes, I admit it is, but what you

didn't mention was your personal experience with the card."

"Because I'd had the wind knocked out of my sails, Harry. It was a bad memory of a terrible night in the life of a nineteen-year-old boy all those years ago in Kilburn. So I got on with the business in New York and tried to push the bad memory away for a while, and then things started to happen. I left Kilburn forever when I went to Belfast for my father's funeral. Frankly, I've always avoided it, and I'd no idea that Murphy was still at Holy Name."

"Well, one thing's for sure, he'll remember your return," Billy said.

"What happened?" Ferguson asked.

"I got angry and, you might say, I let rip, at least that's what Billy would tell you, because he heard. But it was all on purpose. I figured a little acting job was called for. So if you'll all take your seats and Roper turns on his recorder, we'll begin."

It took no more than twenty minutes, and when they were finished Roper switched off and Ferguson said, "Extraordinary. I find particularly interesting the remark Murphy made to you when he gave you the card. That it would be a comfort for all victims of a great cause. It certainly indicates where his political sympathies lie then, and no doubt still do."

Miller put in, "But it's hardly illegal. So it influenced an impressionable youth, which was what Dillon was then, and now he's angry about it. Most people would say so what?" He turned to his sister. "Come on, Monica, as an archaeologist, you constantly have to analyze the past based on very little. What have you got to say?"

"It seems simple to me. So far, four people are dead and various others have been put in harm's way, and the one constant has been that prayer card."

"Which first turned up in Frank Barry's wallet at the Plaza Hotel," Miller said.

"No, Harry," she said. "As far as I'm concerned, it first turned up on that evening in 1979 when Father James Murphy gave it to Sean. He's the one we have to look at next."

"I absolutely agree." Ferguson turned to Roper.

"I'll get right on to it."

Monica said to Miller, "I'd like to go to Dover Street now, Harry, and settle in. Is that all right with you? We could see Kurbsky, Svetlana, and Katya off later."

"A good idea."

She brushed Dillon's cheek with a kiss and went out, followed by her brother. Billy decided to pay a visit to the Dark Man, and Ferguson retired to his office. It was suddenly quiet, only a low hum from the equipment.

Roper said, "You're too wound up, Sean. Relax, go and have a sauna."

"It wasn't good," Dillon said. "I was surprised how violent I felt towards him and that bloody woman. I don't know a thing about her except what the old lady next door to Pool's house in Green Street said about her. A hard bitch, I know that having met her, but the old woman described her as a kind of Mother Teresa."

"Well, we'll see who's right, so off you go, and leave it to Uncle Roper."

Dillon returned to the computer room, hair damp but looking refreshed, wearing an open-necked black shirt, black bomber jacket, and black velvet jeans.

"Not bad," Roper told him. "But it's time you saw the barber."

"Never mind that." Dillon poured two whiskeys and handed one over. "What have you got for me?"

"You're going to love it. I've found a good deal about Murphy and the lady, who's fifty, by the way."

"Good God." Dillon was genuinely astonished. "I'd never have believed it. She's a handsome woman."

"I agree with you. Her picture's coming up now from an identity card. There she is. At least she doesn't look like a prison warden. To summarize, her mother, Mary Ryan, was born in Derry in 1934, she trained as a nurse, married a Patrick Daly when she was twenty-five. Caitlin, her only child, was born in 1959. In 1969, with the civil rights business, there was serious marching in Northern Ireland. The Dalys were in a mixed housing area, and armed men in hoods broke in one night and shot Patrick Daly dead in front of the mother and Caitlin, who was ten at the time. The family had friends in London, so they fled to Kilburn."

Dillon looked grim. "Not good, not good at all."

"Her mother—a trained nurse, remember—got a job

at the Cromwell Road Hospital, and they lodged in Kilburn with a cousin, who was a widow. As Caitlin is a year
older than you, I wonder if you ever knew each other?"

"I came to Kilburn later than that, when I was twelve,
but I can't recall a Daly. What did she do then?"

"Went to St. Mary's College, London, to train as a
teacher. Member of the students' union, president of
Fairness for Ireland Committee, left-wing activist, vice
president of the Civil Rights Committee, third-class honors degree in English, teaching certificate."

"Spent too much time marching," Dillon observed.

"Teacher in various Catholic schools. Then, in 1984,
her mother packed it in as a nursing sister and took the job
of housekeeper at the church, and they moved in together,
and so continued until the old lady died last year."

"And Caitlin is still there, still teaching it would seem,
and still without a man."

"Not true. She's got one, in a way. Listen to Murphy's
story and her position is explained, but not in the way
you might think. I'll roll his file round and read it, particularly 1979."

"The year my father was killed."

"Can you remember the date?"

"Of course I can. November thirteen. How could I
forget that?"

"Well, Murphy went on secondment to Londonderry
in January for six months to be a priest with them at the
Little Sisters of Pity's St. Mary's Priory. Read it."

Which Dillon did. He shook his head. "I never realized

that. I'd stopped going to church, and I was finished at RADA by then. Kilburn was pretty working class, so I was used to keeping my head down about being an actor."

"So you lost touch with him. But I've got a report he sent to his bishop, telling him how bad it was in the war zone and how impressed he'd been with the priory as a nursing home and the efforts of the nuns to help the sick and needy against the odds. His intention was to have a hospice called Hope of Mary, and he intended to re-cruit nuns from the Little Sisters of Pity. This would cost money, but the bishop responded to his enthusiasm. Murphy registered a charitable trust, called Requiem, and the church agreed to buy a suitable house on mortgage for him on the condition he was responsible for raising the operating costs."

"And he has, presumably?"

"In spades. See the photo of him here in full rega-lia, another when he was made Monsignor. He proved irresistible to many businessmen and a sensation in the city. The hospice is paid off, including all improvements, and they've started ones in West Belfast, Dublin, and now one in the Bronx in New York."

"That's a hell of a lot of money, when you look at it. A hell of an achievement. I wonder where it came from?"

"He certainly seems to have the golden touch."

"And where does Caitlin figure in all this?"

"Her mother worked at the housekeeping post at the presbytery till she was seventy. At that time, Caitlin just carried on, obviously by arrangement with Murphy, help-ing out but still teaching. When her mother got cancer, she packed in her job to nurse her, becoming more and more involved with Hope of Mary. The old lady died over a year ago, and Caitlin is still doing her job, but twins it with being executive director at the hospice."

"Fascinating stuff. What else have you got?"

"Costello-cum-Docherty, who tried to torch the Dark Man. Inspector Parkinson recognized him as a petty thief and drunk named Fergus Costello who'd apparently gotten religion over twenty years ago at a refuge for drunks and down-and-outs in Wapping High Street. It was interfaith, but Parkinson spoke of a charismatic priest who turned up there on occasion. So guess who it was?"

"Oh, I'm at the stage where I'm prepared to believe anything you say. But why the fake Irish passport?"

"I don't know. He had a prison record as Costello, maybe he wanted to start fresh."

"He must have known the right people. The passport was an absolute ringer. But our Irish connection falls down when we consider Henry Pool, doesn't it? I know his wife was from Cork, but his father was a cockney soldier, as I recall, so badly wounded in April 1945 in Germany he was immediately discharged and went to live in Kilburn with his wife, who produced Henry in 1946."

"Poor old Ernest, he died of a stroke two years later. But I've discovered an Irish connection that wasn't immediately apparent. His wife, Mary Kennedy? Her father was killed by the highly irregular British police force known as the Black and Tans."

"God help us," Dillon said. "The scum of the trenches. They'd frighten the Devil himself."

"So when we consider Pool and the life he led at the beck and call of an embittered old woman who probably blamed him for being half English and drummed guilt into him every day of his life, I suppose you could say he'd be capable of leaving a bomb in the back of an English general's limousine."

"I take your point. But Pool was the driver."

"Yes, but Ferguson did say Pool appeared to be running away."

Dillon sighed. "A hell of a tragedy it would have been, Charles Ferguson's sainted mother being from Cork herself."

"Actually, I did know that, but they say there are round eight million people of some sort of Irish extraction in the English population."

"Exactly," Dillon said. "More than there are in Ireland itself." He shook his head. "So where does it all lead?"

"God knows," Roper replied, and then Ferguson walked in.

"There you are," Dillon said. "When do we get going for Farley?"

"We don't," Ferguson said. "I decided a little extra security was called for, so I did a little sleight of hand. I apologize for not telling you, but I figured the fewer people who knew, the better. Svetlana, Katya, Alexander, and Bounine were all picked up by an emergency ambulance from the Royal Marsden Hospital, transferred to an anonymous people carrier, and delivered to RAF Biggin Hill in North London. They took off about twenty minutes ago. So that's that. Now, I've contacted Miller and the Salters and suggested that they join us to go over the new information. I asked Monica, too, but she's not feeling too good. She took a bit of a battering, remember. She thought she'd have an early night."

It was no more than half an hour later that the Salters arrived in the Alfa, and, as they walked in, the gate opened again behind them, and Fox delivered Miller, who followed them in to the computer room, where they found Ferguson, Roper, and Dillon talking quietly.

"So what is all this?" Harry Salter demanded. "What about Kurbsky and the ladies?"

"Departed some time ago, and, if you'll all sit down, I'll explain the circumstances."

He repeated what he'd told the others, emphasizing that what had alarmed him was the intruder at Belsize Park. "He was not an ordinary thief bent on burglary, we know that because of the prayer card. Kurbsky's makeover was very effective, so I'm inclined to believe that he wasn't the target. Cochran was probably intent on obtaining what information he could from the women. How he learned about them, I don't know, but that's why I felt we had to take extra precautions."

"I agree," Dillon said. "The Russians were behind the plot for Kurbsky's original false defection. Since then, they haven't heard a word from him or Luzhkov or Yuri Bounine. It must be making someone very angry indeed."

"And angry enough to do something about it?" Ferguson said. "So you think it is the GRU seeking revenge if they can't find answers?"

"It's the GRU I've always worried about, because Russian military intelligence is as good as it gets." Roper nodded. "There are six of us sitting here, and four have experienced serious attempts to kill them. Blake and Monica make six."

Miller said, "You and Dillon must feel left out."

"Well, it would be difficult to get at me here in my wheelchair, but I'm always ready." He produced a Walther from the side pocket of his chair and turned to Dillon. "Why they're leaving Sean alone, I don't know."

"I've already told you," Dillon said. "If I hadn't gone to New York at the last minute, it could have been different."

"So that's it, the bleeding Russians again," Harry Salter said. "What are we going to do about it?"

"Hold on, there's something I'd like you to see first," Ferguson said. "Dillon and Billy visited Kilburn earlier in the afternoon to explore the Irish connection."

"And where's this taking us?" Harry Salter asked.

"To a hospice known as Hope of Mary, which has a website, if you can believe it, featuring a familiar prayer card. It has an executive director, Caitlin Daly, a charity called Requiem behind it, and a priest responsible for the whole package called Monsignor James Murphy. Roper's prepared a very interesting fact file, so watch and learn."

As they pulled chairs forward and Roper adjusted his equipment, Harry Salter said in a low voice to Dillon,

"Waste of time, all this. There's got to be more to it than Kilburn."

"You think so?"

"Of course I do." He sat down. "Shooting Blake on Long Island, bombing the General's car in London, all these other things—this is major stuff, and it takes organization. I think you're absolutely right, Dillon. It's the GRU getting their own back for Kurbsky, and I bet they've been planning it ever since he scarpered."

And he was absolutely right.

IN THE BEGINNING

THE KREMLIN

5

Two weeks before Prime Minister Vladimir Putin's appearance at the UN and the events surrounding it, Colonel Josef Lermov of the GRU had been enjoying a six months' leave of absence to work on a book on international terrorism, a subject on which he held a formidable reputation in Russian security circles. Lermov had had scholarly leanings as a younger man, but he came from a military family—his father had been an infantry general, in his time—and so in spite of Lermov's undoubted promise, the army it had to be.

His wife had died at forty from breast cancer, he was childless, and his parents were both dead, leaving him with nothing to do but devote himself to his duty. A basic knowledge of Arabic had, on three occasions, led to covert operations, and his actions during them had left no doubt of his courage, with the decorations to prove it.

He was sitting at a desk in the university library now, auburn hair falling over his forehead, steel-rimmed glasses on his nose, an air of weariness with life in general about him, when a young GRU captain tapped him on the shoulder and whispered in his ear.

"I regret to disturb you, Colonel, but I've orders to take you to the Kremlin? I have a car waiting outside."

"The Kremlin?" Lermov didn't understand. "What on earth for?"

"The Prime Minister wishes to see you."

Lermov was shocked, and said the first thing that came into his head. "But I'm on leave."

The young Captain smiled slightly. "It would appear not, Colonel."

"Of course. Then if I may retrieve my greatcoat and briefcase from the cloakroom, I am at the Prime Minister's orders."

Twenty minutes later, after a drive through miserable weather, the Captain at the wheel, early winter at its worst, sleet and rain, he was delivered to the rear of the Kremlin. The Captain, whose name was Ivanov, knocked on a small postern door, which was opened by an armed soldier who said nothing and stood to one side as the Captain brushed past him and led the way along numerous corridors until they reached one with an armed guard sitting on a chair with a machine pistol on his lap. The Captain opened a door into an unexpectedly grand room furnished in the French style of the seventeenth century, painted walls and fine paintings.

"This is rather remarkable, I must say," Lermov commented.

"It was the office of General Volkov," the Captain said. "Special Security Adviser to the Prime Minister. Unfortunately, no longer with us."

"I had the pleasure of knowing him. His death will make him sorely missed by all in the GRU."

There was a sideboard with drinks of most kinds available, and a fine desk close to the fireplace with a DVD on it, a TV in the corner.

"The information on the DVD is classified on a strictly eyes-only basis. The Prime Minister's orders are that you should watch it, and take on board all the facts. When you feel you know what you're talking about, press the button on the desk. He will discuss the matter with you then."

"Do you know what's on it?"

"I helped put it together, Colonel."

"What's it about? Just tell me briefly." Peter Ivanov hesitated, and Lermov said, "Humor me, Captain."

"All right. To put it like the Americans would, there's been a 'turf war' going on in London for the past four or five years, and our people have not been doing very well."

"The opposition being British intelligence?"

"An elite group known as the Prime Minister's private army." He quickly ran down its members for Lermov and gave him a precis of the bloody history of the past few years.

"All leading up to the current state of play and the disappearance of Kurbsky, Luzhkov, and Major Yuri Bounine. But there's more on the DVD. Judge for yourself."

"I will." Lermov moved to the sideboard and, as Ivanov left, helped himself to vodka, then sat down to watch. Ivanov had been right, there was a great more detail, and it was a good thirty-five minutes before it finished.

He pressed the button on the desk, and it was surprising how quickly the door in the paneled wall opened and Vladimir Putin himself entered. He was wearing an excellent black suit, a white shirt, and a conservative striped silk tie.

"Prime Minister," Lermov said. "It's an honor to be here."

"I'm a great admirer of yours, Colonel. You have a remarkable mind. Now, sit and tell me what you think. I haven't got long, I'm meeting the French Ambassador."

"This feud with Charles Ferguson's people in London, it's better than a movie, though the body count has been appalling on our side. Then this whole thing with Kurbsky. He arrives in London—and then, three days later, he vanishes. Two days later, Colonel Luzhkov and Major Bounine disappeared."

"Five days for the whole thing. Quite a puzzle." Putin stood up.

"And what would you like me to do about it, Prime Minister?"

"Solve it for me. The Ministry of Arts has put out a

story that Kurbsky is somewhere in the depths of the country working on a novel in private. Likewise, the word on Luzhkov and Bounine is that they have been withdrawn from London to work on secret assignments at GRU headquarters."

"Which means London will need a new Head of Station."

"That's you," Putin said. "I authorized your appointment this morning. Your colleagues will envy you. But you're not there to enjoy yourself, Lermov. You're there to find out what the hell has been going on, and that's not all. I also expect you to find a way of ridding ourselves of the curse of Ferguson and company—permanently."

"I'll do my best," Lermov told him.

"I expect you to do better than that. I expect you to give me exactly what I'm asking for. But there is no need for you to go to London straightaway. Take your time, use our resources, learn the enemy."

"Of course," Lermov said.

"I've arranged for Ivanov to assist you. He's clever, but also quite ruthless and ambitious, so watch him. If you find him satisfactory, you can take him to London with you." He took an envelope from his pocket. "I think you'll find this of great assistance. Use it well." He opened the door in the paneling and was gone.

Lermov opened the envelope, took out the letter, and read it. *From the Office of the Prime Minister of the Russian Federation at the Kremlin. The bearer of this letter acts with my full authority. All personnel, civil or military, will assist Colonel Josef Lermov in any way demanded. Signed, Vladimir Putin.*

The door opened, and Ivanov entered. "I hope things went well?"

"I think you could say that." Lermov offered him the letter, which Ivanov read.

"You *are* in favor, Colonel."

"I've also just been appointed Head of Station for London." Lermov plucked the letter from Ivanov's hand, put it back in the envelope, and slipped it into a breast pocket.

"The Prime Minister has given me quite straightforward orders," he continued. "I am to solve the mystery of Kurbsky, Luzhkov, and Bounine."

"Is that all?" Ivanov's smile was slightly mocking.

"No, he also expects me to come up with a way of ridding us of what he terms the curse of Ferguson."

"Oh, dear." Ivanov sighed. "Based on past history, I'd say that will prove difficult."

"Apparently. Meanwhile, I'm going to go over everything again, all the information we have. I'll need a hotel as close as possible to GRU headquarters."

"There's an old hotel called the Astoria close by, which was taken over especially to accommodate GRU personnel. I'm already billeted there. The limousine we came in is allocated to you. I'm yours to command."

"Yes, so the Prime Minister said. He also said if you prove satisfactory, I can take you to London. Would you like that?"

"Like it?" Ivanov's eyes sparkled. "Colonel, five years ago, the GRU sent me there supposedly as a student on a six-months total immersion course in English for foreigners. It was a pure pleasure. I'd be happy to return."

"Well, let's get started," Lermov said.

The Astoria was acceptable, far better than most army accommodations. There were individual bedrooms with showers that worked, dull but functional. What had been the restaurant was more like a canteen now and run by the military, and the food was simple and sustaining, as you would expect it to be. In Lermov's case, he had an excellent goulash with a glass of a rough red wine to wash it down. He sat there, thinking about things over a second glass, and Ivanov appeared.

"Did you want lunch?" Lermov asked.

"I grabbed a couple of sandwiches and went up to headquarters. I've booked us an office for privacy—the main records department is about the size of a cathedral and just as public. Every file there ever was, lines of computers, poor sods in uniform hunched over. It looks like some Stalinist movie."

"God forbid," Lermov said, and stood up. "Let's get going and see what we can do."

Ivanov had been right about the central research hall, but it was surprisingly quiet—disciplined, really—the occa sional voice in the distance, a constant low hum from the machines. The office was fine, two desks, each with a computer.

"Most of the data obviously is on computer these days," Ivanov said. "Even the old stuff has been transferred, but we can explore original documents if we want, it's still stored elsewhere. Now, where do we start?"

"I'm interested by the speed at which events moved. Kurbsky arrives in London, he's received at Holland Park, and then he's out on the street, walking round and speaking to Bounine. Twenty-four hours after that, he's in Mayfair and shooting some Chechnyan named Basayev with whom he's apparently had history. He calls Bounine afterwards, tells him what he's done, and says he's returning to Holland Park. Bounine tells Luzhkov and Luzhkov tells Putin. And then Kurbsky vanishes, and, two days later, so do Luzhkov and Bounine." Lermov stood, concentrating. "You have a look at all the traffic to and from the London Embassy, starting with the Thursday Kurbsky was received and the few days after. Transcripts of every kind. If a conversation looks odd or interesting, listen to the recording."

"And you?"

"I'm going to find out more about Kurbsky."

He switched on his computer and went quickly through Kurbsky's life. In January 1989, Kurbsky, aged nineteen, had been staying in London with his aunt Svetlana, a famous Russian actress and defector, when news came of student riots in Moscow, blood on the streets and many dead, amongst them his sister, Tania Kurbsky.

Their father, a KGB colonel, had used his influence to have her buried in Minsky Park military cemetery to cover his shame. Apparently too late for her funeral, Alexander Kurbsky's response had been to join the paratroopers in the ranks and go to Afghanistan and then Chechnya, and then Iraq. He'd excelled. Then, Boris Luzhkov had recruited him for his mission to penetrate British intelligence. His bait? That Tania Kurbsky wasn't dead at all but sentenced to life in the worst gulag in Siberia, Station Gorky. If Kurbsky cooperated, his sister would go free.

He sat thinking about it, and then, using GRU operational passwords, accessed prisoners' lists and files at Station Gorky. When he tapped in the name of Tania Kurbsky, however, the screen said *Code 9 Restriction*. He turned to Ivanov, busy at his own computer, and asked, "What's a Code 9 Restriction?"

"Ah, you've got to Tania Kurbsky. I ran into the same roadblock. It means above most secret, which, when I inquired of Major Levin out there in the end office, means you can't have it, whoever you are and whatever it is."

"We'll see about that. Let's go and have a word."

Major Levin was impressed enough when faced with a full colonel of GRU to get to his feet. "Can I assist in any way, Colonel . . . ?"

"Lermov. I'm engaged in an essential intelligence matter, and my inquiry is blocked by the words *Code 9 Restriction*."

"I'm afraid it would be impossible to help you, Colonel."

Lermov took the envelope from his pocket, extracted Putin's letter, and passed it across. Levin read it, eyes bulging.

"Of course, you could phone through to the Prime Minister's Office in the Kremlin or you could simply unlock the information. Right here on your own screen would do."

"Of course, sir, I'm most happy to oblige. If you would be kind enough to show me what it is you seek, I can insert the correct password."

"Excellent." Lermov turned to Ivanov. "You will oblige me, Captain? I wouldn't look if I were you, Major."

Ivanov's fingers flew expertly; the prisoners' lists at Station Gorky appeared with Tania Kurbsky's name, again blocked. Major Levin scribbled a password and passed it over, and Ivanov tapped it in. The screen was filled with the sad, haunted face of a wretched woman looking about a hundred years old. It read: "Tania Kurbsky died of typhoid, aged 28, on March 7, 2000."

"Have you got what you wanted, gentlemen?" Levin inquired.

"Yes, I think so."

He got up, and Levin said, "Is there anything else I can do?"

"Yes, make sure you forget about this. It would seriously displease the Prime Minister if he heard you'd been uncooperative at first."

They returned to the office, and Ivanov said, "I don't think I'll forget that face in a hurry. She was only seventeen when she went in. That means she endured that place for eleven years."

"I agree. So Luzhkov was lying when he said she was still alive."

"Do you think the Prime Minister knew?"

"I'd like to think he didn't, but who knows? The real question is this: what would Alexander Kurbsky do if he found out? The fact that his old bastard of a father had lied when he said she was dead in the first place must have deeply shocked him, but to discover the awful truth about his sister and realize how cruelly he had been duped . . ." He shook his head. "I don't think angry would be strong enough to describe how he would feel. And how he would react is anyone's guess."

"Do you think that perhaps he did find out?" Ivanov asked.

"That's what we need to discover. Did you come across anything else?"

"Just one thing. You remember the Big Four meeting the other month?"

"Of course." The American Vice President had unexpectedly flown in from Paris for top secret talks with the Prime Minister, the Israeli Prime Minister, and the President of Palestine to broker a deal on Gaza.

"You remember they met on a large boat on the Thames? Well, according to some reports, it got a little dangerous out there in the mist. Some small riverboat exploded, an overheated gas tank or something."

"And the point?"

"It was the last day anyone at the Embassy saw either Luzhkov or Bounine."

"Interesting," Lermov said. "You think it was related?"

"You said to look for anything odd," said Ivanov. "And here's another thing. Apparently, Luzhkov *knew* the Vice President was flying in. I found a message about it from the Paris Embassy at approximately midnight on the night before. It was received by a junior lieutenant named Greta Bikov—and signed for by Boris Luzhkov."

"Hmm. That doesn't really tell us anything, though. Tell me, who's been holding the fort for GRU in London since the disappearances?"

"A Major Ivan Chelek. They sent him over from Paris."

"I know him, he worked for me in Iraq some years ago. Slow but sound. You speak to him, explain you're acting under my orders. Find out what he's been doing to investigate, and inquire about Greta Bikov."

"Any special reason?" Ivanov asked.

"Because she was there, Peter, received that transcript as night duty officer and conveyed it to Luzhkov. What was his reaction? Was there anyone with him? Bounine could have been there, for all we know. You were right to bring this matter to my attention."

"At your orders, Colonel." Ivanov produced an encrypted mobile, and Lermov got up and wandered outside.

There was something here, just below the surface of things, he was certain of that, and that feeling tantalized him. An old woman with her head in a scarf and wearing a white coat pushed a tray along the walkway as he leaned on the rail and smoked an American Marlboro. There was a samovar on the trolley that looked as old as her, and sandwiches and pies. She paused and looked at him, a leftover from another age.

"You're not allowed to smoke here, comrade."

"Just give me a hot cup of tea with lemon, *babushka*, and a currant bun, and you can have these. They're American. I shouldn't be smoking them anyway."

She smiled. "You're a good man, I like you." She pocketed the cigarettes, gave him what he'd asked for, and pushed her trolley away. Lermov ate the bun, which was excellent, and was drinking the tea when Ivanov found him.

"You might have got me one."

"Never mind that. What did he say?"

"No sign of any of them. He's even had assets we can rely on in the London underworld to check the morgues, but they've gotten nowhere. He congratulates you on your elevation to Head of Station and says please come soon, as he misses Paris."

"And Greta Bikov?"

"It seems she was very upset by the whole business of Luzhkov and Bounine. She took it badly, cried a lot, and went round looking stressed and anxious. Other staff said she was a favorite of Luzhkov, and the general opinion was that he was having it off with her."

"How delicately put," Lermov said. "Did you speak to her?"

"I couldn't, she wasn't there. She got very depressed, so the Embassy doctor decided to place her on sick leave."

"And when was this?"

"Four days ago. She's right here in Moscow. Her mother is a widow. Lives in an apartment on Nevsky Prospekt, overlooking the river."

"Some fine old houses there," Lermov said. "Okay, let's say she was a naughty girl and Luzhkov's bit of skirt, as her colleagues seem to think. She was used to being overfamiliar with her commanding officer, in and out of his office, putting up with the older man's indifferent kiss, the quick grope."

"I think I see where you're going with this," Ivanov said. "Bad things happen, the boss disappears, a lot of pressure and questions coming your way."

"Leading to considerable stress of the sort induced by fear, so you show that face to the doctor, who puts you on sick leave."

"And sends you home to Mummy and all the comforts of home." Ivanov grinned. "But what is it she's afraid of?"

"I would imagine her overfamiliarity with Luzhkov led to her sticking her nose into things she shouldn't. She may have enjoyed having him on a string, leading him on, if you like. Taking advantage of an aging fool who couldn't keep his fly closed."

"And now with this strange business of his disappearance, she's seriously worried about her misdeeds, whatever they are, surfacing."

"Then it's time to find out what they are." Lermov took the Putin letter from his pocket and passed it to him. "Go down to the cell block, order the commanding officer to provide you with two military police sergeants, women, but the type who look like prison officers. Proceed to Lieutenant Greta Bikov's home. You will remind her she is still an officer in the GRU and that duty calls. The sergeants will assist her into her uniform, if necessary."

There was a kind of admiration on Ivanov's face. "Of course, Colonel."

"I'll give you an hour, then I'll present myself in the cell block and start her interrogation. So get on with it."

Ivanov went away, almost running, and the old tea woman came back along the walkway. She paused. "Another tea, Colonel, you look stressed. What's wrong?"

"It's the acting, *babushka,* it always takes it out of me playing somebody I'm not," Lermov told her.

"What you need is another glass of tea."

"I don't think so." He smiled. "But you can give me one of those cigarettes, if you like."

The house overlooking the river was definitely tsarist in origin, as Ivanov had expected. The Bikov apartment was on the top floor and served by an ancient lift with a metal lattice door. Before going up, Ivanov gave his two forbidding-looking women police sergeants instructions.

"I doubt if you will ever handle a matter of greater importance than this." He produced the Putin letter, opened it, and held it before them. "We are here at our Prime Minister's bidding to arrest a serving officer of the GRU who needs to answer grave charges, one Greta Bikov."

Neither woman showed any emotion, not a flicker on the face. The senior said, "How do we handle the matter, Captain?"

"No need to get too physical, Sergeant Stransky. Let's just frighten the hell out of her, put her in the right frame of mind for her interrogation."

The bell sounded like a distant echo from another time, but the maid who answered it was young, dressed in jeans and a smock, rubber gloves on her hands, obviously engaged in cleaning. A look of dismay appeared on her face.

Sergeant Stransky barked with infinite menace, "Lieutenant Greta Bikov." She moved straight past the girl and led the way along a short corridor. Which opened into an arched entrance with drapes on either side and, beyond, a large sitting room.

There was a piano, a fine carpet, too much old-fashioned furniture, and wingback chairs. Having studied Greta Bikov's service record, Ivanov knew that the woman in the wheelchair beside the fire was the mother, crippled with rheumatoid arthritis in spite of being only fifty years of age. Greta was sitting opposite her, wearing a bathrobe and what looked like pajama bottoms. She'd been holding a cup in both hands and, in scrambling to her feet, spilled some of its contents. Her face was wild with fear.

Her mother cried out, "Who are you? What do you want?"

Peter Ivanov saluted with infinite courtesy. "You must excuse the intrusion, madam, but your daughter must return to duty."

"This is nonsense," Mrs. Bikov told him. "She is ill."

To Greta, confronted by Ivanov in that magnificent uniform with all the medals, it was as if the Devil himself had come to fetch her.

She said desperately, "I'm on indefinite sick leave."

"Terminated on the orders of Colonel Josef Lermov, now Head of Station for the GRU in London."

"No, surely it cannot be?" she said faintly.

Ivanov took out the Putin letter, unfolded it, and held it up in front of her. "The Prime Minister himself requests your presence."

She seemed to stagger, clutching at the back of her chair. Ivanov nodded to Stransky and her partner, who came forward and took an arm each. "Don't be alarmed. These women are simply here to assist you to dress. You must make your appearance in uniform. Go with them now."

They took her away to her bedroom. Her mother had started to weep, holding a handkerchief to her mouth. She said brokenly, "But what has she done?"

"That is not for me to say, madam, it is what a military inquiry will decide."

She buried her face in her hands, crying even more, but he ignored her. There were various bottles and glasses on the sideboard. He selected a bottle of vodka and poured one, drank it, then beckoned to the maid.

"Does she drink?"

"Yes, Captain."

"Do you live in?"

"Yes, I have a room upstairs."

"Excellent. Make sure you keep the vodka flowing and look after her. See to her now. I'm going to make a call."

He went into the kitchen, closed the door, called Lermov on his mobile, and described what had happened. "So what's your opinion of her state of mind?" Lermov asked.

"Very fragile and frightened to death. There's something worrying her, I'm sure of that, it just needs the right shove."

"Well, let's see if we can't give it to her. I'll see you soon."

Ivanov noticed another bottle of vodka on the side by the sink, obviously the maid's, and poured another, thinking about Greta. It wouldn't be necessary to get physical with her. From what he'd seen, she would break very quickly.

There was a knock on the door, and Stransky looked in. "We're ready for you."

"Excellent," Ivanov told her, and went out.

6

What Lermov found when he went downstairs to the cell block was pure theater. The two female police sergeants were supremely menacing as they stood on each side of the door, Ivanov had a look of the SS about him, and Greta Bikov seemed terrified as he walked in.

Ivanov saluted. "Reporting as ordered, Colonel," h barked. "With Lieutenant Greta Bikov." He turned her. "On your feet."

She managed to stand, trembling with fear, p enough, with tightly bound blond hair, undeniab tractive in uniform. One could understand her ap most men. Luzhkov had probably found her irres Her face told it all, a touch of the Slav to it.

She sat there, shaking a little, confronted by this unusual man, someone with the gravitas of a sch university professor perhaps, the world-weary face of a man who had seen most things that life had to offer and had long since ceased to be amazed.

She took a deep breath, which seemed to steady her a little. My God, she's assessing him, Ivanov thought, trying to make sense of what kind of man he is, but it's his rank that's giving her pause for thought. Full colonel. Then the medals, including the one for bravery under fire when he volunteered for that Spetsnaz job in Iraq. Nothing comes higher than that. She tried a shy smile, and Ivanov felt like smiling, too, his thoughts confirmed. Silly girl, this one isn't another Luzhkov to be charmed by you crossing one silk knee over the other and allowing your skirt to slide a little.

Lermov sat opposite her, Ivanov leaned against the wall to the left side, arms folded. Lermov started, "Lieutenant Bikov, there is no specific charge against you, but I am under orders from Prime Minister Putin to investigate the disappearance of Colonel Boris Luzhkov and his second-in-command, Major Yuri Bounine. Captain Ivanov has shown you the warrant signed by the Prime Minister, indicating that I operate with his full authority?"

"Yes, Colonel."

"To business. You were posted to London nine months ago, which was when you first met Colonel Luzhkov?"

"Yes, Colonel."

There was a kind of impatience in her voice. Lermov made eye contact with Ivanov, who moved in. "And Major Bounine, what about him?"

"He only appeared a few weeks ago, a posting from

Dublin." Her impatience broke through, obviously fueled by anxiety. "I've been asked these questions before, Colonel, by Major Chelek. He was very thorough and appeared perfectly satisfied that I had no idea what happened to either of them."

Ivanov, playing the bad guy to the hilt, homed in on her harshly. "If you think that Major Chelek is perfectly satisfied with you, you're very much mistaken, not when he discovered that most of your colleagues were of the opinion that you were having an affair with Colonel Luzhkov."

Her face became very pale. She hammered on the table with a clenched fist, but it was unconvincing, and her voice was weak when she said, "I protest, Colonel. Malicious lies and rumors put about by those who envied my friendship with Colonel Luzhkov. He was the kindest of men."

"Leaving all that to one side, let's have a look at one of your dealings with Colonel Luzhkov. Now, your main duties were as an intelligence assistant in the code room where your expertise was necessary to handle transcripts, encrypted material, and so on."

"That's what I was trained for at GRU headquarters."

"And you acted as Colonel Luzhkov's personal secretary some of the time?" Lermov asked patiently.

"Quite frequently, but much of the work in the code room tends to come in at night, so I often operated the night shift. I was the highest-rated code expert on staff." There was a touch of defiance there.

Lermov took a sheet from the pile in front of him

and passed it across. "Do you recall receiving that transcript? It has your name and also Luzhkov's signature of receipt."

She glanced at it. "I remember very well. Do you want me to read it out?"

"No, just tell us the gist of it." He leaned back and waited.

"It came in minutes before midnight on a Sunday, and I was on the night shift. It was a most-secret from the Paris Embassy. The American Vice President was in Paris for a UN thing and was flying back to Washington on Monday morning, next day. Once in the air, the plan was to divert to London for a meeting with the British Prime Minister, the Israeli Prime Minister, and the President of Palestine to try and broker a deal for peace in Gaza."

"And you took it straight to Luzhkov?"

"I knew he was in his office with Major Bounine, having a drink."

"And what did he say?"

"He couldn't believe it, asked me if I was sure it was true, but I pointed out that, as you can see in the second half of the transcript, the information came from a highly regarded asset in French intelligence who was on the GRU payroll in Paris. It also said the word was that the meeting was going to take place on a riverboat on the Thames for security reasons, but the source didn't know which boat."

"And what was his reaction to all this?"

Greta paused for a long moment, as if suddenly realizing where things were going, and it was Ivanov who jumped in.

"You heard the Colonel. It's a simple enough question."

"He was very excited. He . . . he said what a sensation the death of the four of them would make. It would rock the world."

The silence was so heavy it filled the room, and then Lermov said, "And Major Bounine's reaction?"

"He said surely you're not thinking of something like that, and Luzhkov cut him off and made an amazing speech about the Wall coming down and the death of Communism and the evils of Capitalism. He kept saying things like 'the Communist order must be restored.' He was quite drunk."

"And you were still there listening?" Ivanov asked.

"I felt as if I'd been forgotten and asked what he wanted me to do, and he said the moment we knew which riverboat was being used, I had to notify him at once. I got the impression that Major Bounine wasn't very happy, but he told me to go and get on with it. On my way out of the door, I heard Luzhkov say to Bounine, 'We need a man to deal with our problem satisfactorily,' but that was as the door was closing." She sat there, strangely composed, that edge of defiance again. "So there you are."

Lermov turned and raised his eyebrows to Ivanov, who came and put both hands on the table, his face only a couple of feet away from her. "What do you mean, 'there you are'? That's total nonsense. There isn't a human being in the world who, having heard what Luzhkov was beginning to say, could have resisted holding on for a few seconds to hear the rest. So don't be stupid, and tell the Colonel what it was."

She came apart, tears starting. "All right, then. He said we need a man to deal with our problem satisfactorily, a bad man who is also a madman, something like that. It sounded crazy, but, like I said, he was drunk."

She paused, and Ivanov pushed her again. "Go on."

"Bounine said, 'Do you know of such a man?' and Colonel Luzhkov said that he did, and he told Bounine to go get his coat and put a pistol in his pocket and he would introduce him to the man. I closed the door at once and hurried away to the code room. I was worked up by the whole business, so I opened the door to a small balcony by one of the code-room windows and lit a cigarette, and I saw them go down to the staff car park, get in Luzhkov's Mercedes, and drive away."

"And that was that?"

"No, actually, you should have another transcript in the file. It came in about an hour and a half later from the same source, saying that the riverboat was called the *Garden of Eden* and they would be boarding her at the Cadogan Pier, Chelsea, have the meeting, go downriver and disembark at Westminster Pier, and that preparations were already in hand to prepare the boat at Chelsea."

"And you forwarded it to Luzhkov?"

"I called him on my mobile but Bounine answered, and I gave him the information."

"And you've no idea where they were?"

"I swear on my life, I don't know. There wasn't even traffic noises. It had started to rain incredibly that night and continued for twenty-four hours. The whole thing the following day was bedeviled by rain and heavy mist. You couldn't see across the river."

"And you didn't see them again?" Lermov asked.

"I'd worked the whole night shift, remember, I needed sleep. I went to my room in the staff block down the road. The two of them just disappeared, as I understood it, sometime in the afternoon. That's all I can say. Look, I'm tired, I need the bathroom."

"Of course you do." Lermov got up and said to Ivanov, "A word."

They went out, and Ivanov said, "This is quite a story."

"If it's true, I want you to contact Major Chelek in London. She's just told us she didn't see them again after their night on the town because she'd gone down to staff quarters and gone to bed. See if he can confirm that. Also ask him to confirm the question on this slip of paper."

"I'll see to it. Anything else?"

"Yes, tell Sergeant Stransky to commiserate with her, woman-to-woman, let her have a shower and general cleanup and see that she gets a decent meal and a drink. Have her back here in an hour and a half."

"What for?" Ivanov asked.

"Because there's more, Peter, much more, and I haven't got time to waste. I'm trying to think of absolutely the worst consequence I can threaten her with. I'll let you know when I've decided what it is."

Ivanov said with awe, "I'm beginning to think I don't know you at all, sir."

"Frequently, I think I don't know me," Lermov said.

"But, for now, I'm going back to the office, where, with luck, the old tea lady may be operating."

And she was there, still plying her trade. He purchased two ham sandwiches made with rough black peasant bread, had scalding tea in a tall glass, and sat in the office and went through the loose file from beginning to end, feeling already that he almost knew it by heart.

Academic work was all he'd had time for when it came to writing books, but he loved fiction at any level, had considered it an essential part of his work in the intelligence field. It had taught him that individuals were what they were, could continue to act only in that way, so that it was possible to tell in advance exactly how they would behave in any given situation. He was absolutely certain that applied to Greta Bikov.

The door opened, and he glanced up. Ivanov moved in and dropped a transcript on the desk. "How the hell did you know? When you leave the code room, you sign out if you are junior staff. You also sign out at the front door of the Embassy. Just down the road are staff quarters, and you sign in there and sign out when you leave and sign in again at the Embassy. Here's the answer to your query, too."

"Stupid, stupid girl." Lermov sighed as he read it all.

"What are you going to do with her?"

"Make her tell the truth," Lermov said. "All of it."

Greta was standing by the desk when they went in, Stransky and her colleague on either side of the door, and she looked renewed again, her hair bound, a touch of lipstick, trim and attractive in her uniform.

"Sit down, Lieutenant. I trust you feel refreshed?"

"Of course, Colonel, you've been very kind."

"And you've been very stupid," he said softly, took off his glasses, and polished them.

"What is this?" She was angry now, and allowing it to get the better of her.

"You lied to me. You didn't go off to the hostel to go to bed. The only place you booked out of when a colleague took over was the code room. We've been on to London and had your comings and goings checked."

She was thoroughly unsure now. "I was in the canteen."

"Enough of this. I'll tell you what you are. A tramp who has shared the bed of an infatuated fool who's indulged you at every turn. You stuck your nose into everything, indulged yourself by perusing documents that were eyes-only or most-secret, listened in on his telephone calls. Oh, yes, I've had that aspect of Luzhkov's office and the outer office checked by GRU in London. There are three different systems linking both offices that would allow someone to eavesdrop."

She was thoroughly worked up now. "It's not true, I swear it."

"And then there's the safe, I'm sure he showed that off to you, stuffed with thousands of pounds sent to fund covert GRU operations. I would imagine you purchased your underwear at Harrods."

"Damn you to hell," she screamed.

"No, hell is where you are going." Lermov took a folded document from his breast pocket and opened it on the desk. "You are dismissed from the GRU with disgrace and sentenced to life imprisonment in Station Gorky."

If ever there was horror on a human face, it was on hers. "You can't do that." She broke down, sobbing uncontrollably. "What can I do to stop this dreadful thing happening?"

"Admit everything, and not just what we've been talking about but anything else that you overheard in the past."

She tried to compose herself. "But I wasn't always acting as his secretary. All right, there were some other strange things that happened. He was crazy in a way, and a great drunk, but most of the time I was in the code room."

"Start by telling us what happened on Monday morning. You weren't in the code room then. Tell me exactly what you did."

"The second transcript that came from Paris, the phone with the information about the *Garden of Eden* and Chelsea, came in when I was still on duty."

"You've told us that you called Luzhkov and Bounine answered, and you didn't see them again. I presume that wasn't true."

"I was curious about the whole business, there was no way I could have gone to sleep. There was no sign of the Mercedes in the car park. It's not against regulations to take a restroom break, which I did, and had a shower while I was in there to liven myself up, and I had my alarm which would alert me if anything came through. I returned to the code room, looked out at the car park, and saw the Mercedes was there again. It was just before my six a.m. relief, and another transcript came through from Paris."

"And what was that?"

"A confirmation that the *Garden of Eden* would host a party for a hundred people and would slip its moorings at one-thirty for the trip to Westminster."

"And you, of course, passed it straight on to him?"

"I wasn't sure if he might have gone to his quarters down the road, but, when I tried the office, he was there and told me to read the transcript over the phone."

"So what did you do after that?"

"As I told you, I was intrigued about the whole business, so I went and got a tray at the canteen, coffee, and so on, an excuse to go to the office."

"And?"

"I saw Major Bounine approaching. He was in a robe, a towel round his neck and his hair damp as if he'd been in the shower, and he looked angry. He totally ignored me and went straight into the outer office."

"And you, of course, followed?"

"Yes."

"And you operated one of the recording devices in the outer office that enabled you to eavesdrop. What was being said?"

"I can't remember everything, but the Colonel told Bounine about the time the *Garden of Eden* was leaving, and Bounine said, 'Have you informed Ali Selim about that?' Luzhkov said he had, and that Selim was very happy about it. A hunter scenting his prey."

Lermov glanced at Ivanov. "What do you think, Peter?"

"That, incredible as it sounds, Luzhkov was planning some sort of a hit." He turned to Greta. "How did Bounine react to all this?"

"He brushed it aside and said he had something more important to discuss." She shook her head. "Look, I wasn't making notes, so I can only recall the gist of it."

"Go on," Lermov said. "Just do your best."

"Well, it seemed to concern Alexander Kurbsky."

"It what?" Ivanov was astounded.

"Major Bounine asked the Colonel if he was aware that Tania Kurbsky had died of typhoid in Station Gorky in 2000. The Colonel said that was nonsense, and Bounine told him the Putin files and the DVD were all fake. The Colonel sounded upset and said something about Kurbsky having done everything for nothing."

Ivanov was looking stunned by now, and Lermov said to her gently, "My dear Greta, Station Gorky recedes already. Now, carry on. Did anything else strike you about that conversation?"

She frowned, trying to think back, and then nodded. "I remember now. Bounine said to the Colonel that the man in the black hood who saved Blake Johnson wasn't Dillon at all, it was Kurbsky, who couldn't stand the idea of someone else ending up in Station Gorky like his sister."

"And that was all."

She frowned, trying her best, and then smiled in a kind

of triumph. "Bounine said that Ferguson and Roper had probably found out that Kurbsky's defection was false."

"Incredible," Ivanov said.

"And what happened then?" Lermov asked.

"Bounine walked out, ignoring me, so I took the coffee in to Luzhkov. He was drinking vodka, as usual, and thanked me for the coffee. The fact that I was still there didn't seem to surprise him. I went back in the office, busied myself with some filing, and then he got another call, and I checked it out."

"And who was it?"

"General Ferguson. It was a shouting match, and he called Colonel Luzhkov a bastard." She shook her head. "I only remember bits. He threatened to have a lot of GRU people packed off to Moscow. He said he knew all about Kurbsky and intended to help him in any way he could. He said Kurbsky had already done the United States a big favor by saving this Blake Johnson."

"And afterwards?"

"He was sitting in there drinking vodka for ages and then he sent for Bounine."

"And you listened again?"

"He said to Bounine that in view of what had happened, that maybe it would be a good idea to cancel Ali Selim, and gave Bounine fifty thousand pounds to give Selim for his time."

"And Bounine went?"

"Yes, I was at my desk. He left without a word, carrying a holdall with a shoulder strap." She was obviously uncomfortable again. "I need a rest, Colonel, please."

"We're coming to the end. You've been very good. Bounine returned, did he?"

"Yes, the morning had flown, it was certainly past noon. He came straight through my office and went in to the Colonel."

"And once again you listened?"

"Bounine said Ali Selim had told him he had cancer and had only three months to live and wasn't interested in the money or canceling. He'd go out in a blaze of glory."

She paused, and Lermov said, "Go on, girl."

"I'm sorry, Colonel. Through the glass windows to the corridor, I saw Olga, the staff supervisor, approaching. She was obviously going to come in, so I switched off."

"Dear God, don't let it be true," Ivanov put in with great emotion.

"Calm yourself, Peter," Lermov told him. "Give her a chance." He leaned forward. "How long did she stay?"

"Three or four minutes, and, as soon as she'd gone, I switched on and heard Bounine say, 'You must face him.' The Colonel said that Bounine must go with him and find an opportunity to shoot Selim."

"And what did Bounine say?"

"He agreed to go, said they'd leave in twenty minutes, and went out."

"And Luzhkov?"

"Followed him a bit later, telling me that he and Major Bounine had an appointment and he'd be back later in the afternoon. I left the office and went upstairs to a window overlooking the car park, saw them walk to the Mercedes, get in, and drive away, Bounine at the wheel."

"Well, he would be," Ivanov commented, "Luzhkov awash with vodka like he was."

Greta Bikov seemed to straighten her back, and clasped her hands together on the table in front of her. "And that, Colonel, was the last time I clapped eyes on Colonel Boris Luzhkov and Major Yuri Bounine, so help me God."

Lermov smiled. "I believe you completely, Lieutenant Bikov."

"All sins forgiven, Colonel?" she asked.

"To be frank, I would find it difficult to recommend you to any officer of rank for secretarial duties, but I will overlook that, as your misconduct has provided me with information beyond price. We are not finished yet, of course, but I think you've earned another break."

Lermov sat opposite Ivanov in a secluded corner of the officers' bar and indulged in the finest vodka to be had and cold as ice.

"Excellent," Lermov said as he drank the first one. "I really needed that."

"It surely freezes the brain," Ivanov told him. "Your threat to send her to Station Gorky for life was what did the trick. The silly girl fell for it."

"But I meant it, Peter. There is no room for empty threats in my world. People imagine physical force is always necessary to break down the subject of an interrogation."

"And you don't agree?"

"In the years of the Third Reich, the Germans were the masters of Europe from the English Channel to the Urals, and yet in Britain, where the Nazi spy system was totally destroyed, torture was unthinkable, no physical force used at all."

"So what was the secret?"

"The double-cross system. They turned spies so that their German masters thought the spies were still working for them and believed in their radio traffic."

"How did the British do that?"

"Certainly not torture, and, according to their ethos, you could never depend on any kind of physical force. Their spy catchers offered a simple choice, delivered in the English of the upper classes."

"Saying what?" Ivanov asked.

Lermov delivered his answer in English so perfect there was only the hint of a Russian accent. "'Sorry to hear you can't help us, old man. Too bad. They'll take you back to your cell now. No point in prolonging things. You'll be hung in the prison yard at nine o'clock in the morning.'"

"Good God," Ivanov replied in reasonable English, though not as excellent as Lermov's. "They actually did that?"

"Oh, yes, the salutary-shock approach. The knowledge of that nine o'clock appointment concentrated the minds wonderfully."

"I see now where you were coming from with Greta Bikov. You scared the pants off her."

"Don't feel sorry for her, Peter. Her behavior in London was appalling. Who else has she been listening in on?" He shook his head. "She's not fit for anything as far as the GRU is concerned."

"But still is for us?"

"Of course, but let's review what we've learned so far. Boris Luzhkov, who appears to have been a drunken idiot most of the time, heard of the unexpected meeting of the Big Four and decided to cover himself with glory by arranging to have them assassinated by a man called Ali Selim whom he'd obviously dealt with frequently. I get a hunch that Bounine was not too happy about this but agreed to go along, not really having any choice. After midnight Monday morning, they met Ali Selim, the hit was set up, and they returned to the Embassy. What's the next step?"

"Bounine appeared in Luzhkov's office to ask him if he knew that Tania Kurbsky, who was supposed to be alive, had actually died of typhoid in January 2000, and Luzhkov said he didn't."

Lermov said, "Let's accept that Luzhkov genuinely didn't know that Tania was dead, which would mean Bounine didn't either, so where had he got the truth about Tania from?"

"I'd say from Kurbsky," Ivanov said. "He and Bounine were comrades in Afghanistan, he had access to Bounine's encrypted mobile phone. He phoned Bounine with news about a shooting in Mayfair. They may have been more in touch than we realize."

"And where did Kurbsky get it from?" Lermov nodded as if to himself. "But of course. Major Giles Roper, no one more qualified to unlock the secrets of cyberspace."

Ivanov smiled wryly. "I shouldn't imagine a Code 9 Restriction held up Roper for very long."

"I agree," Lermov said. "And then we have the shouting match with General Ferguson, who threatens the Embassy with reprisals and says he knows all about Kurbsky, would help him in any way he could, and mentions that the Americans were grateful he'd helped Blake Johnson. We know how valuable Johnson is to the White House. So where are we?"

Ivanov said, "I tell you one thing. I'm certain Alexander Kurbsky is out there in the hands of Ferguson and his people. Luzhkov and Bounine, I'm not sure. What do you think? You're the expert on terrorism and covert operations."

"Kind of you to say so, but I've always fancied the idea of writing a novel, and this whole business would be a thriller. Kurbsky, the gallant hero, blackmailed because the sister he thought dead is serving life, and he agrees to infiltrate the enemy elite group, his reward being her release."

"Who turns out to be dead."

"Not really very funny, when you think about it," Lermov said. "A man like Kurbsky, what would he do when he found out that he'd been used so badly?"

"Go on the warpath, I'd say."

"Of course he would, and, like you, I believe he's out there and very probably with Ferguson and his people.

Bounine was his close friend, we know that, so perhaps he's gravitated to Kurbsky. Luzhkov is a total mystery still, but we can find out about this Ali Selim. It's a common name, but he probably has a record. Go and get that moving."

"And you, Colonel?"

"I'm going to have another session with Greta. I'm intrigued by this Blake Johnson business and the man in the black hood not being Dillon but Kurbsky. What's that all about? Be off with you, and you can join me when you've seen to the Ali Selim thing."

So once more to the interrogation cell, where Greta Bikov waited under the impassive gaze of Sergeant Stransky and her colleague. She was seemingly calm, and yet a nerve twitched in her right cheek, and she stirred in her chair as if uncomfortable. She made the mistake of starting before Lermov did.

"I don't think there's anything more I can tell you, Colonel. I seem to have covered everything."

"You will allow me to be the judge of that," Lermov said, and the door opened behind him, and Ivanov entered. He took up his position again, leaning against the wall.

"Everything's in order, Colonel. They're processing the Ali Selim query now. As soon as anything turns up, we'll know about it."

"I'm obliged to you, Captain Ivanov." Lermov opened his file and gave Greta his full attention. "Everything you've told us so far has made sense, though aspects of it can't be fully confirmed. Now I would like you to cast your mind back to tell us how Bounine told Colonel Luzhkov of the death of Tania Kurbsky. You said that he also referred to a man in a black hood."

"Yes, but I've already told you about that."

"Refresh my memory," Lermov said.

"He said the man in the black hood who'd saved Blake Johnson wasn't Dillon at all, it was Kurbsky, who couldn't bear the idea of someone else ending up in Station Gorky like his sister."

"And had you heard any reference to a man in a black hood before?"

"Yes, it was earlier, I think. Something had gone wrong involving two GRU guys called Oleg and Petrovich, a moronic couple who provided a little muscle when it was needed. The Embassy has a deal with a private airfield in Essex called Berkley Down. We book Falcons out of there for the Moscow run. Luzhkov told me to have one standing by on Sunday and said Oleg and Petrovich would be escorting somebody there for an onward flight to Moscow."

"And you've no idea who?"

"God, no, it was a high-security thing, but late on Sunday night when Bounine was with him I listened in."

"Why?"

"Oleg and Petrovich had phoned in from out of town asking for transport and, when they arrived, they were in a damaged state. Petrovich had an injured hand, and Oleg was holding a bloodstained rag to his right ear. They ended up in sick bay."

"And what did you hear Luzhkov say?"

"He was very angry and threatened to have them transferred to a penal regiment. Bounine asked him if he believed the man in the hood was Dillon, and Luzhkov said that Dillon was famous for shooting off half an ear."

"And that's all?"

"Absolutely."

Lermov nodded, thinking about it, then said, "That will be all—for the moment anyway."

Suddenly, her anger flared. "You're not putting me into a cell overnight?"

"Lieutenant, you are a serving officer in the Russian Army. We may not have penal regiments for females, but there are other things that could happen to you, so take care."

"I'm sorry," she said desperately.

He ignored her. "Take her."

She went out, totally dejected, between the two sergeants.

Ivanov said, "What now?"

"Check with London again. I'd be interested to know if Oleg and Petrovich are still on the roster."

"We should be able to get that on our computer staff records, Colonel. It will only take a minute."

He hurried out, and Lermov sat there, thinking about it. Things were certainly coming together, but of course you always needed luck in any kind of investigation, and he got exactly that a few minutes later when Ivanov returned.

"Excellent news, Colonel, Oleg and Petrovich were transferred from London two months ago. Indifferent fitness reports. They're right here in Moscow, attached to the field infantry training school on general police duties."

"And still GRU?"

"Yes, Colonel."

"Something of a comedown, I would have thought. Go and arrest them, Peter, and, if anyone objects, use this." He produced the Putin letter and passed it over.

"My pleasure, Colonel," Ivanov told him, and rushed out.

7

A little later, Ivanov called in. "I've got them, Colonel, a thoroughly unpleasant couple. Greta Bikov was right to describe them as moronic."

"Did they give you any trouble?"

"Not really, they've been drinking and they're generally surly and cocky. The duty officer at the training school was only a lieutenant, so as I outranked him, he accepted the situation without fuss. I didn't have to use the letter."

"Where are you?"

"Almost with you. I'm in a standard military police secure van. I'm up front with the driver. I've put them in the rear with two police sergeants, and they thought that was a great joke. It's the booze, of course."

"Well, let's try to wipe the smiles off their faces. I'll wait for you in the interrogation cell we used for Greta Bikov."

He went out on the walkway and found the old tea lady pushing her trolley towards him. She stopped and poured a glass of tea from the samovar without a word. He accepted it and gave her a banknote.

"I can't change that," she said.

He drank the hot tea gratefully. "That's all right, *babushka,* maybe you still have a cigarette to spare from that packet I gave you."

She produced the pack of Marlboros from her smock pouch and extracted one carefully. "They won't like you smoking it."

"Then they can lump it, *babushka.* I'm a colonel, a full colonel."

She produced a plastic lighter and flicked it on for him, and, as he blew out smoke, she smiled for the first time since he'd known her. "I like you, *tovarich,*" she said.

"And why do you like me, *babushka*?"

"Because the truth about you is that you don't give a toss."

"Absolutely right, *babushka.*" He was laughing as he walked away.

When he went into the interrogation cell, he found a police sergeant on either side of the door and Oleg and Petrovich sitting behind the table, still handcuffed. Ivanov was sitting near the door and jumped up.

"Prisoners present as ordered, Colonel."

They were so drunk, they started to laugh, and Oleg said, "Is he taking the piss? I mean, this has gone far enough. We're lieutenants in the GRU, or hadn't you noticed?"

Lermov walked around the table slowly, the cigarette still in his mouth, and stood looking down at them, then gently stubbed it out, and said to the two sergeants at the door, who were looking grim and flexing their clubs, "The left leg first on each of them, if you please."

They moved in, clubs swinging, and both of the men howled and went down. The sergeants pulled them on their feet. Ivanov had seldom seen two drunks sober up so fast. Oleg was actually sobbing.

"Let's get one thing clear. The sergeants will be quite happy to move to your right leg and then each arm in turn, but I detest violence, so listen carefully. Captain Ivanov, if you please!"

Ivanov read the letter. When he was finished, Lermov said, "My warrant from Prime Minister Putin gives me total authority over your destiny. I shall now question you on certain matters relating to your service in the London Embassy that involved you. If you do not tell me the exact truth about what happened, you will be reduced to the ranks and posted to a penal regiment."

They stared at him dumbly, total dismay on their faces. Lermov held up the Putin letter. "This warrant from your Prime Minister gives me the power to do this. I have no more time to waste. Give me your answer."

"Anything, Colonel," Petrovich mumbled.

"That's right, sir," Oleg joined in. "Just tell us what you want to know."

"Then sit down and let's get started."

———————

From then on, it was easy, and they fell over themselves to pour out the truth. Colonel Luzhkov had offered them this very special job to kidnap an American, Blake Johnson, who had just arrived in town and was staying in a top-floor suite at a hotel in Mayfair. A truck that did laundry pickups in the area was available to them, and uniforms to go with it. They explained how they'd gone up in a service elevator, abducted Blake Johnson, returned to the truck, hid him in the rear, and driven away, their destination a private airfield at Berkley Down, where a Russian Falcon was waiting to fly him to Moscow and onwards to Station Gorky.

Then came the business of the truck being forced to stop, an unexpected passenger in the rear, the man in the black hood, who spoke the kind of Russian you'd expect from a Mafia lowlife, who shot Petrovich in the hand and blew away half of Oleg's right ear, then drove off with Blake Johnson in the truck and left them to phone the Embassy for help. Luzhkov had been furiously angry, had referred to the man in the black hood as someone named Dillon, because this Dillon had a reputation for shooting half an ear off people who offended him.

So that was it, all there, a perfect piece of the jigsaw. They sat there, broken and humble, and Lermov didn't even feel grateful. *Animali,* the Italian word for "scum," was the only way to describe them. Blake Johnson was the enemy, and Lermov knew him only by reputation, but that didn't mean one couldn't feel distaste for what had been planned for him.

He considered it all, then stood and said to the sergeants, "Take these men to a holding cell." He turned to Ivanov. "Put the necessary documentation in hand for their demotion to the ranks and transfer them to an appropriate penal battalion."

Both men gasped in disbelief. "But you promised, Colonel, that if we told you the truth, we'd be all right."

"Yes, I lied, but you thoroughly deserve it." He went to the door, which one of the sergeants opened for him, and walked out.

Back in the corner of the officers' bar, he sipped tea and reviewed the situation. It was certainly all coming together, thanks to patient questioning and sound detective work. They were almost there, and then Ivanov came in and sat down opposite him, an edge of excitement to him. He put a transcript on the table.

"Just in from London. Excellent stuff, so I spoke to Major Chelek to confirm."

Lermov poured another glass of tea. "Just tell me."

"GRU computer experts said the London Embassy can access Scotland Yard files, and no one named Ali Selim has a criminal record. The computer checked on other people of that name resident in London and found several, but one seemed particularly interesting—because he was dead."

Lermov said, "Explain."

"Remember the *Garden of Eden* sailed downriver on Monday afternoon? Well, this Ali Selim was fished out of the river at Wapping two days later."

"Drowned, of course."

"No, his throat was cut."

"I see. What is the source of this information?"

"Grafton Street Morgue in Wapping, where the body was delivered by the paramedics who recovered it. It's all there in the morgue records. A brief report of the recovery of the body, identity and address in a wallet found on the body. He lived at a place called India Wharf on the Thames. The autopsy report indicated that due to possible contamination of the body, cremation was urgent, and this took place at the morgue facility the same day."

"I must say, Ferguson is definitely turning out to be the ruthless bastard of legend. Is that everything?"

"Major Chelek has gone down himself to this India Wharf where Selim lived to see what he can find out. He'll be in touch as soon as possible."

"Then let's have something to eat until he does."

An hour in the canteen, a heavy vegetable broth that was a meal in itself with black bread, and, once again, a glass of the rough red wine.

"Peasant food," Lermov said. "In spite of the delights of the modern world, we still love the kind of food our grandparents enjoyed."

They went back to the office, and, ten minutes later,

Ivanov's secure mobile sounded. "Put it on speaker," Lermov ordered.

Ivan Chelek's voice was clear and firm. "Well, here I am on India Wharf, looking out over the Thames, Ivanov. It's raining."

"I'm here also," Lermov told him. "We'll make this a conference call. So where are we at?"

"It seems to be an anchorage surrounded by old Victorian warehouses, most of them boarded up just waiting for a developer to knock them all down. Four motorboats tied up for the winter with canvas covers. No sign of any kind of habitation."

"So Ali Selim didn't live there."

"Oh yes he did. There's a lane at the top with a few old terrace houses and a corner shop. I walked up, tried the shop, and struck gold."

"Go on," Lermov told him.

"The people living in the houses are all Islamics of one kind or another, and the shop was their general store, run by an aging Arab named Hussein. We had the place to ourselves. I'm an old Iraq hand, as no one knows better than you, so I went and locked the front door, took a pistol from my pocket and five hundred pounds in fifties, and put them on the counter. I told him in Arabic that he had a clear choice. He could answer my questions or I would blow his brains out."

"And?" Lermov said.

"Proved a mine of information. Ali Selim was born in London. His father was a seaman off a freighter, in the old days when the Pool of London was thriving. He met and married a cockney white woman. It seems Ali was a very frightening and violent man from his youth. He went to prison on many occasions for robbery, assault, that kind of thing."

"And yet there is no police record on him at Scotland Yard," Ivanov observed.

"Obviously, his record had been wiped clean," Lermov said. "As if he never existed."

"He existed all right," Chelek said. "Apparently, he had relatives in Afghanistan who helped with the poppy trade, and he was into the drug business and made big money."

"Was he interested in the Islamic movement?"

"Not at all. He drank very heavily and made strange remarks when he was drunk, deriding Islam, and mocking such things as the bombing attacks in London by British-born Muslims, saying that he'd done far more than they ever could imagine. He once said to Hussein that they should have come to Belfast with him in the old days and seen some real action."

"Did he indeed?" Lermov said. "So we've established that he was a thoroughly frightening individual who would appear to have some sort of terrorist links in his past, and that's if he is to be believed. Is that it, then?"

"Not quite. Ali Selim lived in a barge anchored in the basin here. He also had an orange motorboat with a huge outboard motor. It was called *Running Dog,* and he boasted it could do forty knots. Both vessels have disappeared."

"Has Hussein got any explanations for that?" Lermov asked.

"Yes, he sometimes looks after an old greyhound for his son. On the Monday that the meeting was taking place on the *Garden of Eden,* he locked up his shop at one o'clock and walked the dog down the street, leading to the wharf. As he got to the end of the wharf, he drew back because he saw two men in fluorescent-yellow-and-black jackets being urged off the barge by Ali and pushed towards the *Running Dog.* The thing is, their hands were tied. Ali was wearing a similar jacket and carrying a large canvas bag."

"Were they talking?"

"It looked like it, but Hussein couldn't hear a thing. He said the weather was terrible, pouring rain, and mist so thick that the *Running Dog* disappeared as it roared away."

Ivanov said, "And Hussein turned right round and went straight back to the shop and minded his own business."

"I'd say a sensible thing to do, considering his experience of the kind of man Ali Selim was," Lermov told him.

"So what does all this say to us?" Chelek asked.

Lermov said to Ivanov, "I recall you telling me about a small riverboat exploding, an overheated gas tank or something."

Chelek said, "You think that was the *Running Dog?*"

"I've never been so certain of anything in my life," Lermov said. "This is how I write the story. Ali Selim sets out in the *Running Dog* to attack the *Garden of Eden,* probably with a bomb of some kind. I feel that his two prisoners were Kurbsky and Bounine."

"But what happened to Luzhkov?" Ivanov demanded.

"I cannot answer that."

"But what do you feel most probable?"

"Ali Selim is the person most likely to have had the answer. His barge has obviously been spirited away by Charles Ferguson, who has also had his criminal file at Scotland Yard wiped clean. It's as if he never existed. The crematorium at Grafton Street Morgue has taken care of that, reducing him to six pounds of gray ash. It was possibly an oversight on Ferguson's part not to have the morgue records wiped out, too."

"So it's all over?" Chelek said.

"Not at all," Lermov replied. "I must make my report to the Prime Minister, but what do I tell him? That Alexander Kurbsky is alive and well and safe in the hands of a most bitter enemy of Russia, and that Charles Ferguson has won again?"

"When can I expect to see you in London?" Chelek asked.

"I'll only know that when I've seen him and he confirms my task. Then I'll need time to work out a plan of action. In the meantime, you must continue to run things over there, Ivan. How did you end things with Hussein?"

"I told him that I had it on good authority that Ali Selim was dead."

"And what did he say to that?"

"He shrugged, and said in Arabic it was his time."

"I suppose it was. Take care, old friend."

Ivanov switched off his mobile. "So what now, the Prime Minister?"

"No avoiding it." Lermov patted him on the shoulder. "You've done well, and I definitely intend to take you with me to London when I go, but there's still work to be done here, so let's get started. I'll summarize what's happened, and you can take it down on your laptop."

"Then what?"

"Forward it to the Prime Minister's Office and request an interview."

It was lightly snowing on the way to the Kremlin but pleasantly warm in what had once been Volkov's office. They'd presented themselves in good time for the interview, but were still waiting an hour after the designated time.

"Do you think he's making us wait deliberately?"

"We're not important enough, Peter."

"Well, I believe that we are still one of the greatest nations on earth," Ivanov said. "And considering the state of the world today, that he has time for us at all surprises me."

"I agree, but I think it only proves how passionately he is involved with events in London."

The door in the paneled wall swung open, and Vladimir Putin entered, immaculate in the black suit and white shirt he favored.

"My apologies, gentlemen, one economic crisis after

another seems to be the norm for the world we live in. I did find time to read your résumé of the Kurbsky affair. Succinct and to the point, Colonel."

"Captain Ivanov's help has been invaluable, and I intend to take him with me when I take up my duties in London."

"Excellent." He sat down at the desk. "I agree with the conclusions in your report, Colonel. Luzhkov was foolish and stupid, and, like you, I believe he has paid the ultimate price. Kurbsky and possibly Bounine are alive and well and in the care of Charles Ferguson and his people. They have all been a thorn in our side for too long. One attempt after another to eliminate them has failed, and it's time we do it right."

"So what do you want me to do?"

"As I said before, Colonel, destroy them, Charles Ferguson and all his people. Finish them off, Colonel, once and for all. The British are not our friends, they grant asylum to dissidents, traitors to our country. The British Government allows their territory to be used as a launching pad to fight Russia. This will send them a message."

"If I may, there are still many Russians living in London, many of them oligarchs and friends," Lermov said. "But the world financial crisis has altered things. Many who had billions have lost billions. They're keeping their heads down and trying to recoup. They wouldn't like an ill wind blowing in from the Motherland."

"I haven't the slightest sympathy for those bastards. If you do need help in that area, remember that the State owns Belov International, and the chief executive officer is Max Chekhov. He's the only oligarch I have any time for and that's because he's in my pocket."

"I'll bear that in mind."

"Think of the Moscow Mafia, Colonel. Someone tries to rock the boat by moving into someone else's territory, and what does the boss do? He sends for an expert, a specialist, usually a stranger from out of town, to handle it."

"I'll take that on board and consider it, Prime Minister."

"But at your soonest, Colonel, at your soonest. You have my letter. Use it. Don't allow anyone to stand in your way." He got up to go, opened the door in the paneling, and paused. "Those fools, Oleg and Petrovich, I approve of you dumping them in a penal regiment."

"It seemed appropriate," Lermov said.

"But what about this Greta Bikov? That her confessions have been of great assistance can't be denied, but she is totally untrustworthy. Her behavior speaks for itself."

"And what would you suggest, Prime Minister?"

"I have a perfect solution. There is a small GRU detachment at Station Gorky, am I right?"

"I understand so."

"Transfer her to it on a one-year detachment."

He was gone. Ivanov turned. "Poor, silly little bitch. Will you tell her or do you want me to do it?"

"I'll do it, and, in a way, Putin's right. It could be the making of her. At least she's not being kicked out of the army. Let's get out of here. We've got a lot to do."

"Anything special for me?"

"Yes, Max Chekhov. Dig out everything about him."

"And what are you going to do?"

"Give Greta Bikov her new orders."

Which was not as bad as he expected. Sergeant Stransky had brought her into the interrogation cell again, where she had found Lermov waiting, and he told her the worst.

Her face was blank, eyes fixed and staring, as he delivered the news. "This is the personal decision of the Prime Minister."

Of all things, there was not only a kind of relief but a slight smile. "Putin himself? I'm honored. I'm sure that he's only thinking what's best for me. I know I did wrong." She smiled fully. "After all, it's only a year. You've been very kind, Colonel."

She rose and turned to Stransky, who took her arm and led her away. "My God," Lermov said softly. "She thinks she's got away with it."

He laughed wryly as it suddenly occurred to him that she had, and he got up and went in search of Ivanov.

He found him sitting at his computer. Lermov paused, and then asked, "How did it go with Greta?"

"I got the impression she thinks she's come up smelling of roses. God help the male members of staff at Station Gorky, she'll wreak havoc. What have you got?"

"Max Chekhov, age fifty, married but no children. Wife lives with her widowed mother in St. Petersburg, but he never visits. A university degree in general engineering, He worked as a road builder and military engineer in Afghanistan. Wounded in a roadside ambush and sent home when we still thought we were winning the war. Worked for many construction firms, and then came the crazy years, oil and gas in Siberia and all the other things. Like with most oligarchs, it just happened, and, there he was, a billionaire. He loves London, booze, and women, in that order, but he's a shrewd operator, which is why Putin made Chekhov chief executive officer when the State took over Belov International."

"I suppose the argument is that as a rich man in his own right, he's to be trusted," Lermov said. "Where does he live?"

"There's a company house off South Audley Street in Mayfair, which he never uses personally but leaves to visiting dignitaries. His personal treat is an exclusive apartment on Park Lane—where, apparently, he was shot in the knee one night by a hit man delivering flowers. It's thought to be the work of these gangsters, the Salters."

"Well, they do get round, don't they? Anything else?"

"A place off the West Sussex coast called Bolt Hole. It's reached by a causeway passing through a marsh, and it's private. There was an article about Chekhov buying the place and wanting to build a helicopter pad and the authorities forbidding it because of the marsh and the birds being protected. There's a photo of him, if you want to see it. He agreed not to build the helicopter pad and said he's fallen in love with the island."

"Show me," Lermov said, and Ivanov obeyed. Chekhov wore a reefer coat and leaned on a walking stick, had long hair and dark glasses. "He looks pleased with himself."

"Well, he would be, having bought that place," Ivanov said. "It looks bloody marvelous to me. Here's another photo from the same newspaper. A strange name, Bolt Hole. I wonder what it means?"

"Probably Saxon or something like that," Lermov said. "I think I'd like to see Chekhov. Handle it for me. Speak to him and get him here. Now, let's go have a drink."

In the bar, Ivanov said, "So it seems the Prime Minister won't be content with anything less than the destruction of Ferguson and his entire group."

"Which has been tried before."

"And failed."

"But it doesn't have to. You just need the right weapon. If you want to be certain of hitting the bull's-eye, you must be able to put the muzzle of your weapon against it and pull the trigger."

"Difficult when the target is people."

"Not really. The man who tried to assassinate Ronald Reagan walked right up to him and fired, in spite of the crowds and the security people," Lermov pointed out.

"But that implies sacrifice," Ivanov suggested.

"Of course, the principle beloved of suicide bombers, but your truly professional assassin plans to perform the act and survive to do it again, like Carlos the Jackal. Look how long he lasted."

"I see what you mean," Ivanov said.

"My studies of revolutionary movements and terrorism covers anarchist bombings in tsarist times, Fenian dynamiters when Queen Victoria was on the throne, and, in the twentieth century, everyone from the IRA to Al Qaeda. One thing is clear. Except for religiously motivated suicide bombers seeking an imagined salvation, the majority of terrorists would much prefer to survive."

"And live to fight another day?"

"Exactly."

"So how many are we talking about? Ferguson, Roper, the Salters, Dillon, and Miller . . ." Ivanov began.

"Plus Miller's sister, Monica Starling. She's Dillon's girlfriend now but working for Ferguson." Lermov nodded. "Blake Johnson."

"That adds up to eight," Ivanov said.

"Ten, if Kurbsky and Bounine are still alive and well and in Ferguson's hands."

"An invitation to a dinner party and a bomb under the table would take care of it," Ivanov said.

"Very amusing, but nothing is that certain in life. Somebody tried a bomb under a table at Wolf's Lair in the hope of catching Hitler out, and it was a conspicuous failure."

"Sorry, Colonel, I was obviously joking and the Prime Minister isn't. What do you make of that advice he gave you, when he said think of the Moscow Mafia and what they do when somebody's giving them a problem?"

"Send for an expert, a specialist, usually a stranger from out of town who nobody knows? Yes, I've been thinking about that."

"It sounds like a plot from a movie."

"But life often is," Lermov said. "Because cinema, in its simplicity, gets straight to the point by leaving out all the boring bits."

"I'm not certain what you mean, Colonel," Ivanov said warily.

"That the Prime Minister could be right. What we need is just such a man . . . and I know where he is."

"And where is that?" Ivanov was totally bewildered.

"The Lubyanka Prison. His name is Daniel Holley."

"He's British?" Ivanov asked.

"Oh, yes, an extraordinary man. And an even more extraordinary killer."

DANIEL HOLLEY

HIS STORY

8

Looking back at his life, Daniel Holley always felt it had started when he was twenty-one, when he had gone to Belfast to take a master's degree in business, but that was only because what had happened before was so ordinary.

He had been born in the city of Leeds in Yorkshire, where his father, Luther Holley, taught at the grammar school, an occupation he could afford, for there was money in the family and he had inherited early. At a rugby club dance one night, he had met a young nurse who had just finished her training at Leeds Infirmary. Her name was Eileen Coogan, and she came from a town called Crossmaglen in Ulster, a hotbed of nationalism, just across the border from the Irish Republic.

In spite of the fact that she was a Roman Catholic, he married her, for, as his first name implied, he was a

Protestant, though no one had ever known him to go to church. It was enough to make him refuse to allow the boy to be christened into the Catholic faith. "No Popery here," was his rather illogical cry, but his wife, well used to his bullying ways, let it be.

She exacted payment from him when she discovered that she could have no more children and insisted on returning to nursing—a kind of victory, as it turned out, for she did well over the years, and was a nursing sister when her husband suffered a pulmonary embolism one night, was rushed to hospital, and pronounced dead on arrival.

Daniel, a bright boy, was accepted at Leeds University at seventeen, and, by the time he was twenty, he was halfway through his final year, studying business and financial planning. He took those subjects not because they were the greatest things in life but because he seemed to have a talent for it. In actuality, having served in the OTC at school, he was attracted to the idea of joining the army and entering Sandhurst, for the weapons training he'd undergone in OTC appealed to him. But, once again, his father had said no. And then his father had died.

There was a good turnout at Lawnswood Cemetery, where they had the funeral, a few teachers from the school and old pupils. Through the forest of umbrellas, as people paused outside the entrance to the crematorium, he noticed a stranger standing on the edge of the crowd, about thirty years old from the look of him, with a handsome, rugged face. He wore a raincoat and tweed cap, and he looked like he was waiting for someone, and then Daniel's mother rushed to him, flung her arms around his neck, and hugged him fiercely. Daniel hesitated, then approached.

She turned, crying, "Oh, what a blessing this is. My nephew, Liam Coogan, come to pay his respects all the way from Crossmaglen."

He was smiling as he took Daniel's hand in a strong grip. "A bad day for it with the rain, but grand to see my only aunt after all these years, and to meet you, Daniel." He gave Daniel a strong hug. "To be honest, I didn't make a special trip. Your mother phoned mine with the news, and me on the ferry from Belfast to Heysham en route to London. Lucky I called home. They gave me the sad news, so I've diverted, as you can see."

"You'll stay the night with us," Eileen said.

"God bless you, I can't even come with you for the wake. I'm delayed already for important business in London, so I must be away. It was just that, as I was over by chance, maybe it was a sign from God that I came to you in your hour of need."

"And bless you for a kind deed." She kissed him, and turned to Daniel. "Take the car and see your cousin to the railway station."

"Now, that would be wonderful," Liam said. "There's an express to London in forty-five minutes."

"Then let's get going," Daniel said, and led him to the car.

As he was driving, Daniel started to speak. "There's something I want to get straight," he said. "All these years when we never saw you, never had any contact—that wasn't us, my mother and me. It was my father and his obsessive hatred of Catholics."

"Daniel, don't we all know that at Crossmaglen? God help us, but the old bugger must have really loved her to marry her in the first place."

"He was an overbearing bully who liked his own way, but I never doubted his love for her and hers for him."

"He never allowed you to be christened, I heard."

"That's right."

"Jesus, I've got a bloody Prod for a cousin. Your mother did keep in contact over the years. Writes regularly to my mother, always telling her not to write back, but she made telephone calls."

"Maybe they can get together now," Daniel said. "My mother could visit in Crossmaglen."

Liam was still smiling but different now. "You wouldn't want to do that. Crossmaglen is IRA to the hilt, Daniel. It's what the army calls bandit country. It'd be a bad idea to come back to Ulster at this stage of the Troubles." He changed tack. "I heard some of the guests talking, and you were mentioned. Only a few more months to your graduation, and you only twenty. Business and financial planning. Well, that's useful."

"What about you?"

"I went to Queen's in Belfast. Economics, politics. I taught for a while."

"And now?"

"This and that, wheeling and dealing." They drove

into the car park at the main railway station. "You have to turn your hand to anything you can in Belfast these days." He took out a wallet and produced a business card. It said "Liam Coogan, Finance & Business Consultant." "You can get me at that number anytime. It's an answering service."

For some reason, Daniel felt emotional. "If I'm ever over there, I will. It was kind of you to do that for my mother."

"You and she are family, Daniel, and that's the most important thing in the world."

He was out and gone, hurrying through the crowd, and Daniel switched on the ignition and drove away.

In 1981, with a first-class honors degree under his belt, it seemed natural to proceed to an MBA, and when he checked a list of suitable universities Queen's at Belfast jumped out at him. He was, after all, a half Ulsterman, though not born there. But there were roots, and perhaps it was time he sought them out.

His mother, recently appointed a matron, was slightly dubious. "Some terrible things happen over there," she said. "God knows, it's the country of my birth, but I'm happy to be out of it, and that's the truth."

"Well, let me see for myself," Daniel told her. "I'll get in touch with your nephew and see what he thinks."

It was three months since his father's funeral, and he had never tried to call the number on the card his cousin had given him. As Liam had said, it was an answering service, but it took his message, and Liam called back an hour later.

"It's grand to hear from you, and congratulations on your first-class honors."

"How did you know that?"

"Your mother talking to mine. They're at it all the time since your dad passed away. So what are you going to do? She was saying if it hadn't been for your dad, you'd have tried for Sandhurst and the army."

"Yes, I enjoyed my time with the OTC at school, but that's all in the past. I'm thinking of coming to Queen's and doing an MBA. What do you think?"

There was a long pause, then Liam said, "Jesus, Daniel, with your academic success you could take your pick of universities where life would be a lot less stressful. I'm not knocking Queen's, it's a damn good university, but Belfast is still a war zone, and you're English."

"No, I'm not, I'm half Irish," Daniel said.

"You're English every time you open your gob," Liam said. "And that won't go down well with a lot of people."

"So you're telling me not to come over?"

"Now, why would I do that? The Coogans have never taken kindly to being ordered what to do, and you're half a Coogan. Let me know when it's definite, but let me give you a piece of advice: make sure you have a passport with you when you come."

"But Ulster is part of the United Kingdom. Surely you don't need a passport when you enter the country?"

"Security is the name of the game here. The police and army have got complete power to stop, search, and question you anytime they choose. It's useful to have your passport with you as an identity card. Take care—and let me know what you decide."

"I'm going to come, Liam, that's a given."

"Stubborn young bastard, aren't you? On your own head, be it. Just stay stum when you come, and don't tell people what you are."

He started his course at Queen's later than usual, at the beginning of November, winter on the horizon. It seemed to rain a lot, although he didn't let that put him off, venturing downtown with a raincoat and umbrella, obviously sticking to the city center at first. In spite of the bad weather, he found himself enjoying what many people called the most dangerous city in the world. That was a matter of opinion, of course, but it was true that the Europa close to the railway station was the most bombed hotel in the world. He ventured in for a drink one time, and marveled at the extraordinary feats of bravery that had taken place there on the part of bomb-disposal experts.

His room in a hall of residence was a short walk from the university. A great deal of his work was personal research, but there were occasional seminars and lectures, so he did get the chance to sit in with people. There were students from all over the world and from all over England, but, for the majority of them, the accent of Ulster was unmistakable. You couldn't tell who was Catholic and who Protestant, and yet the war being waged in the streets outside was as much about the religious divide as anything else. Sitting in the common room of the students' union, or drinking in the bar and observing his fellows, there didn't seem to be any difference, but there was, and occasionally it surfaced.

After a general seminar one day, he stayed on to discuss something with his professor. Visiting the bar afterwards, he was hailed by two third-year students named Graham and Green who'd also taken part in the seminar. They were local students from Derry, which was all he knew about them except that they didn't appeal, particularly Green, with his greasy, unkempt hair and shabby jeans. His liking for the drink was also clear. A nasty piece of work, Daniel had decided, and he tried to avoid him.

"Come on, man," Green said. "You need a drink. What a bloody bore Wilkinson's seminar was. He gets worse all the time. Get us some beers, why don't you?"

Daniel joined them with reluctance, returning with three bottles from the bar, determined to be off of there in ten minutes. Green was already edging into drunkenness. "How's it going, my English friend? Someone said you were from Yorkshire."

Remembering Liam's advice, Daniel hadn't advertised his Ulster roots. "That's right."

"Are the girls any good where you come from?"

Daniel shrugged. "The same as they are anywhere, no different."

"Nice girls, are they, decent? Not like those cows over there?"

He indicated two girls sitting in the corner, chatting over coffee. They were perhaps eighteen, in denim skirts and jumpers.

"I don't understand," Daniel said carefully.

"They're Fenian sluts," Green said. "They'd shag anybody."

Graham nodded seriously. "You'd need a condom there, they've probably got the pox."

"Because they're Catholics?" Daniel asked.

"It's a known thing," Green said. "So watch it."

"But how do you know I'm not a Catholic?"

Graham said, "Well, you've got a Yorkshire accent." He roared with laughter, then paused. "Here, you're not, are you?"

"What the hell has it got to do with you what I am?" Daniel turned and went out, angry and thoroughly depressed.

He walked back to the residence hall and discovered a message for him pinned to the bulletin board. It was from Liam, asking him to get in touch, so he did, and waited, and Liam came back to him half an hour later.

"How's everything?"

Daniel took a deep breath and swallowed his anger. There was no way he could tell Liam what had happened. "Fine, Liam, it's working out very well."

"That's good. Listen, I've a surprise for you. My wee sister, Rosaleen, is in town this weekend, staying with friends. She's a teaching assistant in an infant school. She's coming home Monday, but she's free Sunday night, Daniel, and a charmer. She'd love to meet you."

"And I'd love to meet her. Let's make it at my residence hall since we've never met, that's the easiest. I'll give you my verdict."

And she was a charmer, young and pretty, with black hair, reminding him totally of the dark Rosaleen of Irish legend. They called his room to tell him he had a visitor, but, as he was going downstairs, he knew it must be her the first time he saw her. She carried an umbrella, for it was raining outside, and wore a dark blue overcoat over a dress and ankle boots, a bag hanging by a strap from her left shoulder.

She smiled as he took her hand and reached up to kiss his cheek. "It's so grand to meet you, Daniel."

The only flies in the ointment were Green and Graham, who appeared from the common room at that moment. They looked astounded. "What's this, Holley, where have you been hiding it?"

Obviously the worse for drink again, and he took her hand. "Come on, Rosaleen, we'll go down the road and have a bite to eat."

As they wandered out, behind them Green said, "Rosaleen, did you hear that? She's a fucking Fenian."

Daniel started to turn, and she pulled him around. "Never mind them, they're just Protestant shites that can't keep their gobs shut."

She was calmly fierce, so he gave in, offered his arm, and they went down the road together. "Where would you like to go?"

"Oh, fish-and-chips in a café will do me fine, with a cup of tea, and you can tell me all about yourself."

They spent two hours enjoying the simple meal and discovering each other. He was extolling the joys of Wharfedale in the West Riding of Yorkshire, she the beauty of the South Armagh countryside, and they vowed to exchange visits. It was ten o'clock when they left. The rain had stopped, but the streets were Sunday-night empty.

"If we walk back to my residence hall, I could call a taxi," he said.

"Belfast taxis anytime of night cost a fortune, and that's when you can get one. It's not all that far to where I'm staying, fifteen minutes." She laughed. "Well, maybe twenty."

"Nothing at all," he said, offered her his arm. They waited for a white van that had been parked across the street to start up and drive past them, and then they began to walk.

It began to rain again, and she got the umbrella up, laughing, and they hurried on, and there was only the odd car passing, and then nothing, as they turned into an empty street, its shops locked up, with their lights on, and bare of parked cars, a police regulation to discourage bombers. A white van—was it the same one?—eased out of a street behind them, passed, and then braked, the driver and his passenger wearing black hoods. The rear doors burst open, and two more men jumped out wearing hoods, one of them holding a revolver.

Rosaleen cried out, and Daniel closed in on the man holding the revolver, grabbing for it with one hand and, in the struggle, tearing off the hood, revealing Green. Daniel shoved him away, still trying to wrench the weapon from Green's grasp, but another man had run around the van and grabbed him from behind.

"What the hell do you think you're doing?" Daniel shouted as he struggled, but Green, laughing madly, cried, "I'll tell you what we're doing, you fugger. We're Red Hand Commandos, and we're going to teach you and that Fenian bitch some manners."

Behind him, Green struggled to force Rosaleen into the back of the van, and Daniel heard it and her cry of despair, and then Green reversed his grip on the gun and struck Daniel a heavy blow across the side of the head, and that was the end of it.

Daniel came to in subdued darkness, his head throbbing and matted with blood, and discovered that he was in the back of the van, street light filtering in from the windscreen. He tried to sit up and found that his wrists had been tied in front of him with some rough cord. Raising his hands, he could see that the knot was large and had obviously been done in a hurry. He had no difficulty in getting his teeth into it and was free in a couple of minutes.

Heavy rain drummed on the roof, and he slid to the

rear and pushed open the doors with his feet, aware of the van's tool kit to one side. He opened it and found a tire iron. He hefted it in his hand for a moment, then got out.

He was in a cobbled courtyard, a wide gate behind him standing open, a streetlight beyond showing old and towering warehouses. He turned and found a four-story building. A light over a large painted sign revealed "Bagley Ironworks, White Lane, Belfast." The whole place looked old and decrepit, but there was a dim light inside, and he went up some stone steps and pushed the door open.

There were workbenches, a jumble of machinery, hoists hanging from above, rain drifting in, and a woman crying, then begging and pleading. He stood there frozen. Then she screamed, and somebody shouted, "Be quiet, you bitch," and there was the sound of a heavy blow.

As he started upstairs, the tire iron ready in his hand, he heard a sudden, desperate cry. "No, please, not that."

"Shut your gob" was followed by sustained blows, and a voice saying, "Stop it, you bugger, you'll kill her."

Daniel reached the top of the stairs and found the door half open. Green was sitting at a table, an open whiskey bottle beside him, fiddling with the Smith & Wesson. A door was open behind him, and suddenly it seemed very quiet.

A voice said, "Jesus, you fool, you *have* killed her."

Green turned to the open door. Daniel lurched forward and smashed him across the skull with the tire iron, then picked up the revolver just as Graham appeared in the doorway and shot him in the heart at point-blank range. As Graham was hurled backwards, Daniel took two quick paces forward and shot the next man he saw in the back of the head as the man started to turn.

The fourth man was old and wizened and shaking in terror. "For pity's sake, don't, I never laid a finger on her."

"Then why's your belt undone and your fly open, you lying bastard?" Daniel stepped close and put a bullet between the old man's eyes.

The sight of Rosaleen now was something that would stay with him always and change his life forever, make him a different man, for dead she was, beyond any doubt, and lying on what was presumably some janitor's bed. He found an old rug to cover her broken and defiled body.

He went back into the other room and he heard a moan. Green was stirring, and, almost without thinking about it, Daniel shot him in the head. He picked up the open bottle of whiskey, raised it, swallowed some down, and emptied the rest of it over Green's corpse.

"You Prod bastard, Green," he said. "Well, I'm a Prod bastard, too."

Looking around, he realized the place must have been an office of sorts in its day. There was a wall phone by the far door, and he went and tried it and, by some miracle, it still worked, so he did the obvious thing and called Liam.

Liam called back surprisingly quickly, for once. "Now then, Daniel, how are things going with you and Rosaleen?"

And Daniel told him.

He was sitting at the table, clutching the revolver, the blood oozing from the side of his skull, when Liam arrived almost an hour later, patted Daniel on the shoulder, and went straight into the janitor's room. When he came out, the look on his face was terrible to see.

There were half a dozen hard-looking men with him and two paramedics in green. Liam kicked Green's corpse, and said, "Get rid of this rubbish and his pals. Round the back in the river will do." He eased the gun from Daniel's grip. "I'll have that now, son."

"I couldn't save her, Liam."

"You did your best. I'd say four kills is a remarkable number for a beginner."

"And you're an expert, so you would know?"

"That's right, cousin. I've been with the Provisional IRA since the beginning. Red Hand Commandos are Protestants closely linked to the UVF. We'll make them pay."

"Nobody can make them pay for what they did to her."

"I know, son, I know." Behind him, two men brought Rosaleen out in a black body bag, supervised by a paramedic.

"What is this?" Daniel asked.

"We have an ambulance below. The police don't stop ambulances at night. We're going to take you to a convent down in the country, where the nuns are a nursing order and good friends of ours."

The other paramedic came forward and examined his head. "That's not good at all. We've got to do something about that and fast." He called to a couple of men. "Just take him down."

Which was really the end of it, because although Daniel remembered being on a stretcher in the ambulance across from the black bag, he couldn't recall a single thing about the journey afterwards.

St. Mary's Priory, it was called, and the Mother Superior, a Sister Bridget Blaney, was a qualified surgeon, for they were Little Sisters of Pity, a nursing order whose help was there for all who needed it, and, in troubled times, that was bound to include the IRA.

Coming to his senses, Daniel found himself coming out of an anesthetic in a recovery room. Sister Bridget herself, still wearing scrubs over her habit, was smiling gently, Liam anxious behind her.

"You'll be fine, Daniel," she said. "The faintest of cracks on the side of your forehead. Fifteen stitches will give you an interesting scar, but what you need is a solid week's rest in bed. Liam has told me of the circumstances here."

"Everything?" Daniel said weakly. "Rosaleen?"

"God rest that child's soul, for I knew her well. She is in heaven now, and I shall pray for her, and so must you."

He smiled weakly. "I'm not baptized in the faith, Sister, my father wouldn't have it, but my mother is a good Catholic and a matron at a hospital in Leeds."

"Well, I'm sure she mentions you in her daily prayers, and I will, too."

"Even though I'm a Protestant?"

"Even that," she said cheerfully. "But you must rest

now, and Liam has to leave to take Rosaleen home to Crossmaglen and her family, so say your good-byes."

She went out, and Liam said, "Now, do as she says and take it easy. I'll be back."

Daniel said, "Just tell me one thing. You and Provos . . ."

"What about it?"

"You're not just another volunteer, you're bigger fish than that?"

Liam took his right hand and held it tight. "After what you did for my beloved sister, I count you closer than any brother. No secrets between us ever, so, yes, I am."

Daniel nodded weakly. "I understand Éamon de Valera's father was Spanish, and it was his mother who was Irish. It's the same for me, if you think of it, except my father was Yorkshire."

Liam frowned slightly. "What are you saying?"

"That maybe you could use me. I know I'm still on morphine and things are a little fuzzy, but I don't think there's a place in my life for the old Daniel anymore. I killed four men a few hours ago, face-to-face and as close as you could get, and it didn't bother me. God bless Rosaleen, and I hated them for what they did to her, but to be able to do what I did, Liam." He shook his head. "There was a devil inside me, deep and hidden, but he's found his way out."

Liam's face was grave. "Rest, son, that's what you need. I'll take your love to the family, and I can tell you now you have theirs for eternity."

Rosaleen's funeral was on Wednesday afternoon, three days after Liam left with her body, and the following morning, to Daniel's astonishment, there was a knock on his door, it opened, and his mother entered, Liam behind her.

"My God, I can't believe it," Daniel said.

She kissed him, and pulled a chair forward. "Your aunt spoke to me the moment she received the news from Liam. There's a direct flight to Belfast from Leeds Bradford Airport. I was able to be at the funeral. I know, Daniel, the whole dreadful story and what those swine did to my beloved niece."

"And what I did to them?" Daniel said.

"Trouble, violence, the gun, is the history of Ireland, Daniel. I was born to it, and the history of the Coogan family is full of it. What you did had to be done, a terrible deed. How could I love you the less for it, but I agree with Liam. It's best you go away for a while, leave the country, in case there's even the slightest chance of this being held at your door."

It was interesting that Liam had said it to her, but he let that go as she got up. "You're away, then?"

"Yes, Liam has one of his men taking me to the airport now. I love you dearly. Keep in touch any way you can," and she was away.

"The shock of my life, that," Daniel said. "Now, what's all this about me going away?"

Liam now took the chair. "What you were saying about joining us? Now that your head's clear, do you still feel the same way?"

"More than ever."

"I have a suggestion. We can't manage Sandhurst for you, though I know you had an interest in going there, but we do have good relations with our Islamic friends. We've sent people with great success to Algiers, where we have an excellent contact. All this costs money, but we have plenty of that coming in from the States, and Qaddafi's been more than friendly to us."

"What happens when I get to Algiers?"

"You'll be passed from hand to hand until you reach a training camp deep in the desert. By the time they've finished with you, you'll be an expert in weaponry of every description, explosives, the mechanics of bomb making, hand-to-hand fighting, assassination." He shrugged. "What else can I say? You're academically gifted, you could get a job in the City of London anytime you wanted. Or you could do this."

"That was then, this is now. My path has changed, Liam. I must follow it."

"Your choice, Daniel. I've had one of my people in Belfast remove your things from your room, and we've dropped a beautifully presented letter with a scrawled signature to Professor Charles Wilkinson, saying you're having to leave for urgent family reasons."

"Well, that's it, then." Daniel smiled. "When do I go?"

"As soon as Sister Bridget says you're fit."

"Can I keep in touch with you?"

"No problem. I'm your control. You have my card, remember. It was a good thing you had your passport in your pocket that night. I'll be back for you as soon as she agrees, and then it's over the border, and we'll see you off from Dublin."

The person who emerged from the desert oasis of Shabwa at the age of twenty-three bore little resemblance to the Daniel Holley who had entered it. He was a thoroughly dangerous man in every way, as he reported as ordered to the man in Algiers who had received him in the first place, one Hamid Malik, a shrewd businessman whose line was general shipping in the Mediterranean. It was a front for darker matters, and he handled the needs of a number of organizations involved, as he liked to describe it, in the "death business." The PIRA were clients, and their money was good, which was all that mattered, for he was never a man to make judgments.

Sitting opposite Daniel in the heat of his office in Algiers, with an electric fan spinning on the desk, he said, "Remarkable, Daniel. You went in a troubled boy, and the reports from the camp say you are now a man to be reckoned with."

"So what comes next?"

"Thanks to the good offices of Colonel Mu'ammar Qaddafi, the *Kantara,* with a substantial cargo of assorted weaponry, is waiting in the harbor now for you to board her. Her destination is the coast of County Down in Northern Ireland." He pushed a large canvas bag across. "There are fifty thousand pounds in there, Qaddafi's gift to your cause, and the arms are free. There's also a letter from Liam Coogan for you."

"Which you probably opened?"

"I am a careful man, Daniel, and you have much to prove. Allah protect you."

The *Kantara* proved to be a rust bucket, with a crew of ten reasonably villainous Arab seamen who showed a certain amusement when he boarded. The captain was named Omar, and he smiled a lot.

"Ah, the moneyman." He nodded at Daniel's bag. "A little large for my safe, but we can squeeze it in." They were standing at the bridge rail.

"That's not necessary," Daniel told him. "Presumably, there's a key for the cabin door?"

"Certainly, you will find it on the inside."

The crew, grouped below, seemed to find the whole thing funny, muttering amongst themselves and laughing. One of them, a Somali in a soiled white T-shirt and jeans, said, "A chicken for the plucking, this one. What will they send next?"

Daniel didn't react. He understood exactly what the man had said and the implied threat. A legacy of his time at the training camp was reasonable Arabic, but, as his chief instructor had always said, it was sensible to keep quiet about it, prepared for trouble armed with information an enemy didn't know you had.

On the first day at sea, lying on the bunk in his cabin with the bag in a locked cupboard underneath, he listened to the drunken voices of the crew, who were squatting under deck lights in the stern. It was obvious that, as far as they were concerned, he was never going to reach his destination. He reached under his pillow, took out a Browning pistol, pushed it into the waistband at the back of his linen slacks, and went out.

The ship's bosun, Hussein, had the wheel, and Omar was in the stern, having a drink and laughing with the men. Daniel slid down the short ladder, hands on the rails, and they all were suddenly aware of him.

The Somali spoke before anyone else. "So here he is, the boy trying to do a man's job."

Daniel produced the Browning and shot him between the eyes, knocking him against the rail, the skull fragmenting. The shock was complete, and the crew cowered, not knowing what to expect. The *Kantara* itself started to veer to port, and Daniel swung around to find that Hussein had left the wheelhouse and was raising an AK-47 rifle. He shot him twice, and Hussein bounced against the front of the wheelhouse, the rifle flying from his hands. He fell across the bridge rail and tumbled to the deck.

Daniel turned to Omar, and said in Arabic, "I'm sure you like a neat and tidy ship, so I suggest the crew dispose of these two over the side and wash the deck down, and that you get up that ladder and behind the wheel. We appear to be going round in circles, and that won't do, because my destination is Northern Ireland."

Eight days later, they drifted in to the County Down coast, fishing nets draping the deck as per Liam's instructions in the letter that Malik had given Daniel. In the early darkness, two trawlers came alongside and tied up, Liam leading the way, the man with him joining with the crew of the *Kantara* to transfer the cargo.

Liam embraced Daniel and followed him to his cabin, where the bag was passed over. "What the hell's been going on? This radio message to Malik? 'Two men lost overboard but proceeding'?"

"I had trouble with the crew, but I made my point early."

"You mean the two over the side had a bullet in them?"

"I do. Anyway, I don't feel disposed to the return passage."

"That's fine, we can send you back by air. I don't know what happened here, Daniel, but Malik is straight as a die."

"Then he should take more care about who he hires in future. Can I stay, Liam? Is there anything active I can do?"

"Not in Ireland. We invented the term 'informer,' and, sooner or later, most things surface. If what you did at the Bagley Ironworks that night ever came out, there are those on the other side who'd hunt you down if it was the last thing they ever did. In any case, the army is bringing in the SAS more and more, and we're feeling the effects, good men being killed or ending up in Maze Prison."

"You've trained me to be a soldier, remember that."

"Yes, and a hard man you can be, we know, but you've a top brain in that skull, especially in the ways of business, finance, and the like. You can serve us in other ways. There are people like us all over the world with aspirations in their own country. I want you to go into partnership with Hamid Malik. He's got a genuine business, and one that makes money, but with something else underneath, as you know. You're too valuable to be a foot soldier."

"And what will Malik think about the idea?"

"I think you'll find he'll discover it impossible to resist."

They walked out on deck, Liam carrying the bag, and found one trawler sailing away, the other still alongside. Someone shouted, "Are you coming or not, Liam? We're loaded."

"We're on our way." Liam crossed to the other deck, and Daniel glanced at Omar, standing at the bridge rail. "Look for me in Algiers, you bastard, and behave yourself."

As Liam had said, Hamid Malik agreed to the idea at once, and Daniel proved his worth very quickly, reorganizing the administrative side of the shipping business, introducing modern methods, technology, and computers. It meant a growth in the company's legitimate side that Malik had never anticipated. There were plenty of old-fashioned freighters available—rust buckets, perhaps, but improved at small cost—and they were perfect for the trade that Daniel expanded, working every port in the Mediterranean.

Underneath, with much assistance from Libyan sources,

they supplied more arms to the PIRA, to ETA in Spain, and, on one memorable occasion, dealt with a contract brokered by Liam for a weapons expert to go to South America on behalf of the Colombian terrorist organization, FARC.

Daniel had gone himself, invoking Liam's wrath. He had ended up on the run in deep jungle, engaged in one firefight after another with pursuing Colombian special forces, and finally managed to escape across the Peruvian border.

Back in Algiers, it was business as usual, the rise of Islam inexorable. Pushed by their contacts in Libya, the firm had to concentrate on supplying the demands of people like the PLO and Fatah, and Ireland was less and less important. Besides, the SAS special forces of the British Army had affected the PIRA so much that seventy to eighty percent of the latter's planned operations had to be aborted.

The First Gulf War came and went in 1991, and, in February of that year, an attempt to fire rockets on Downing Street from a parked van narrowly failed. Daniel read about it, then phoned Liam on the same old number. It was an hour before he called back.

Daniel said, "The Downing Street business. Is it one of yours? It looks like a typical PIRA hit." Over the years, their calls had been sparing.

"Absolutely not. We've no bloody idea whose it is. How're things at your end?"

"How do you think? The death business has been booming in the Middle East, haven't you noticed?"

"I've been thinking we might have to consider taking the fight to the British mainland again. The SAS are bleeding us dry. We may have to try something else."

"Such as?"

"Hitting at the British economy. I've got sleepers in London, Daniel, people who have ordinary jobs, ordinary lives, who just wait."

"For what?"

"To be needed. Over the years, many of them have attained a reasonable level of expertise in weaponry and the handling of explosives, by spending what we call a holiday at one of our training camps in the remote part of the west of Ireland."

"And you have lists?"

"I have indeed. The thing is, if there was ever a special job, when we needed to call some of them to action, would you be interested in being their controller?"

Daniel answered without hesitation. "Of course. When would it be?"

"Perhaps never. I just wanted to know what you thought. Have they got those newfangled mobile phones in Algiers yet?"

"Not that I've seen."

"Well, we've got them here, and they'll change your life. Stay well. I'll be in touch."

But it was November 1995 when he heard from Liam again. "A long time since you called," Daniel told him.

"I've been banged up in Maze Prison for four years,

missed out on the City of London bombing, but they gave me a compassionate early release. Lung cancer."

"Dammit, Liam, you should have told me. What are you up to?"

"The usual thing, organizing trouble for the enemy. We're going ahead with the idea we talked about before, a campaign in London next year that will shock the world. There's a courier package on its way to you."

"It was just delivered. I haven't had a chance to open it."

"Years ago, I organized my sleepers in cells of seven. There's one in particular, a woman and six men. I last activated them four years ago. Twelve small explosions rocked the West End of London for a two-week period. They got away with it, and I closed them down. The effect was incredible. People were walking on tiptoe for months. They all live in the Kilburn area of London. The package gives you their names and last-known addresses. I want you to go to London, speak to the woman in charge, and activate the cell. At this stage, I can't give them details of what they are required to do."

"Just hold themselves ready?"

"That's right. The whole purpose of the cell system is to maintain absolute security. I share no information about my sleepers with anyone on the Army Council, even the chief of staff."

"How do I persuade this woman I am from the right people?"

"She knows my name. What you say is: 'Liam Coogan sends you his blessing and says hold yourself ready.'"

"And that's all?"

"Tell her that when the time comes to strike, the word will be: 'The day of reckoning is here.' I'll call you and you will pass it on." He had a fit of coughing. "Jesus, I should give up the smoking. Do this for me, son."

"Of course I will, Liam."

"Take care."

Daniel thought about it for a while, then phoned the airport and booked a flight, trying to open the package with one hand as he did so.

It was Saturday, and Caitlin Daly was in the kitchen at the presbytery, enjoying a cup of tea with her mother, when the phone rang. She answered, and the voice with the slightest touch of a Yorkshire accent said, "Caitlin Daly?"

"Yes, who am I speaking to?"

"Liam Coogan sends you his blessing and says hold yourself ready."

The shock was immense, and she put a hand on the table to steady herself. "Who are you?"

"Just call me Daniel. I'm Liam's cousin."

"You don't sound Irish."

"My mother was from Crossmaglen. I'm sitting in a rear pew in the Church of the Holy Name. It's very peaceful, and not a soul here. Can I see you? My time is limited. I have a plane to catch to Algiers."

"Five minutes." She put down the phone, and her mother said, "Who was that, dear?"

"Business," Caitlin told her. "I've just got to go round

to the hospital." She reached for her coat and put it on. "I shan't be long."

Reading the notes on Caitlin Daly, her tragic experience as a child in Derry, her life till now in her mid-thirties, Daniel had expected to find her interesting, but he hadn't been prepared for her beauty. It left him momentarily speechless. But not Daly.

"What's going on?" she demanded.

Recovering his wits, he said, "I'm only here as a mouthpiece for Liam. I'm to tell you that you must consider your cell activated. There will be a campaign in London next year that will shock the world, though at this stage he can't give you details of what you are required to do."

"And how will we know?"

"When the time comes to strike, the word will be: 'The day of reckoning is here.' He will tell me, and I will pass on the order to you. Those are his instructions."

"So we wait?"

"That's what he told me, and this list for you, the members of your cell. Do the names of these six men still make sense?"

"Oh, yes, they are all members of the Hope of Mary circle at the refuge here at the hospice."

"Some sort of a club?"

"Much more than that. The sound basis for all our lives. I will call them together tonight and inform them of the situation."

He stood up. "You're a remarkable young woman, Caitlin."

"And you are a remarkable young man, Daniel."

He left her then and went out, the door banging, and she stood there, leaning on the back of the pew, shaking with emotion. The vestry door opened, and Monsignor Murphy came out. "Oh, it's you, Caitlin. I thought I heard voices. Who was it?"

"A stranger from a far-off land, Monsignor, who wandered in by chance. He's gone now. I sent him on his way." She took his arm. "Let's go to the presbytery and join Mother for a cup of tea."

That evening, having called the other members of the cell in turn, she met them in the chapel at Hope of Mary. Barry, Flynn, Pool, Costello, Cochran, and Murray joined her, and, filled with excitement and awe, they recited their own special prayer together at roughly the same time that Daniel Holley arrived in Algiers, although it would be many years before he discovered that meeting had taken place.

Two months later, Liam Coogan died of a sudden heart attack. Daniel was in Hazar at the time, brokering an arms deal for the Bedu Army in that region. Malik reached him on his mobile, but protocol was a delicate matter with Arab rulers, and it was a week before Daniel could get down to the port by Land Rover and find a plane to fly out. There was no possible way he could have got to Crossmaglen to attend the funeral, and there would have been great danger for him anyway. The funerals of Provo leaders like Liam were always very public affairs and attracted a great deal of media attention.

The real shock hit him when he went in the office, and Malik said, "A terrible tragedy, Liam going like that, but maybe it was a blessing, with a prolonged death from cancer to look forward to. At least, he'll have a smile on his face, wherever he is now."

"What's that supposed to mean?" Daniel asked.

"The Provisional IRA bombed the Canary Wharf business district in London two weeks ago."

Daniel was stunned. "I can't believe it. Is my mail here?"

"On your desk."

There was no message of any kind from Liam, but, on the other hand, if he'd wanted to speak to Daniel, he could have made contact by mobile, even in such a remote country as Hazar. The truth was that if Liam had been responsible in any way for the London bombing, he would have contacted Daniel and told him to activate the cell. He hadn't, because somebody else had been responsible. The chief of staff knew Liam was a dying man and had probably taken appropriate steps. So there'd been no message to Daniel to pass on to Caitlin Daly. Her cell would doubtless have taken pleasure in the news from London but been disappointed in their failure to be a part of it.

Should he phone her? He toyed with the idea and

dismissed it. The bombing had had nothing to do with Liam, that was the truth of it. He was a sick man, a dying man, and others had taken care of it.

So he put his sorrow behind him and got down to work, busy with deals to Pakistan, and then in June 1996 the Provos struck again, the center of Manchester devastated. But in the end, enough was enough, and the cease-fire of 1997 became peace the following year.

How had Caitlin Daly felt, he used to wonder, waiting for the call that never came, the call that was obviously so important to her? But it was over now and done with, until the next time. He smiled, wryly admitting to himself that nothing had changed, not really. There might be "peace," but the PIRA still ran the largest crime syndicate in Europe, so to hell with it.

Wars and rumors of wars, world terrorism, Islam on the march, Chechnya, Bosnia, there was no end to it. Business was business, as far as Malik was concerned, and Daniel went with the flow, operating on the theory that a good product and a pistol in the pocket was all you needed to get by. The life he had led had made him a total cynic, and that was all he believed in anymore.

His luck ran out in 2004. Always take care in the Balkans, Malik used to say, they kill each other at the drop of a hat. That was certainly true enough for Kosovo. Its Muslim citizens hated Serbs beyond anything else in the world and wanted independence.

Daniel had brokered three previous deals in Kosovo, for the Muslims had plenty of money to spend on arms, supplied by sympathizers in the oil-rich Gulf States. A Bulgarian agent named Kovac made the arrangements, and they were simple enough. All Daniel needed in the wild backcountry was a smuggler who knew the forest area and a suitable old Land Rover.

The driver's name was Mahmud, and he didn't speak, instead concentrating on his driving on the narrow mud tracks of the forest, a rifle at his feet. He was about fifty, unshaven, and with a walleye. Daniel had met him on one previous occasion and remembered that he'd been surprised at how good his English was, and Mahmud had explained that at nineteen he had gone to England, to Manchester, where his uncle lived.

"How far to this Lamu place?"

"Not long now," Mahmud said.

"I saw you a year ago. How are things now? Do the Serbs still raid the villages?"

"Sure they do. They rape our women, kill the children."

"Burn the mosques?"

"All those things, and sometimes the Russians come."

Daniel frowned. "I hadn't heard that. The Russians aren't supposed to be here. The United Nations wouldn't sanction it."

Mahmud shrugged. "They stay round here in the border country, special soldiers they call Spetsnaz."

Daniel sat there thinking about it and wondering what the Russian game was. That they were strong supporters of the Serbs was a given, so their presence in this Muslim part of Kosovo gave him pause for thought.

"Lamu, now, just up ahead." Mahmud pointed to a crossing of tracks where the trees thinned out, and there was a sudden engine roar as a large armored vehicle plowed through small trees from the right and braked to a halt. It was a Russian storm cruiser. Daniel recognized it at once.

"We've got trouble," he said as two armed men in uniform leapt out.

Mahmud picked up his rifle and scrambled out, firing a wild shot, then turning to run and was immediately shot down.

The soldiers walked forward slowly, weapons ready. Beyond them, several more had emerged from the storm cruiser and stood watching. Daniel opened the door and got out.

He'd picked up enough Russian over the years to understand it when one of the soldiers said, "Who are you?"

So he responded as a reflex, pulling the Browning from his pocket and shooting both of them in the heart, double-tapping, first one and then the other.

As he turned to run into the forest, there were cries of dismay from the other soldiers and a fusillade of shots as they ran forward. He was hit in the right thigh, he was aware of that, and then the left shoulder. He went down, and they were on him in seconds, boots swinging.

And then somebody shouted—a voice of real authority, he knew that—and then there was only the blackness.

He came to on a bed in a room with a beaded ceiling, feeling no pain, only a general numbness. He was heavily bandaged, and a man was sitting at his bedside in a high-back chair, smoking a cigarette. He wore combat fatigues with the tabs of a full colonel, and, when he spoke, his English was excellent.

"So you return from the dead, I think, Mr. Holley?" He smiled and held up Daniel's passport. "What an interesting man you are, but then I've heard of you before. In fact, many times over the years."

"Who are you, Spetsnaz?" Daniel croaked.

"The unit I'm with is, but I'm Colonel Josef Lermov of the GRU. Both of the men you shot have died."

"They usually do."

"My men wanted to kill you, but we can't have that. I'm sure you have a fascinating story to tell. The unit paramedic has patched you up, and we'll be returning to our base in Bulgaria, where you can have proper treatment. People like Kovac are seldom trustworthy, I find."

"My own fault," Daniel said. "I've taken the pitcher to the well too often. What happens now? A short trial in Moscow?"

"Oh, we don't do that these days. Very counterproductive. Moscow, certainly, but I fear it likely to be the Lubyanka. Not the death sentence. It is unfortunate that you killed those two men, but your death would be such a waste. I'm sure you tell a good story, and I look forward to hearing it. Sleep now."

He went out, clicking off the light. Daniel lay there, trying to make sense of it all, but his brain was befuddled by morphine. It was over, that was all he could think of, after all these years it was over, and he closed his eyes and drifted into sleep.

MOSCOW

9

A hell of a story," Ivanov said when Lermov was finished.

"He's been in the Lubyanka five years now. I did his first interrogation when we got back from the Kosovo mission, which was a highly illegal affair anyway, so he couldn't be put on trial in any public sense."

"Which explains him serving life imprisonment at the Lubyanka?" Ivanov said.

"Exactly. For the good of the State, rubber-stamped in some office."

"So he just sits there in his cell going slowly mad?"

Lermov shook his head. "I've kept watch over him. When we first got down to business, I pointed out that the usual prospect for a man like him would be a transfer to Station Gorky, where all he could expect was treatment of a kind that would shorten his life considerably. On the other hand, if he cooperated with me, he could enjoy privileged-prisoner status at the Lubyanka, his own cell and a job in the library."

"And he proved sensible?" Ivanov said. "But, then, who wouldn't?"

"No, it was more complicated than that. You could say he was just being sensible, a pragmatist, but I soon discovered it was subtler. I never had the slightest difficulty in getting answers to my questions from him."

"That's extraordinary," Ivanov said. "But why?"

"I'll tell you later. I have to speak with the governor of the Lubyanka. I'm going to get him transferred here to my authority."

"And what do you want me to do?" Ivanov asked.

"Make sure Max Chekhov gets here soon."

In London, Max Chekhov was in his apartment in Park Lane, standing in front of a mirror in his dressing room and adjusting his bow tie, when his mobile sounded.

"Who is it?" he asked in English.

The answer came in Russian and used his old army rank. "Major Chekhov?"

"Yes."

"Captain Peter Ivanov calling from GRU headquarters in Moscow on behalf of Colonel Josef Lermov."

Chekhov was immediately wary, for, as an old military hand with connections at the highest level of government, he knew the name Lermov was one to take seriously.

"What is this about?" he demanded. "I'm due at the Royal Opera House in a couple of hours to see *Carmen*."

"Well, I'm afraid she'll have to wait," Ivanov told him. "Your presence is requested in Moscow. By the Prime Minister, no less."

Chekhov was shocked and also immediately worried. "Why? What's this about?"

"You'll find out soon enough. There's a plane waiting for you at Berkley Down. I suggest you don't keep the Prime Minister waiting."

He clicked off, and Chekhov called Major Ivan Chelek at the Embassy and, when he answered, told him what had happened.

"Have you any idea what's going on, Ivan?"

"I can't say, Max. I do know that Putin's appointed Josef Lermov as Head of Station here. He's also given him the task of solving the Kurbsky riddle. I've been helping the investigation at this end as much as I could."

"And what have you found?"

"That's not for me to say, Max. If I were you, I wouldn't linger."

He switched off, and Chekhov unfastened his bow tie and started to unbutton his dress shirt, angry, but frightened as well. What the hell did Putin want him for?

The reason for his unease was a dark secret. Sometime before, Charles Ferguson had ordered his kidnapping by the Salters, and Chekhov had ended up at the Holland Park safe house. Chekhov was not a brave man, and he had spilled the beans about various matters to earn his release.

If it ever got out at the Kremlin, he was not only finished, he was a dead man. On the other hand, Ferguson had never approached him again. Maybe nobody knew? With a sinking sense of dread, Chekhov began to dress appropriately for winter in Moscow.

Ivanov found Lermov in the bar, vodkas waiting in a bucket of crushed ice. The Colonel toasted him. "How did it go with Chekhov?"

Ivanov took his vodka down in a single gulp, and told him. "I got the impression the summons worried him," he said.

"The mention of Putin's name worries a lot of people." Lermov swallowed another vodka.

"What about you?"

"Daniel Holley, you mean? I spoke to the governor at the Lubyanka, and faxed him a copy of the Putin letter. Holley is on his way here."

"You were going to tell me more about his interrogation."

"Yes, I was. When I told you that I had no difficulty getting answers to my questions, you sounded a little disappointed. It was as if you expected more from him."

"You could be right, I suppose," Ivanov admitted.

"It took me a long time and many interviews to really get to the truth about him. He told me his secrets, but it wasn't because he was afraid of the threat of Station Gorky."

"What is he afraid of, then?" Ivanov asked.

"Nothing." Lermov shrugged. "He is a nihilist."

"And what would that be?"

"A common philosophy in tsarist times. A nihilist is someone who believes that nothing has any value—in his case, that nothing has any value *anymore*."

"I'm not sure I follow," Ivanov said.

"The rape and murder of Rosaleen Coogan, and his execution of the four men responsible—I think it completely changed him. I don't think he's been able to take anything seriously since then. To him, it's all a violent game, in a way."

"And you think that's the way he secs it?"

"Yes, I do." Lermov took off his glasses and pinched his nose. "And if he doesn't care about anything, that includes himself."

"Come in, Dr. Freud."

Lermov's mobile sounded, and he answered it, listened, and nodded. "We'll see you in two minutes." He gave Ivanov a brief smile. "Holley is at the main entrance. I'll leave you to do the honors. Just bring him up to the office, and we won't need a guard."

As Ivanov approached, he saw a man in a black tracksuit standing between two prison guards and chatting with them. To Ivanov's surprise, he didn't have the shaved head of a prisoner, which was privilege indeed. His dark brown hair was reasonably long, with no sign of gray in spite of his age. He looked fit and well in the tracksuit. His good, strong face wore a slight smile, the smile of a man who couldn't take anything too seriously.

"Mr. Holley, I'm Peter Ivanov." The two guards put their heels together, and Ivanov signed for him.

"God bless, lads," Holley told them in very acceptable Russian. "Don't do anything I would." They went away smiling, and he turned to Ivanov. "What happens now?"

"I take you to Colonel Lermov. I've been working with him on this case by order of the Prime Minister."

"I am impressed." Ivanov led the way, and Holley said, "You'll know all about me, then?"

"You could say that."

"So you'll know what dear old Josef wants with me?"

"Of course I do, but I think he'll prefer to tell you himself. This way." He gestured up the stairs to the walkway and followed Holley up.

Lermov was standing beside the old tea lady, and she was filling a glass for him.

"Just in time, Josef," Holley said. "I'll join you."

"Another for my friend, *babushka*," Lermov told her. "You look good, Daniel. They've been treating you well, I think."

"Six months since you last saw me," Holley said. "I've been promoted. Looking after the accounts in the general supply office. A corrupt lot, the staff in there. Thieves and chancers. Most of them merited a cell themselves."

"Yes, the governor told me how pleased he was. Didn't want to part with you."

Holley sipped the tea the old lady had given him. "And is he going to part with me? How can he? Who says so?"

Lermov took the letter from his pocket and unfolded it. "Captain Ivanov and I have several copies between us. It's proved to be an open sesame everywhere we've shown it."

Holley held it in one hand and studied it, still sipping his tea. "Well, it would, wouldn't it? Vladimir bloody Putin himself." He handed the letter back. "Your chum here dismissed the guards. What was that all about?"

"We don't need them," Ivanov told him. "What are you going to do, Daniel, suddenly make a run for it? Where would you go?"

"Daniel, now, is it?" Holley said. "We are getting friendly." He switched to English, and the Yorkshire accent was obvious. "I'll say it again, Josef, what goes on?"

Lermov answered him in English. "It's a miracle you're here at all, Daniel. Five years ago, when you killed two of my men in Kosovo, the rest wanted to execute you. I kept you alive, with two bullets in you, for moral reasons, then discovered we'd captured someone very special indeed."

"Someone worth saving," Holley said.

"Absolutely—an open window on terrorism and the death business. Over twenty years of hard experience. You were beyond price, and the knowledge I've gained from our many talks has been invaluable."

"Happy to have been of service, but I didn't have much of a choice about that, did I?"

"Station Gorky?" Lermov shook his head. "At least be honest with yourself. You had a choice of a better option and took it. Whatever else you are, you're no martyr, Daniel, and shall I tell you why? You have to believe to be a martyr. You, my friend, don't believe in anything."

Daniel Holley changed, something dark passing on his

face like a shadow over the sun, an elemental force there that had Ivanov reaching for the flap of his holstered pistol, and then Holley actually laughed.

"You want to know something, Josef? I think you might well be right. What happens now?"

Lermov nodded to Ivanov, who said to Holley in English, "You and I will go into the office opposite, where I'll show you a DVD and offer you certain files on the computer—"

"Some of which is information gained from you from our conversations over the years," Lermov cut in.

"—Then we'll have a look at a situation that is giving us trouble, and we'll see what suggestions you might make to rectify the matter," Ivanov finished.

"That's what you were always good at, Daniel, isn't that so? Analyzing the situation, assessing the risk? You're a master at that sort of thing," Lermov said.

"If that's supposed to make me feel good, you're wasting your time. What is the point of this exercise, Josef?"

"Your sentence, Daniel. You've done five years so far. You're forty-nine and look forty on a bad day. But as the years roll on, that won't last. Maybe we can do something about that."

"Your logic is irrefutable." Holley turned to Ivanov. "So let's go into the damn office and see what you've got."

"I'll leave you to it," Lermov told him, and went along to the walkway to where the old tea lady had pushed her trolley, when Holley's mood turned black.

"Tea, Colonel?"

"No, *babushka*, I need vodka . . . a lot of vodka."

"The one with the accent? He's a little mad, I think."

"Aren't we all, *babushka*?" Lermov told her, and went down the stairs.

But instead of the bar, he went to his room, sat at a desk by the window, got out the manuscript of the book he was working on, and read through the current chapter, which had been cut off in midsentence by a tap on the shoulder by Ivanov in the university library. It was good stuff, but it was unfinished, there was no ending, but, then, there seldom was in his business, the life he'd chosen instead of a calm and scholarly career in the academic world. It suddenly struck him that he'd never really had a choice. He glanced at the final page of the chapter, then closed the manuscript with a kind of finality and put it in his briefcase.

"So what next?" he asked himself softly, and the knock on the door answered him.

Holley wore a cord around his neck, a red-and-gold security tag dangling from it of the kind worn only by senior staff members.

Lermov pointed to it. "What's this?" he asked Ivanov.

"I thought people might wonder who he was when he's walking round."

"You know, like going to the lavatory or down to the bar, Josef," Holley told him.

He pulled a chair forward, sat opposite Lermov, and Ivanov leaned against the door. Lermov said, "So you've gone through everything, Daniel?"

"Absolutely. You don't seem to have missed much, you and the boy wonder here."

"So what do you think?"

"About the fact that the boss man wants Charles Ferguson and his people eliminated and doesn't care how you do it?"

"Yes," Lermov replied calmly.

"Well, I like his advice about that Moscow Mafia hit man. It's almost flattering. I've been called many things, but Mafia has never been one of them."

"Get on with it."

"All right. If we take Ferguson's immediate clan, that means Roper, Dillon, Miller and his sister, the two Salters, and Blake Johnson. Eight in all," Holley said.

"Don't forget Kurbsky and Bounine," Ivanov put in.

"Silly me," Holley said. "I was forgetting the greatest novelist Russia's produced in modern times, a possible Nobel Prize winner. So ten in all."

"So it would appear. Peter joked that all we needed was a dinner party and a bomb under the table."

Holley glanced at Ivanov. "It's the real world we're talking about here." He turned back to Lermov. "So the man in the Kremlin wants no hint of any Russian influence in this whole affair?"

"If possible."

"So if there was a hint of PIRA about what takes place, that would be just the thing?" Daniel asked.

"Exactly." Lermov leaned forward. "I was thinking of Caitlin Daly."

Holley allowed his anger to show. "Damn you, Josef, I should never have told you about her."

"You told me many things, Daniel, it was part of our agreement."

"This is ridiculous. I visited her only once, Lermov, in November 1995. That's fourteen years ago. She could be dead, for all I know."

"She is alive and well, living and working exactly where she was then." Lermov smiled. "I had Major Ivan Chelek at the London Embassy make inquiries."

Holley said, "He went to the church, I suppose?"

"Something like that. He said she was a very attractive lady."

"She would be about fifty now," Holley said.

"Chelek said you could take ten years off that."

Holley suddenly got up. "I don't know about you two, but I need a drink. I can't get my head round this."

He turned to the door, Ivanov barred his way for a moment but Lermov nodded, so Holley pulled it open and went out.

Ivanov said, "He doesn't seem keen."

"He'll come round. We've talked so many times over the years, I feel I know him." He shrugged. "At least, as much as one can ever hope to understand another human being."

"Forgive me, Colonel, but I'm a cynic," Ivanov told him. "I often experience considerable difficulty in knowing myself."

"I admire your honesty. Tell me something: how often have you killed?"

"I was too young for Afghanistan and the First Chechen War, but I was bloodied in the Second. I was twenty when I went to that. Field intelligence, not infantry, but it was a desperate, bloody business. The Chechens were barbarians of the first order, imported Muslims from all over the place to serve with them. You couldn't drive anywhere without being ambushed."

"Yes, I saw some of that myself," Lermov said, "and know exactly what you mean. Daniel Holley's experience has been different. His killing has been close and personal. Back in Kosovo when my Spetsnaz boys got him, he double-tapped the two men he killed on the instant, no hesitation."

"I wonder how many times he did that on his travels?" Ivanov said. "It stands to reason that as an arms salesman, he kept rough company."

"Exactly." Lermov stood up. "Let's see how he's getting on."

They found Holley sitting in the bar, a glass of beer in front of him and a large whiskey. Lermov said, "I thought you had no money."

"I told the barman I was waiting for you. Have a seat."

Lermov waved to the barman and sat down.

Holley raised the beer and drank, not stopping until the glass was empty. He finished with a sigh, and said in English, "As they'd say in Leeds, that *were* grand." He reached for the glass of whiskey and tossed it down. "And that were even better."

"Would you like another one?" Lermov asked.

"Not really. It'd be nice to have a rugby match to go with it. But this is Moscow, not Leeds, and Russia, not Yorkshire, so let's get down to brass tacks."

"And what would that be?"

"Why do you think a woman I spoke to fourteen years ago will still be waiting and still interested in a cause long gone?"

"But that's what sleepers do, Daniel, they're always the chosen ones, the believers, and they wait, no matter how long it takes, even if they're never needed at all."

"A gloomy prospect," Holley said.

"And let me remind you what Caitlin Daly did back in 1991—the bombs she and her cell set off in London. The general panic, confusion, and fear she caused lasted for months. A considerable victory."

Holley said, "I know all that. Anyway, there's not just her to consider. What about the men in her cell? Alive or dead, who knows? I can't even remember their names."

"I can help you there. I have a fax all the way from your old partner in Algiers, Hamid Malik. I got in touch with him when you fell into my hands five years ago. He's proved a valuable asset to us," Lermov told him.

"You clever sod," Holley said. He waved to the barman.

"Yes, I am, aren't I? Anyway, he had the original correspondence from your cousin Liam, and I have all the names."

"It means nothing. Even if these men are still round,

there's no way of knowing if they feel the same way about dear old Ireland."

"True, but I've given the list to Chelek, and he'll trace them."

"You said you didn't want any obvious Russian involvement in this business."

"Absolutely right, but it'll save you time, and, once you get there, it'll all be in your hands. It'll also be of assistance to Caitlin Daly if she has lost touch, but you won't know that until you've seen her."

"Don't you mean *if* I see her?" Holley asked, and drank his new beer down.

"No, I mean when you see her, so make your decision now."

"To arrange the deaths of ten people, one of them a woman, isn't what I planned to do when I got up this morning."

"You mean, when you got up in your cell at the Lubyanka, where Captain Ivanov will certainly return you if I order him to. And then I'll give him another order."

"To do what?"

"To get your head shaved, your belongings packed and ready for the early-morning flight to Station Gorky."

There was a pregnant moment, and Ivanov looked wary. Holley said, "So in the end, Josef, you're just as bad a bastard as the rest of us."

"I've no intention of having my head served up on a plate at the Kremlin."

"I can see that, you're not the John the Baptist type. So you want me to play public executioner again?"

"I suppose I do."

"And can the hawk fly away to freedom afterwards?"

"I should imagine that is exactly what he would do if this matter was resolved to our mutual satisfaction."

"Excellent." Holley tossed his whiskey down. "If you'd said yes, I wouldn't have believed you anyway." He got up. "Right, I don't know what you are doing about my accommodation, but I presume I can use the office, so I'm going to go up now and knock out some sort of plan of action."

"A room will be arranged for you," Lermov told him. "But the office is yours. You may use my authority to extract any information you like from the GRU computers."

"And this Max Chekhov who's on his way from London? I know we're supposed to keep the Russian influence out of things, but he's floating along on a sea of money, booze, and women. I bet he could be useful."

He went out, and Lermov said, "So, Peter, are you disappointed again?"

"No," Ivanov said. "I think he's a thoroughly dangerous man."

"I know, and he looks so agreeable. Let's have another vodka on it."

There was snow mixed with sleet in the evening darkness as the Falcon carrying Max Chekhov landed at the Belov International private-aircraft facility close to the main Moscow airport. When the plane pulled in to the entrance of the terminal building and Chekhov came down the steps, Lermov was waiting for him in full uniform, fur hat, and fur collar. He saluted, giving Chekhov his title, one soldier to another.

"Major Chekhov . . . Josef Lermov."

"Kind of you to meet me, Colonel."

"A pleasure but also a duty. The Prime Minister is waiting for you now."

For a moment, Chekhov was terrified again and fought to control his shaking. He stumbled slightly, mounting the icy steps leading into the terminal, his walking stick sliding.

Lermov caught him and laughed. "Take care. I wouldn't want you to fall and break a leg. The Prime Minister doesn't permit excuses."

"That is my experience of him, too."

They reached the limousine, a porter following with Chekhov's bags, and found Ivanov waiting. Lermov made the introductions, then he and Chekhov sat in the rear and Ivanov got behind the wheel and drove away.

The snow was falling lightly now, and it was really rather peaceful. Chekhov said, "It's a great pleasure to meet you. Your name is certainly familiar to me. Could I ask what this is all about?"

"General Charles Ferguson."

Chekhov's sudden anger blotted out any fears he was going through at that moment. "That bastard! I'm half crippled, as you may have noticed, and it's all his fault. A shotgun blast in one kneecap delivered by gangsters in his employ."

"Yes, I'd heard something of the sort. Well, the Prime Minister's had enough. He's entrusted me with the task of doing something about it. He wants them finished off."

With his rather unique experience of the ways of General Charles Ferguson and company, Chekhov had reservations about Lermov's prospects but felt it politic to offer only enthusiasm. And he was relieved to hear that they didn't seem to know anything about his other past history with them. This could work out nicely.

"I will tell you, Colonel, and with all my heart, I would like nothing better than to see those swine wiped off the face of the earth."

"Then we must do our best to oblige you."

Twenty minutes later, they were sitting in the same office where Lermov had met Putin before, the one that belonged to General Volkov, once head of the GRU. As they waited, Chekhov said, "A great man, Volkov, did you know him?"

"Not intimately."

"Disappeared off the face of the earth. I wonder what became of him?"

"Oh, I think it highly likely that he and his men were murdered by this man Dillon on Ferguson's orders," Lermov told him.

"Good God." Chekhov crossed himself.

"Yes, they fully deserve killing. And the Prime Minister has told me I may rely on you for any help I need."

Before Chekhov could reply, the wall panel opened, and Putin appeared in a tracksuit. "There you are, Chekhov. Good flight? Is your leg improved?"

"Excellent, Prime Minister, really excellent," Chekhov gabbled.

"Has Colonel Lermov explained the task I have given him?"

"Yes, sir, he has," Chekhov managed to say. "I completely agree with everything you have ordered. He may rely on me totally in London."

"Good." Putin turned to Lermov. "How's it going?"

"Very well, Prime Minister. I was inspired by your advice to think Moscow Mafia and how they would handle it."

"And you've come up with an answer."

"A man, Prime Minister, and just the one for the job."

"Don't tell me," Putin said. "Just get on with it, and let the result speak for itself. Good luck."

He moved, the door opened in the paneling, and he was gone. Chekhov heaved a sigh of relief. "Thank God. Let's get out of here. Where do we go now?"

"The Astoria, the staff hotel for GRU headquarters. It's not exactly the Dorchester, but you'll be amongst friends."

Chekhov accepted the Astoria with good grace, for an old soldier amongst soldiers again usually fits in. Ivanov helped him settle in, and suggested meeting downstairs in half an hour for a meal.

Chekhov said, "Look, Captain, I was wounded in Afghanistan, so I'm not just a rich fool like some of my fellow oligarchs. Your colonel has told me about your plan, and the Prime Minister's just confirmed it to me."

"Do you have a problem with it?"

"Of course not, those bastards crippled me. But just sit down for ten minutes and tell me exactly what's happening. Would that be asking too much?"

"Not at all," Ivanov said, and told him everything.

Afterwards, he left Chekhov to unpack and went in search of Holley, whom he found in the office, working away on the computer, papers spread around, sometimes making notes by hand.

He sat down for a while, watching him. "I see you still like doing things the old-fashioned way."

"It may seem strange," Holley said, "but I find that no matter how much information I accumulate electronically, I can extract the essence of things with a few brief notes by hand."

"And what are you searching for?" They turned and found Lermov standing in the doorway, Chekhov peering over his shoulder. "Max Chekhov . . . Daniel Holley."

Holley nodded, and said, "Anything and everything about all the individuals involved in this affair, their comings and goings, their timetables. Take Lady Monica Starling, for instance. I've now got her family home in Essex, her brother's house in Dover Street, her rooms in Cambridge. I've got a full schedule of her lectures and seminars online. And I've got pretty much the same for most of the people on our list, as much as is possible."

"So when do you think you'll be ready?" Lermov asked. "To give Daly a call and tell her the day of reckoning is here?"

"Oh, very soon, I should think. First, I need something from you: encrypted mobiles, one for each of us, and a spare for Caitlin Daly."

Lermov said, "See to that, Peter. Anything else?"

"You'll have my passport on file somewhere. I'd only just renewed it in 'ninety-four when you grabbed me in Kosovo."

"You want to have it back?" Lermov asked.

"It would be nice. And, don't forget, I was always a highly successful businessman in the world's eyes, although a trifle disreputable because of the arms dealing. The darker side of my record has never been in the public domain. I even have a bank deposit in London. If you can find the passport, your people could put a stamp or two in it to fill in the five-year gap." Holley nodded, looking thoughtful. "And while you're at it, prepare another British passport to go with it. Daniel Grimshaw, a good Yorkshire name. I can thicken my accent to go with that."

"Is that all?" Lermov said. "If it is, I suggest we go down for dinner."

Holley shook his head. "I'll join you a bit later. I still need to check a few things about the opposition. I need to know exactly what their schedules are." He smiled. "You said that if you want to assassinate ten people, invite them round to dinner and explode a bomb under the table. Obviously, we can't do that. But assassination victim by victim has its problems also. It's like a warning light to anyone else connected."

"I can see that, but what's the answer?"

"To hit everybody at once, no matter where they are."

"That would take some planning," Ivanov told him.

"You could say that. So leave me to it. And I'd appreciate the encrypted mobiles at your soonest."

They left, and Holley cut to the news on television. They were talking politics as usual, and there was some fuss about Europe's cry that the Russian Federation was depriving them of gas and oil, turning off the pipelines. They cut to Putin vigorously defending himself, blaming America for interfering in European affairs, castigating Britain for supporting them. It seems there was some meeting of the UN in just a week, and Putin was going there to defend his point of view.

Holley switched off, smiling slightly. "Clever bastard," he said softly. "Daring the President and the Prime Minister to show up and face him. Which, of course, they won't." And then a switch clicked in his head. What was it he had seen? He quickly paged through his notes and— yes, there it was. Harry Miller's Parliamentary diary: *6th February, visit to the United Nations, New York, on behalf of the Prime Minister.* It was the date of Putin's intended appearance.

He pushed a bit further and found a booking for Miller at the Plaza Hotel in New York, a place he knew well, looking across Central Park. And there was something else he'd noticed before. What was it, what was it?

———

And then he had it. His fingers danced over the computer keys again, accessing the White House administrative logs. Yes, Blake Johnson would be spending a three-day weekend on Long Island and in New York City: *On Presidential business at the United Nations.* And the first day of Blake's holiday was February 6th, a Friday.

Miller & Johnson. Holley smiled.

10

After a while, Ivanov entered the office, a bag in one hand. He opened it and produced two mobile phones with their chargers.

Holley examined one. "It looks good, small, light."

"It's called a Codex, produced by British intelligence. To be honest, we've simply stolen it and manufactured it for ourselves. It's totally encrypted. The number for each one is on the sticker on the back. You just peel it off."

"Excellent."

"And I've gone round to records and found your passport. I'm having the forgery section bring the passport up-to-date with a few entry stamps, as you wanted, and they're creating a new one for Daniel Grimshaw." He held up a small camera. "So don't smile, please, just look solemn."

He took what he wanted, and Lermov came along the walkway and opened the door. "What's all this?"

"Forgery, need a passport photo," Ivanov told him.

"I see. Chekhov's gone to bed. I think we all should."

"One more thing," Holley said. "I need some clothes."

"I suppose we could find something suitable enough for flying in the Falcon—" Ivanov began, and Holley cut him off.

"Don't be stupid. I am not flying in the Falcon. British intelligence monitors your planes in and out of the country. I can't afford to be seen anywhere near you, and, to be frank about it, neither can Chekhov. He shouldn't be observed getting off a Russian flight in the company of important GRU people. It's too political a statement."

Lermov nodded. "You're right, of course. I see you have the mobiles you wanted. We have them now, too, so we can keep in touch at all times. Ivanov will take you shopping for clothes tomorrow."

"But what guarantee do we have that, once out of our sight, he won't do a runner, Colonel?" Ivanov demanded.

"Don't be silly, where would he go?"

Ivanov went out, and Lermov turned and smiled. "So it's coming together for you, you think?"

"I think so. I know how the game should proceed, the moves the players would be required to make, but until I have spoken to Caitlin Daly and checked whether her cell has survived I can give you no assurance of anything."

"I understand. When do you want to leave?"

"The sooner, the better. The day after tomorrow, if possible, certainly no longer than the day after that."

"I'll leave you now, to make your call."

He opened the door and paused as Holley said, "And which call would that be?"

"Daniel, as the Americans say, 'You can't kid a kidder.' You haven't asked for mad money to survive on, for accommodation while you're in London, or, most important of all, for weaponry. This can only mean you have a source in mind, someone with an encrypted mobile like you have now. Amazing things, mobiles. Within two minutes, you can be talking to someone anywhere in the world. Algiers, for instance."

"You wily old fox," Holley told him.

"It's been said before. I'll leave you to it."

In the old Moorish house on the hill overlooking the harbor of Algiers, Hamid Malik lay on the bed in his bedroom, the windows open to the night air, the light wind stirring the fragrance from the garden below. He was reading a day-old copy of the *Financial Times* and wondering what the world was coming to. And then his mobile sounded.

"Who is this?" he asked in Arabic.

Holley replied in English, thickening his Yorkshire accent. "It's me, you daft bastard. I can't remember the exact words, but somewhere in the Bible it says: 'For this my son was dead, and is alive again.'"

Malik, bursting with emotion, replied in Arabic, "Praise be to Allah. I have always known what happened to you in Kosovo long ago. A man named Lermov got in touch with me."

"So I understand. He tells me you've been a valuable asset."

"Purely business. Arms for Somalia, or wherever the Russians are stirring up trouble."

"So the death business is booming?"

"As always, partner. So when can I see you back in Algiers?"

"I'm not sure. There's a rather unusual mess in London that the Russians want me to clear up."

"Blood in the streets, you mean?" Malik groaned. "Daniel, you are closer than a brother to me. When does it end?"

"As Allah wills, old friend," Holley said. "There's a debt to pay here if I'm to be set free."

"I see." Malik thought about it for a moment. "What if you went ahead with this venture, got to London, and simply disappeared? This would be easy for me to arrange. You know I have blood relatives living in England. Connections of every kind in the Islamic world."

"Russia is one of the most powerful nations on earth, with round sixty thousand GRU members worldwide. One way or the other, I'd be hounded down if I did a runner. I must go with the tide on this one and hope for the best."

"So how can I help you?"

"I'll need a banker, and weaponry. Your cousin with the antique shop in London in Shepherd's Market, is he still alive?"

"Selim Malik? Very much so."

"That would be fine. The Albany Regency is just

round the corner. Tell him to book me a studio suite there from the day after tomorrow. Nothing too ostentatious. I've always found that staying in a reasonably expensive class of hotel is the best cover of all."

"I'll take your word for it. Anything else?"

"They've recovered my old passport for me, but they're putting together another one. Daniel Grimshaw, born in Leeds," Daniel said.

"I must admit that sounds Yorkshire enough. You are presumably using an encrypted phone?"

"A British Codex."

"Give me your number." Holley did. "Now we are truly linked like brothers. Just as in the old days." Malik laughed. "Stay well, my friend, and stay close."

The following day, Ivanov took Holley to GUM, a store which seemed to be able to supply every human need, and, as the clothes had to support Holley's role as a prosperous businessman, he went for top of the range in everything, somewhat to Ivanov's alarm.

"The prices here are shocking."

"You've got the card Lermov gave you, so who's counting?"

He got an excellent suitcase, a black single-breasted suit, a navy blue blazer and gray flannel slacks, four shirts, two pairs of black shoes, underwear, a collegiate-looking striped tie, and a black raincoat that Ivanov said was outrageously expensive but had a reinforced inside pocket lined with soft leather in which to carry a concealed pistol.

"You're sure that's it?" Ivanov asked as he produced the card and paid.

"Why didn't you get something for yourself while we're here?" Holley asked.

"That would be dishonorable," Ivanov said as they walked out, and then he smiled. "Besides, better to wait. The pound was down again in the paper this morning. Much cheaper to shop in London."

"A sensible point of view." They were walking towards the limousine. "Obviously, I haven't fired any kind of weapon recently. Is there a firing range at headquarters?" Holley asked.

"In the cellars. I'll arrange it, but I shouldn't imagine you'll have a problem."

"You're right, of course, but it would be sensible to test myself," Holley said as they drove away.

The firing range was the same as such places the world over. The sergeant in charge was named Lisin, a hard old soldier favoring cropped hair and a GRU tracksuit. There was a bad scar on his left cheek that could only have been caused by a narrow miss—"the kiss of a bullet," as the old-timers put it.

It was a gloomy sort of place, the cellar, the bare lights at the far end picking the target figures out of the darkness, six of them side-by-side.

"Here you are again, then, Captain Ivanov, still wanting to try your luck?"

"That's it, Sergeant," Ivanov told him cheerfully. "What have you got for us today?"

"It's good for you to handle the enemy's preferred choices. There's a Glock here, if anybody fancies it. A Beretta, much used by the American Army in Vietnam. And this Browning Hi Power that's been round in the British Army for years, still the weapon of choice with many members of the SAS."

Ivanov hesitated, a door creaked open behind, and Holley glanced over his shoulder and saw Lermov and Chekhov come in. He turned back to Ivanov.

"Of course, the Glock takes some beating, but the other two have certainly proved themselves over the years." He turned, smiled easily at Lisin, who frowned, suddenly wary.

Lermov said, "Show us how it's done, Sergeant."

"A pleasure, sir." Lisin picked up the Glock, assessed the position, and fired from left to right, deliberately, shooting the first three targets in the heart. He put the safety on and turned to Ivanov. "Three totally dead men, and that's the point, sir, isn't it?" He held the Glock out. "Would you like to have a go? There's still plenty of rounds in it."

Ivanov took the Glock, holding it two-handed, turned and fired quickly at the other three targets. He caught the edge of the heart in the fourth target, the fifth under the ribs, and the sixth in the top edge of the heart.

"Not doing too well today, are we, sir?" Lisin said, a slight smile on his face, and Ivanov was shamed.

Lermov said, "We all have our off days, Peter."

Lisin took the Glock and fired at the three targets again in the same deliberate way, shooting each one in the center of the heart. He emptied the weapon, and turned to Holley.

"Would you like to have a go, sir? If so, I'll put up fresh targets."

"No need," Holley told him. "I've never been in love with a Glock, and the Beretta is a fine weapon, but the Browning has a history to it." He turned, holding the weapon against his right thigh, then his hand swung up, firing single-handed in an oddly old-fashioned way, starting with one and ending with six, shooting each target between the eyes. He ejected the magazine and pulled off his sound mufflers and placed the Browning on the table.

Lisin was dumbfounded. Ivanov stared at Holley in awe. "I've never seen anything like that."

"Because it's a gift." Lermov patted Holley on the shoulder. "From God, like all gifts."

"From the Devil, is more likely," Holley said. "I'm going up to the office now." He walked to the back of the cellar where Chekhov was standing, amazed. "If you can spare the time, Max, I need to talk to you."

When Chekhov joined him in the study, he found him sitting at the computer. "Come and look at this," Holley said.

Chekhov pulled a chair forward. Bolt Hole was on

screen. "Hey, I recognize that, it's a magazine interview I did. I didn't realize it was online."

"There's more, several magazine and newspaper stories. I'll show you."

They sat watching for five or ten minutes. Chekhov said, laughing, "Why are people so interested? I'm not a film star."

"You're an oligarch, a billionaire. You're a curiosity to the English. How did you buy it?"

"It was advertised for sale in *Country Life* magazine. I had my driver run me down to West Sussex and fell in love with it instantly."

"And bought it, just like that?"

"It's what we oligarchs do, Daniel. We have so much money, it has no meaning anymore."

"Do you often stay there?"

"Whenever I can. If they'd allowed me the helicopter pad, I would probably have visited more because of the convenience, but they didn't. If I go down for a while, I take staff from the town house that Belov owns in Mayfair."

"So who looks after the place?"

"I own a cottage a mile and a half down the road on a creek running through the marsh. It's called Patch End, and a local lady, a widow named Lily White, keeps an eye on Bolt Hole and acts as housekeeper. Her son, Jacob, a local fisherman, looks after my boat, the *Mermaid*."

"And what's that like?" Holley asked.

"A bit like a sport fisherman but about twice the size. I like to go for a sail when I'm there."

"If the weather's right?"

"Oh, I don't know. It can be fun, or used to be. I've been limited these last couple of years with my leg."

"Do you go anyplace else?"

"I go to the States every couple of months. Belov has a building in New York, and I visit on business."

Holley nodded. "Okay, that's all good to know. Now, when you return to London, make sure it's by yourself. You shouldn't be seen with anyone like Lermov or Ivanov. I'll do the same. I'll fly business class under an assumed name on a British Airways flight to Heathrow. The only way I will communicate with you is by encrypted mobile. The same rule applies to my dealings with Lermov and Ivanov. I'd advise you to do the same."

For a moment, the memory of his brief kidnapping and interrogation at the hands of Charles Ferguson and his people returned to haunt Chekhov, and he had an insane desire to tell Holley all about it, but that would never do. He was, after all, still in Russia. He would just have to travel hopefully.

"Everything you say makes sense. What happens when we get there, and you speak to this Caitlin Daly woman?"

"I haven't the slightest idea. She might say, 'You're out of your head, get away from me or I'll call a policeman,' which means the whole thing's off. Bizarre, isn't it?"

"It certainly is," Max Chekhov said. "I'll see you later."

Soon after, the door clicked, and Ivanov entered with a large envelope, which he emptied on the desk. There was

Holley's original passport, in very good condition, along with another in the name of Daniel Grimshaw, plus a driver's license.

"I must say, the forgeries are excellent," Holley told him.

"You don't have a credit card."

"I'll take care of that myself."

"And you're not going to tell me how."

"Of course not."

"Nor where you're going to stay."

"That's correct. Now, go tell your boss that I'm ready to go."

He went out. Holley found some plastic envelopes, tidied the desk, turned off the computer, and left the office. In his bedroom, he took the purchases he had made at GUM, laid them on the bed neatly, then put his Holley passport in one of the plastic envelopes, zipped it up, and put it in the inside left pocket of the jacket of the black suit. The Grimshaw passport he put in the right inside pocket. He laid out a white shirt and underwear, socks, a pair of shoes, then packed everything else into the suitcase.

Careful and meticulous, as always, but he liked things to be right, and it meant that he was ready to go and everything else was in his head.

He went downstairs and found Lermov in the bar with Chekhov. As usual, they were drinking vodka. "Everything in order?" Lermov inquired.

"I think you could say that." Holly waved to the barman. "A large scotch over here."

Ivanov came in with an envelope in his hand. "As you ordered, Colonel."

The barman brought the scotch, Lermov opened the envelope and took out an airline ticket. He examined it, then pushed it over. "Ten o'clock in the morning, Daniel, business class, British Airways to London, just as you wanted."

Holley examined it. "Excellent. The only thing missing is a few euros for expenses and a taxi from Heathrow to downtown at the other end. A thousand should do it."

"I would have thought five hundred would be ample." He smiled at Holley. "After all, as I understand it, you have your own banking arrangements in place. Meantime, the Prime Minister has asked me to join his party in New York—he's giving a speech to the UN on Friday. I'll fly to London after that. Captain Ivanov will leave in the Embassy mail plane tomorrow and assist Major Chelek." His slight, weary smile was for all of them. "I think we know where we are with this business, gentlemen."

Chekhov tried to look eager. "The 'game's afoot,' isn't that what the English say? That writer, Conan Doyle?"

"Shakespeare, actually," Daniel told him. "But we'll only have a game at all if Caitlin Daly decides to join us."

"Well, let's travel hopefully," Lermov said, and got up. "I need you in my office, Peter, we have much to do."

"Before you go, let's get one thing straight," Holley said. "As they say in the theater, it's 'my gig' over there, and what I say goes. Max takes his orders from me."

Ivanov was going to say something, but Lermov shut him up. "Of course, Daniel."

They went out. Daniel knocked back his scotch, and Chekhov said, "Let me get you another."

"Why not? But just the one." Chekhov called to the barman, and Daniel said, "Your staff at Belov International in New York, are they mostly Russian?"

"No. The New York branch was an American firm when Belov took it over years ago. But we do have many Russians there. And as you must know, the Moscow Mafia extends not only to London but also New York."

"And you employ such people?"

"On the security side of things. They can be very useful. Our head of security at the Belov building is one such man. Mikhail Potanin."

"Who is, I suppose, capable of most things?"

"Let's say he's very reliable. One has to be practical. Sometimes in business, people must be persuaded to see reason."

"That must be very reassuring for poor put-upon businessmen like yourself." Holley got up to go.

Chekhov said, "So it will be just the voice on the phone over there. You will keep me informed, won't you?"

"As much as I feel necessary. You've got to trust me, Max. After all, I've got to trust you. Lermov will want to know everything I say to you, so try juggling with that. But remember what we agreed. I'm in charge over there. You take your orders from me."

"Of course."

"I'm better for you in every way, Max, better than Lermov, believe me. So be sensible."

"Why wouldn't I?" Max managed to sound indignant.

"Because you couldn't have become a millionaire without being a devious bastard. Play straight with me." Holly smiled. "Or I'll kill you."

In his bedroom, he called Malik in Algiers. "Everything set?"

"Yes. Selim remembers you well from the old days and looks forward to meeting you. The Albany Regency is one he uses regularly himself for overseas agents visiting him, and he's booked you a suite. It's all on the firm. And he uses an encrypted mobile himself. I'll give you the number."

He did, and Holley wrote it down. "I won't call him now, but you could confirm my arrival. Tell him I don't want to be picked up. I'll get a taxi at Heathrow."

"I'll let him know. Stay in touch, and may Allah protect you, my brother."

"I could be spending the rest of my life in the Lubyanka or even Station Gorky. Now I've been offered a chance to earn my way out of it. I'd say the hand of God has got something to do with that. Take care, Malik."

He lay back on the bed, pillowed his head, and stared up at the ceiling, taking a very deep breath, his stomach churning.

"Now it begins," he said softly. "Now it begins."

LONDON

11

It was just after two-thirty the following afternoon when Holley's taxi drew up outside the Albany Regency just off Curzon Street. Stormy weather had caused the flight from Moscow to take longer than usual, but he was here in Mayfair and London in the rain. He had changed the euros Ivanov had given him for sterling, paid the cab-driver generously, and went up the steps to the entrance, where a doorman in a top hat and green frock coat greeted him and a young uniformed porter relieved him of his suitcase.

He found the hotel pretty much as he had remembered it. Slightly old-fashioned, which was its charm, but maintained well, and expensive enough to ensure that the clientele was respectable.

His reservation was waiting, and all Holley had to do was sign the reservation form and produce his passport for identification purposes. The Russians had used the same date and place of birth as on his real passport but hadn't put his mother and her address in Leeds on the next-of-kin page. There would have been no point. During one of his sessions with Lermov during his second year of confinement, the Colonel had told him his mother had died. It was a bad memory and one he preferred to forget.

The young porter accompanied him to the fifth floor and showed him to the suite, which was pleasant and functional, with a sliding window to a small balcony with a good view of Curzon Street and Shepherd's Market. Holley tipped the boy, unpacked quickly, and put his things away. He noticed himself in the full-length mirror when he opened the wardrobe. The black suit, the striped tie, and white shirt made him look exactly right. Banker or lawyer, businessman or accountant. Eminently respectable.

There was a small refrigerator next to the television. He opened it and selected a double-vodka miniature, poured it into a plastic cup, added a little tonic water, and toasted himself in the mirror.

"Here we go, off to bloody war again, old lad." He drank it down and went out.

Shepherd's Market had always been one of his favorite places in London. The narrow streets, the pubs, the restaurants, and the shops selling everything from paintings and prints to antiques. "Selim Malik" was painted in gold above the door of one such shop, a narrow window on each side, one offering a triangle of truly remarkable Buddhas and the other an exquisite Bokhara silk rug. The door was shut, but there was an intercom beside it, and Holley pressed a button, confident he was on camera.

Which proved true, because before he could open his mouth a voice said in Arabic, "Praise be to Allah."

A moment later, the door opened, and he was pulled inside to a tight embrace. "Daniel, it is you. Six years since I've seen you, and you look good."

"Older, Selim, older, but you never change."

Selim was small, perhaps five-five, with long, curling hair that had once been black but was now silvery gray and swept behind the ears, no mustache but a fringe of beard, and a dark olive face. He had good-humored eyes that lit up his personality when he was happy, as he was now. He wore a velvet jacket from another age, a ruffled shirt, and baggy velvet trousers.

"Everything is change, Daniel. I was sixty-five this year, imagine that. Come into my study and have a glass of champagne with me to celebrate."

"So you're still that kind of Arab?"

"Allah is merciful. You've booked in at the hotel? Everything is taken care of? I have a running account there. They're very good."

The study was partly rococo and partly Victorian, with overstuffed chairs and two enormous sofas and an Axminster carpet that must have cost a fortune. A large round table in beaten brass was almost at floor level, and a bottle of Cristal champagne in an ice bucket sat upon it, with seventeenth-century Venetian goblets to drink it with.

"Sit down," he urged. "And you do the honors. I'll be back." He went out, and Daniel thumbed off the cork and poured. Selim returned with a black bag and a laptop, which he put on the table. "A present for you. But let's have a drink first."

He drank it straight down and poured another. "Allah be praised to see you out of that terrible prison. You must feel like Edmond Dantès escaping from the Château d'If."

"I think he did sixteen years, but I may be wrong," Daniel said.

"You haven't seen Hamid?" He chuckled. "Forgive me. To you, he was always Malik."

"An old habit. No, I haven't seen him, but we've spoken. I can buy my freedom. The Russians want me to do them a big favor right here in London. If I can bring it off, I'm rid of them for good."

"You think you can trust them?"

"Not really, but I must go with the flow, and hope."

"You know best. Don't tell me anything—I would rather not know what it is. Please open the bag and see if it's what you wanted."

Holley did and pulled out an ankle holster and a Colt .25 with a couple of boxes of ammunition. "Hollowpoint," Selim said.

Next was a cardboard box containing a Walther PPK with a Carswell silencer, the new, short version. Last of all came a nylon-and-titanium bulletproof vest.

"This is wonderful," Holley told him.

"There should be a knife in there as well."

Holley groped around and found it, slim, dark, and

deadly, with a razor-sharp blade leaping to attention when a button was pressed.

"Excellent. That's taken care of me perfectly."

"Not quite." Selim leaned over and opened a zip to a side pocket of the bag. He took out an envelope. "Expense money. Ten fifty-pound notes, and another five hundred pounds in twenties. There is more where that came from, so ask when you need it. Here's a company credit card. I've taped the PIN number on the back. Learn it and destroy. There's always the chance that you're going to need a credit card these days."

"What can I say?"

"Not much. Have you eaten?"

"No."

"Well, let me buy you a late lunch round the corner at the Lebanese. Great, great cooking, unless you have other plans."

"No, not for a while yet. I'd love to have a meal with you." He stowed the items back into the bag. "I'll leave these here for the moment and get them when I come back."

"That's fine." As they went through the shop, Selim said, "What's the plan, to get started at once or take your time?"

"Actually, I'm probably going to Mass," Daniel Holley said. "But don't ask me to explain."

He left the hotel in the early-evening rain, borrowing an umbrella, walked to the end of Curzon Street, hailed a black cab, and told the driver to take him to Kilburn. Darkness was falling and the traffic busy, but they were there quite quickly, and he asked to be dropped at Kilburn High Road. He walked the rest of the way.

Unfortunately, according to the times inscribed on the board at the gate, he was already too late for that evening's services. He hesitated, but a hint of light at the church windows encouraged him to go forward.

Walking through the Victorian-Gothic cemetery, with angels and effigies of one kind or another looming out of the darkness, he realized that he couldn't remember much from his first visit, but, then, it had been so brief. He turned the ring on the door and went in.

It was incredibly peaceful, the lights very low, and the church smelt of incense and candles, the Mary Chapel to one side. Money had been spent here, mostly during the high tide of Victorian prosperity that had coincided with the church-building period when the anti-Catholic laws changed. The stained-glass windows were lovely, the pews beautifully carved, and the altar and choir stalls ornate. Flowers were stacked all around the altar steps in polished brass vases.

Music was playing very softly and almost beyond hearing, but suddenly it stopped. A door creaked open and closed, the noise echoing, there was the sound of footfalls on tiles, and Caitlin Daly walked in from the right-hand side carrying a watering can, and he recognized her instantly.

Holley stayed back in the shadows and watched. The photo he'd seen of her on the Internet was perfectly recognizable but didn't do her full justice. The woman in the green smock and gray skirt, rearranging flowers at the altar and watering them, had been beautiful when he had last seen her in her mid-thirties. At fifty, she was still attractive, her face enhanced by the copper-colored hair that had been cropped in a style Holley remembered from an old Ingrid Bergman movie.

She finished, bowed to the altar, crossed herself, picked up the watering can, turned, and detected movement in the shadows. "Is someone there?" she called, and her voice echoed in the empty church.

He hesitated, then stepped forward. "Can I help you?" she asked.

"I'm not sure. I last saw you in 1995, when I gave you the message: 'Liam Coogan sends you his blessing and says hold yourself ready.'"

She stared at him for a moment, obviously shocked. "Oh, dear God. Who are you?"

"You asked me that last time, and I said: 'Just call me Daniel. I'm Liam's cousin.' You said I didn't sound Irish."

"You don't, you have a tinge of Yorkshire in your voice."

"That's not surprising, since I was born in Leeds."

She shook her head. "I still can't believe it."

"I phoned you at the presbytery and said I was sitting in a rear pew in the church and asked to see you. I said my time was limited, as I had to catch a plane to Algiers."

She nodded. "Yes, I remember so well, and the thrill of it."

"And the disappointment?"

"Oh, yes, but we can't talk here. Monsignor Murphy is at a dinner tonight. We'll use the sacristy."

It was warm and enclosed in there, a desk and a couple of chairs, a laptop, religious vestments hanging from the rails, registers of all kinds—marriages, deaths—and a church smell to everything that would never go away.

She leaned against the wall by the window, arms folded, and he sat opposite. "Tell me about yourself," she said.

"I'm using an alias at the moment: Daniel Grimshaw."

"A sound Yorkshire name that suits your voice."

"My mother was a Coogan from Crossmaglen, and I was a volunteer with the PIRA."

"So was I, and proud of it."

"I know. Liam told me about your sleeper cell and how he activated you in 1991. Twelve explosions that resonated in the West End of London for months."

Her face was glowing. "Great days, they were."

"Then you went back to waiting? Did that bother you?"

"It's what sleepers do, Daniel, wait to strike again."

"And hopefully for the big one. Back then, Liam asked me that if he activated you again, would I be your controller, and I said yes. Liam died, of course, from a heart attack, but I'm here now."

She nodded gravely. "God rest Liam's soul. He was a good man."

"Were your cell members disappointed not to have a role in the 1996 bombings?"

"Yes, but at least we had the satisfaction of seeing the British suffer such a great defeat. It's strange, but seeing you like this brings your last visit vividly back to me. We always met weekly in the chapel at Hope of Mary. The day you gave me Liam's message, I called a special meeting and gave them the good news."

"And how did they take it?"

"Excitement. Awe. We knelt and recited our own special prayer together."

"'Holy Mary, Mother of God, pray for us sinners, now and at the hour of our death, we who are ourselves alone'?" Daniel said.

She was amazed. "But how do you know that?"

"I just do, as I know the names of those men—Barry, Flynn, Pool, Costello, who changed to Docherty, Cochran, and Murray. A hell of a long time ago. I wouldn't imagine they're still round?"

"Until two years ago, they all attended our weekly meeting, but unfortunately Barry and Flynn had a severe brush with the law. They were both too handy with a gun. Finally, an armed robbery they took part in went sour. They would have probably gotten seven years if caught, but I used a certain influence I have, obtained false American passports for them and other necessary documentation, and packed them off to the States."

"And you stay in touch?"

"On a regular basis. We have a Hope of Mary Hospice and Refuge in New York, too. They are both security men there."

"And the remaining four?"

"We meet as we've always done, united by prayer and a common commitment to the PIRA. I was recruited at London University, the others in various ways. Liam Coogan used to arrange trips to training camps in the west of Ireland. The IRA version of a holiday, he used to say. We did that many times over the years. Bonded, you might say."

"But really only got to do your work with that twelve-bomb jolly in Mayfair in 1991. Was it enough?"

"It always is, if your resolve is strong and you are committed."

"But you need more than that, I think, some deep-seated reason, perhaps some great wrong that urges you on."

"That's true. Take Henry Pool. He's a self-employed private-hire driver. Like you, he had an English father and Irish mother, but her father was murdered by English Black and Tans in 1921 when she was only six months old and her mother fled here to Kilburn. It was a strong motive for him to not exactly care for the English."

"I shouldn't imagine his mother would ever let him forget it."

"Is there something wrong with that?" she asked.

"Not at all. For a ten-year-old child to see her father gunned down by masked intruders in front of her and her mother would, I imagine, be a memory that would last forever."

Her face was surprisingly calm. "So you know about that? Exactly who are you, Daniel, this half Irishman who claims to have been a member of the Provisional IRA? You not only sound Yorkshire, you look like some prosperous businessman. What on earth would ever have made you join?"

So he told her all about Rosaleen Coogan.

Afterwards, she sat down on the other side of the desk from him, her face like stone, her eyes burning, and it was obvious that she accepted the truth of what he had told her.

"Those foul creatures. God's curse on them for what they did to that poor girl."

"Some kind of curse on me ever since," Daniel told her. "I've killed a number of times for the Provos and other times for myself." He stood up, put his foot on the chair, and hitched his trousers up, revealing the ankle holster. "The way of the gun has become rather permanent in my life."

"But you don't regret what you did, you can't!" She banged on the desk with her clenched fist. "Damn all of them."

And now she was really upset, and Daniel said, "Take it easy. It's not always good for us to let the past intrude."

"You don't understand. It's brought it all back to me. The night the men with guns smashed their way in and murdered my father. They forced themselves on my mother, two of them. It was only my age saved me."

Holley, aghast at the horror of it, could only say, "I'm so sorry, girl."

She took a deep, shuddering breath. "What I need is a drink, and I don't think it a sin in the circumstances to raid

Monsignor Murphy's cupboard in search of Communion wine." She found a bottle and two coffee cups and poured a generous measure into each. She handed one to him and drank deeply herself. "Now, tell me everything properly, who you are really and what you're doing here."

"There's a man named General Charles Ferguson who runs a special security outfit for the Prime Minister. His right-hand man is Sean Dillon, once a top enforcer for the PIRA, and a good one. In 1991, he was in a Serb prison when Ferguson turned up and made him an offer he couldn't refuse: to join him or face a firing squad."

"So Dillon chose the traitor's path?"

"You could put it that way."

She poured more wine for both of them. "There's no other way of putting it. Tell me more—everything."

"You're quite a man, Daniel," she said an hour later when he was finished. "Probably the most remarkable one I've met in my entire life."

"So what do you think about the Russians?"

"A means to an end. I've nothing against them. In the early years of the Troubles, they provided arms for the PIRA on more than one occasion. I know that for a fact."

"And Charles Ferguson and company?"

"To hell with him. Over the years, as you tell it, he's been responsible for the death of many of our comrades one way or the other. Major Giles Roper may look like a tragic and romantic hero in his wheelchair, but his exploits in bomb disposal did us great harm."

"By God, but you're a hard woman, Caitlin."

"As for Dillon, a damn traitor, and I've no time for him. The fact that his own father was killed by British soldiers should have been bad enough for him."

"He did great work for the cause for years until Ferguson appeared on the scene."

"He's the worst kind of turncoat, I can't see it any other way, and these gangster friends of his, the Salters, they've done us great harm also."

"And then we have Harry Miller?"

"The Prince of Darkness himself. He appears to have made a hobby out of murdering members of the PIRA for years."

"His luck is obviously good. His wife's wasn't, but that's the price you pay. What do you think of his sister?" Holley asked her.

"From what you tell me, she killed a Provo. The kind of upper-class English woman who thinks everything's a jolly jape. She deserves to meet the same end as everyone else."

"And you really mean that?"

It was as direct a challenge as he could make. She said, "I'm very old-fashioned, Daniel. I still believe in a United Ireland, and the Peace Process hasn't given us that, so to hell with it. You and your problem, if I can put it that way, mean there's a chance to go active once more and dispose of some very bad people who've done my side nothing but harm."

"So you're with me on this?"

"You can depend on it," she said firmly.

"And what about the others? Can you talk them round?"

"I don't think I'll have much trouble. Pool has lived on his own since his mother died. Docherty is on his own. He served time as Costello, so I obtained an Irish passport for him as Docherty. He's a drunkard every so often, so no woman will put up with him. Matthew Cochran lives in one lodging home after another since his wife died of breast cancer, and Patrick Murray is a long-distance truck driver. He's never married. Just has one girl after the other. Barry and Flynn, I've already told you about, but, as they're in New York, whatever you're planning won't concern them."

"An assorted bunch."

"But committed, Daniel, committed. The oath, our special prayer, the comradeship—all these things make us what we are—and going active again would only affirm it."

Daniel said, "I'll take your word on that." He stood and took a Codex and its charger out of his raincoat pocket. "This is an encrypted mobile. I've stuck a tab on it with your number and mine. Memorize them and destroy. Call me anytime, and I'll be in touch with you very soon. When will you speak to your people?"

"I'll start phoning round tonight. Daniel, it's been marvelous to see you again." She meant it, her eyes shining, and actually shook hands.

Outside, it was pouring, so he raised his umbrella and walked down the path through the gravestones and effigies of the cemetery, pausing for a moment in the roofed gateway to the street.

"Dear God," he said softly. "Am I out of my bloody mind or is she?" But there was no answer to that, and he walked down to the main road and hailed a cab.

It was nine o'clock, and a thought struck him. The Salters and their pub, the Dark Man on Cable Wharf. This could be a good time to check it over. It'd be reasonably busy, so he would be able to blend in with the crowd. His knowledge of London, learned on many visits in the old days, stood him in good stead now. He told the driver to drop him off in Wapping High Street, found a lane with a sign that read "Cable Wharf," and went down.

There was a new development of flats on one side, decaying warehouses on the other, eager for the builders, much of the area begging to be developed. He moved out of the darkness onto Cable Wharf, and it was interesting and attractive. The other side of the Thames was a panorama of streetlights, the Dark Man to his right, the sound of music drifting up. Beyond, there was what looked like a multistory luxury apartment development, the jetty of the old wharf running out into the river, several boats moored there. Things were busy at the Dark Man if the car park was anything to go by, and he ventured into the bar.

It was very crowded, a pretty mixed slice of humanity, all ages, men and women, the roar of voices coupled with taped music. It was like a Victorian-themed pub—mirrors, mahogany, and porcelain beer pumps.

Harry Salter and his nephew, Billy, were familiar to him from pictures, and he saw them sitting in a corner booth, seemingly oblivious to the noise. Holley stayed down at the end of the bar, squeezed against it by those standing around and indifferent to him.

A handsome blond arrived on the other side of the bar, and he ordered a beer and a whiskey chaser. She prompted back, "That will put hairs on your chest."

He handed across a ten-pound note, and she tried to give him some change, which he waved away. The noise almost drowned her thanks, and somebody called, "Hey, Ruby, down here."

"There must be a better way." She smiled. "Roll on, eleven o'clock."

"You could go on way after that, couldn't you?" he said.

"Into the early hours if we want, but not in this pub, love. When I call time, out they go. I need to get a life even if they don't."

She turned away. Holley drank his beer, tossed down his whiskey, and left. He walked along the wharf and saw a shed with an old Ford van outside. The door on the driver's side wasn't locked, so he opened it. It smelt like a garage inside, and there was a key in the ignition. Probably used as a runabout on the riverside. He got out, walked to the end of the wharf, and stood looking at the lights for a while. He turned to the pub again, thinking how vulnerable it was, then he went back up through the darkness and hailed a cab in the High Street.

In his suite at the Albany Regency, he checked the room safe in the wardrobe in which he had left the Walther and silencer and all his ammunition. Everything was in order, and he took off his jacket and tie, opened his laptop, and tapped in to some of his files, brainstorming in a way. Miller and Blake Johnson were in New York for the Putin appearance at the UN, that was a fact. That Frank Barry and Jack Flynn were in New York, too, seemed fortuitous. To be candid, it was as if it was ordained. Highly trained in weaponry over the years, "too handy with a gun," Caitlin had said, fleeing to America to avoid the prospect of seven years in jail for armed robbery. A lot could be done with that. He considered it, then thought of his conversation with Max Chekhov about the Belov operation in New York, especially his head of security, Mikhail Potanin. From the sound of him, he'd been Moscow Mafia in his time, which meant he was capable of most things.

Before any final planning was possible, it was necessary for Caitlin Daly to sound out the cell and see what they thought, but the presence of Barry and Flynn together in New York titillated him. If they took care of Blake Johnson and Harry Miller on Friday . . .

He clicked on Charles Ferguson and saw that he was at a dinner at the Garrick Club that evening. Then he checked on Monica Starling and saw that she had a faculty dinner with Professor George Dunkley of Corpus Christi College that night at a country hotel called Raintree House. He looked it up and discovered it was six miles out of Cambridge.

The audacity of what he was thinking appealed to him. He thought some more about it, then sat by the window, looking out at the night and the rooftops of Shepherd's Market, and called Caitlin Daly on his Codex.

She was deeply cautious, waiting for something to be said. "It's Daniel, Caitlin."

She laughed, relief in her voice. "Forgive me, I'll need to get used to this phone. You got back okay, obviously. You didn't tell me where you're staying."

"A nice, quiet, respectable hotel near Shepherd's Market."

"Ah, Mayfair, I like it there."

"I'll get right to the point. Two of the people on our list, Harry Miller and Blake Johnson, will be in New York on Friday, and I was thinking of your people, Barry and Flynn, who you helped to get out of London when prison was in view. 'Too handy with a gun,' you said. How do you think they'd react if you suggested they do the job on Miller and Johnson?"

"They could be up for it," she said. "They've always been hard men. Lucky to stay out of prison years ago. The head of security at our place in New York has told me he's sure that, on the side, they're hoodlums for hire."

"And how do you feel about that?"

"I speak to them most weeks. Their membership in

the cell still means a great deal to them. I'd be willing to put it to them."

"I know it's too late for you to speak to the other four tonight, but it's only six in the evening in New York. I'm not trying to put any pressure on you, but time is of the essence. Could you speak to them tonight? No point in me calling, I'm nothing to them."

"I was always the leader, Daniel, guiding them as I saw fit. As far as I'm concerned, though, the show of hands has to be one hundred percent and nothing less. I have only four to stand in front of now, and if we are to agree to your plan of campaign against Ferguson and his people, it is logical that I should speak to Barry and Flynn. But I must make one thing clear. If we agree and they don't, all bets are off."

"Yes, I can see that. I can also see that I'm in your hands on this. By the way, I haven't asked about your weapons status."

"We were well supplied with small arms, explosives, bomb-making parts. It was a while ago, of course, but it should all still be under lock and key in a large cupboard in the presbytery wine cellar. I'm going to go now, Daniel, think out my approach and speak to Barry and Flynn. If I'm lucky, I might even find them together. You must be tired. You were, after all, in Moscow this morning. I'll speak to you tomorrow."

And she was right. Suddenly, he felt bushed. He poured a whiskey for a nightcap, drank it while peering out of the window. So far, so good, but tomorrow was another day. And he went to bed.

———

The following day, Chekhov phoned him just after breakfast. "Daniel, my friend, how goes it?"

"It goes very well. Where are you?"

"In my apartment. Infinitely preferable to Moscow, I'll tell you. To look out of my window at Hyde Park warms my heart. I love this city."

"Did Lermov say good-bye nicely?"

"Frankly, I think he's more interested in his trip to New York than in your enterprise at the moment. I believe he takes it as a sign of great favor from the Prime Minister."

"You surprise me. I would have imagined him above that sort of thing."

"I'm a true cynic in such matters. People like Lermov, men of huge brain and much learning, often express contempt for the grace-and-favor aspect of success until it's offered to them. I suppose he would love to be a general, if you see my point. Of course, what would really seal it for him would be your success with the business at hand. Can you tell me what's happening?"

Holley had no reason not to. "I went to church, in a manner of speaking, and saw the lady in question. She embraces the idea of activating her cell, listened to what I told her of Ferguson and company, and damned them all. She can't stop hating the British, Max. Her father was killed in front of her when she was ten, her mother raped."

"It sounds like something out of a Bosnian night-mare," Chekhov said. "What do the members of the cell say?"

"I'm waiting to hear. The only problem is that two of them had to clear off to New York with the law breathing down their necks."

"So what are you going to do?"

"Well, everything obviously depends upon what her people decide, but, if it's favorable, I think I'm going to need your help."

"In what way?" Chekhov asked.

Holley explained about Barry and Flynn, and when he was finished Chekhov said, "Where would I come in?"

"The way I see it, one of them will hit Blake Johnson in Quogue and the other take Miller in New York. This guy you employ at Belov . . . Potanin, I think his name was?"

"Mikhail Potanin. What about him?"

"The impression you gave me was that he was capable of anything. I'd like him to monitor Barry and Flynn. Don't even try to say no, Max. I know the way you oligarchs rose to power, and it was on the backs of a lot of men like Potanin."

"So who's arguing? Let's see first if Barry and Flynn agree, and, if so, I'll put it in Potanin's lap."

"I'll be in touch the moment I hear. Is Ivanov in?"

"Making himself at home. He'll have all week to make his move until Lermov gets in at the weekend. He's too eager, that boy."

Half an hour later, Caitlin called. "How are you?" she asked. "Did you have a good night?"

"More to the point, did you?"

"Daniel, they went for it hook, line, and sinker. Flynn lives in Greenwich Village, but Barry has a staff flat at the Refuge. I called him first, and Flynn was with him. Barry put the telephone on speaker, and I was able to discuss it with both of them. They admitted to having done contract work in the past."

"There's an old Yorkshire saying: 'I don't mind a thief as long as he's an honest thief.' From the sound of them, they'll do for me. The Refuge where Barry has staff quarters, I take it they have computer facilities?"

"Of course."

"Look up Harry Miller online and you'll find a photo of him walking along a London street. Send Barry a copy. While I have you, you can give me their addresses and mobile numbers."

"Is that necessary?"

"I can't do everything through you, Caitlin, it'll just be too cumbersome and ineffective. Besides, I've just arranged for someone to monitor them and see to their general welfare. He'll make sure they're all right."

She did as he asked, and he wrote the information down. "When is your meeting?"

"Six tonight."

"Do you want me there?"

"Not really, Daniel. I've been their leader for so long,

THE WOLF AT THE DOOR   251

and the cell is a tight unit psychologically. I think it would be better if you told me what you wanted them to do, and I'll pass it on."

"Fine. I'll allocate the tasks and get a taxi up to the church later this afternoon to give them to you. That means if they do say yes, you can tell them what's expected of them. If they say no, then simply put the stuff in your office shredder. I'll phone you when I'm on the way."

"Daniel, are you sure?"

"Time is going to be very tight. Friday will be a big day and night both here and in New York. If you're going to get anywhere with them, remind them of their years of serving the cause, appeal to their patriotism. Ferguson and his people are the enemy. You've got to sell it."

"I will, Daniel."

As he sat going over a mental progress report, he realized the one issue he hadn't done anything about was the Kurbsky mystery. He looked at his watch. He had time for just a quick look. He left the hotel quickly, hailed the first cab he saw, and told the driver to take him to Belsize Park. He soon found Chamber Court, the residence of Kurbsky's aunt, Svetlana. It was a substantial detached property, early Victorian from the look of it. There was a front gate and a side gate, each with an intercom, but you couldn't see through the gates, and the walls were high, and it looked like an electronic security system ran along the top.

He kept on walking at a steady pace, aware that he

was very probably on camera, and then a strange thing happened. The side gate opened, and a man in overalls emerged. He was completely bald, his cheeks hollow, the eyes sunken and staring. Obviously, someone on chemo-therapy. It seemed cruel to think it, but he looked like a walking ghoul.

The poor sod, Holley thought, as Alexander Kurbsky ignored him and went into the corner shop on the other side of the road.

Holley kept going and found Abbey Road, increasing his pace and turning up his collar as it started to rain lightly. According to the files, Kurbsky's aunt lived in the house with her companion, Katya Zorin, British born but of Russian extraction. When the original plan had been put in place, Kurbsky had told Luzhkov that his aunt was to be left alone, that he would not visit her because he didn't want her in any way to be involved with the plot that had brought her nephew to London. In all the material Holley had studied, there had been no indication that anyone connected with the GRU had made any attempt to check the situation. Could Chamber Court have been housing Kurbsky all along, perhaps under Ferguson's protection? It was an intriguing thought, just as intriguing as the poor wretch he had just seen. Possibly an odd-job man of some sort.

He continued along Abbey Road, caught a cab at Swiss Cottage, and told the driver to take him to the Al-bany Regency. There was work to be done.

———

He sat drawing up the specific plans of action for Caitlin Daly. The number one target was Ferguson. He had that dinner at the Garrick Club, and Henry Pool was the obvious choice there. Pool had been in the private-hire business for several years, and his luxury Amara limousine was already preapproved by the Ministry. It was up to him to discover a way of being Ferguson's driver on Friday night. One of the small explosive devices Caitlin had hidden in the wine cellar would suffice to do the job, aided by an electronic remote control or possibly a pencil timer.

Miller and Johnson in New York were down to Barry and Flynn.

The Salters—he was helped there by the fact that, unusually for such a successful pub, it closed at eleven o'clock, and its comparative isolation would mean it would take time for emergency services to get there. An arson attack after midnight. He wrote down the name John Docherty, and suggested he proceed on foot so that the noise of a vehicle at that time in the early hours would not be noticed in the pub. He mentioned that an old Ford van parked outside the shed had a key in the ignition.

Monica Starling. She would leave Corpus Christi College at seven o'clock and drive six miles to the Raintree House. A photo from Holley's laptop was printed, and he assigned the task to Patrick Murray, the long-distance truck driver. It shouldn't be hard to run Monica Starling's vehicle off a country road.

Finally, Alexander Kurbsky. Something was not right about Chamber Court, he felt it instinctively, and the strange inhuman being he'd seen coming out of the side gate didn't seem right either. So that task he suggested for Matthew Cochran. Cochran would have to get over that wall to discover if it was tenanted only by the two women or not.

He produced each task on a separate sheet and put them together in an envelope with no address on it, as a precaution, and his mobile sounded. He answered.

"It's me, Ivanov. I'm calling from the Embassy. What's happening?"

"I've been busy, that's what's happening. I really haven't got time to talk now."

"Don't give me that. I'm in charge of you until Colonel Lermov gets here on Saturday. I've spoken to Chekhov. He tells me you've contacted the Daly woman and she's interested, but what's all this about New York?"

Holley was angry and bitterly regretted having been so open with Chekhov. "None of your business, sunshine. Don't interfere. If you screw things up, I'll kill you, I swear it."

"You wouldn't dare."

"Try me. Now, be a good boy. You know the rules. We never meet, I'm in charge, and I keep you informed on the telephone."

"Fuck you, you bastard."

"Why, Peter, I didn't know you cared."

Holley switched off. He might have known. That was the trouble with the military, always wanting to show what big stuff they were, always stealing the good work some junior officer had produced and passing it off as their own.

He pulled on his raincoat, stuffed the large envelope in a plastic bag, and went out in search of a cab.

It was late afternoon now, shadows drawing in, and close to five. He was just in time. It would give her a chance to look at his plans. He called her from the High Street in Kilburn.

"I'm here. You don't need to spend time with me. I'll just pass you the envelope."

"Wait for me in the church. I'll walk from the presbytery and come in through the back door."

He did as he was told, pushed the great front entrance open and ventured in. There were five or six people over on the right waiting by the confessional boxes. He stood at the back, and she appeared outside the sacristy and waved, and he went to join her.

She pulled him in, took the envelope, and opened it. "I'll give it a quick read." She finished the sheets in five minutes and put them back in the envelope. "It all seems to make sense. I'm sure Pool can sort something out with the car. He once told me he's very well in with the Ministry. It's a starting point anyway."

"Good."

"What about Roper and Dillon? I don't see them here."

"We haven't got enough manpower at the moment. But we can take them soon. For Roper, I thought we'd blow up the Holland Park safe house. The man in the wheelchair never seems to leave it these days."

"And Dillon?"

"I'll shoot him. He's a loner, which simplifies things. Someone alone in the street on a rainy night, someone behind . . ." He smiled, and she took a step back.

"Someone walked over my grave when you said that."

"Not you, Caitlin, not for years. Call me when you're ready."

He went out and straight up the aisle, opened the door wide, and started down the path. Peter Ivanov, dressed in a trench coat and trilby, stepped out of a monumental archway and faced him.

Holley stood there looking at him. "So you knew about the church and where it was even when we were in Moscow. You're not supposed to interfere, Ivanov. You'll ruin everything."

"Come with me," Ivanov told him. "We're going to have a little discussion. I wouldn't argue with Sergeant Kerimov here. He doesn't like it, and he's bigger than you."

Holley walked towards the car, where Kerimov, large and lumpen, stood on the other side waiting to get behind the wheel. He looked formidable. "Come on, get in." Ivanov opened the front passenger door. "I'll sit behind you."

Kerimov was smiling when he eased behind the wheel. Holley leaned down as if to sit on the passenger seat, pulled the Colt from his ankle holster, and shot Kerimov through the back of the left hand. He cried out, tried reaching for his gun with his right hand, and Holley rapped him across the head. Kerimov slumped across the wheel.

"Oh, dear, you'll have to get him in the backseat and drive him somewhere. Better not make it an emergency room. They call the police to a gunshot wound. Of course, there's always the medical facility at the Embassy," Holley said.

"God damn you," Ivanov told him.

"Next time, I'll kill *you*, remember that. Especially if I find you've come back here and interfered with Caitlin Daly."

He walked briskly away and left them to it.

12

On the way back, he reviewed the situation. He wasn't bothered in the slightest by what he had just done. Ivanov could hardly call in the law. All he could do was haul the wretched Kerimov back to the Embassy's sick bay. Lermov would have to hear about what had happened, of course, but it was obvious that Ivanov had broken the rules they'd all agreed on. What would Lermov make of that? Not very much, Holley concluded. He'd probably tell Ivanov to stop being an ass. Holley had made his point, drawn a line in the sand, and that was that.

He got out at the hotel but didn't go in. There wasn't much he could do right now, waiting on news of the meeting and which way things would swing. He also needed to give Chekhov the addresses and phone numbers of Barry and Flynn so Chekhov could speak to Potanin and get things up and running, but there was the same problem there. Frustrated, he went along to Shepherd's Market to visit Selim.

Sitting in the study, darkness falling outside, a gas fire burning in the Victorian fireplace, Holley fidgeted while waiting for the call. Selim had once again provided champagne, but Holley's was untouched.

"You really should drink up, Daniel," said Selim. "It'll help you relax. What's wrong? Can you tell me?"

"Not in any detail," said Holley. "It's just . . . I'm on the verge of satisfactory resolution to my job here, but—"

"But someone is interfering?"

"How do you know?" Holley asked.

"Because you always do things on your own. You hate any interference, and I can just bet that whoever you're doing this job for doesn't see it the same way."

"We agreed that we should never meet, that we should only make contact by encrypted mobile, and just now I had some eager young bastard, together with a sergeant the size of a brick wall, try to put me in a car in Kilburn."

"Ah, a sergeant. The military's involved, then. Men in uniform, they need to take charge, give orders."

"Well, not to me." Holley took the glass and drank it down in one gulp.

"So what did you do?"

Holley reached to the ankle holster and took out the Colt .25 and laid it on the brass table. "Shot the Sergeant in the back of the hand as he gripped the wheel and left his captain to struggle back to the Embassy with him."

"Wonderful." Selim smiled. "That's the best thing I've heard in years. You're a lone wolf, Daniel, the most dangerous beast in the forest."

Holley's mobile sounded. It was Caitlin. "Can we talk?"

Holley glanced at Selim, who pointed to the kitchen, picked up the bottle of champagne, and went out.

"I'm with a friend, but you can speak now. How did it go?"

"They went for it completely. And listen to this: we've already had a stroke of luck. It seems that Ferguson's usual car was damaged in a minor accident last week, so it's away for repair. Henry Pool said it's common knowledge amongst the other drivers because Ferguson was very angry."

"So he thinks he can be the replacement car?"

"Absolutely certain. Pool says if he asks for it, he'll get it. The dispatcher is an old pal of his."

"He's not concerned about the hazard?"

"He said it's common to leave passengers in the limousine to run errands for them, get a newspaper or cigarettes or sometimes a bottle. He'll nip out, set off the bomb, and no one will be the wiser."

"And the others are just as enthusiastic?"

"Yes, Docherty is quite happy about handling the Dark Man situation. He lived in Wapping years ago and knows his way round down there."

"And Murray?"

"No problem. He's going to put a suit and tie on, drive

up to Cambridge in the morning with the photo, find where Monica Starling lives, and put a face to the name."

"And Cochran?"

"He said that he seemed to have less to do than anyone. If I can't find a way to break into a house inhabited by two spinster ladies, he said, I should be ashamed of myself."

"Excellent. Call Barry and Flynn, too, tell them the good news, and give them the following name: Mikhail Potanin. Have you got that?"

"I've written it down."

"He is a very experienced guy in this kind of business, and he'll be in touch with them. They have nothing to fear. He'll help in any way he can. This Friday in New York is definitely on."

"Yes, I've got all that."

"Get on to them right now. And . . . thanks, Caitlin."

He called Chekhov next. It sounded like there was a party going on in the Park Lane apartment: music, female laughter.

"It's me," Holley told him. "What's going on over there?"

"Daniel, old son. Just a few friends."

"Are you drunk?"

"Never that, Daniel. You insult me as a Russian."

"We need to talk."

"And we shall. I'll go into my study, close the door,

and silence the chattering of fools." There was a movement, a certain banging, and the noise died. "How can I
help?"

"Everything's dropped into place. Caitlin and her cell
will swing into action here on Friday. As we speak, she's
confirming with Barry and Flynn that it's on for Friday.
I'll give you their phone numbers."

Chekhov said, "If I press a button, I'm recording this,
so just tell me."

Holley did. "I'm dropping this in Potanin's lap to
watch over them, make sure they're up to it—and, if necessary, clean up any messes."

"Don't worry, Daniel, he's done this kind of thing
many times before," Chekhov said.

"I gathered that, but make sure he realizes it's serious
business. I hear you had Ivanov on your case?"

"He gave me a call, I asked him if he'd spoken to you,
and he said not yet. I get the impression he doesn't exactly trust you."

"And I don't trust him. He called me, demanding that
I fill him in on everything. I gave him short shrift. I had
a package to deliver to Caitlin Daly."

"And don't tell me: he followed you?"

"He didn't need to. He just popped up. But he wasn't
supposed to approach her or me in any way—that was the
plan. He turned up in the graveyard at the church with
some thug called Kerimov in tow. Tried to force me into
his car."

"Oh, dear, tell me what happened."

"I shot him in the hand, not Ivanov, the large peasant.

I left them there to sort it out, went along to the main road, and hailed a cab."

"If you were here, I would embrace you, my friend," Max told him. "That's the most entertaining thing I've heard in years."

"Glad to oblige. Call Potanin now and tell him to get things moving in New York. I'm relying on you."

"The instant we hang up. What about Kurbsky?"

"I've got one of Caitlin Daly's people investigating the house in Belsize. I've been to have a look. There's something strange there, but I'm not sure what," Holley told him.

"Surely Kurbsky couldn't have been hanging out there. It's too obvious."

"I saw a weird guy coming out, a ghoul, God help him, obviously on chemotherapy."

"That couldn't be Kurbsky. He certainly doesn't have cancer."

"I'm not saying it was him. I just have a hunch about the place, that something's not quite kosher. Anyway, let's get moving. Let me know how things go."

But Chekhov did not immediately call Potanin. He stood there thinking about it, then he sighed deeply, murmured, "I suppose I'd better," and called his contact number for Lermov in Moscow.

The Colonel answered at once. "I wondered when I might hear from you. How's Holley getting on?"

"Quite brilliantly," Chekhov told him. "I've got to

say, Josef, he's a remarkable man. Here's the state of play at the moment."

He quickly went through everything Holley had told him, and when he was finished Lermov said, "He certainly works fast."

"So I should go through with it, call Potanin in New York and tell him to give Barry and Flynn any help they need?"

"Of course you should go through with it! This could be an extraordinary coup. Let me know everything— everything!—as it happens, even when I'm with Putin."

"I will, of course," Chekhov told him. "What do you think of this unfortunate business with Ivanov?"

"I don't know what you mean."

Chekhov told him, delighting in it, because he resented Ivanov's assumption of command and had come to realize that he didn't like him anyway.

Lermov said, "Stupid boy. I had high hopes of him, but there you are. I'll make my displeasure clear when he tells me."

"If he tells you," Chekhov said.

"Oh, he'll tell me all right, Max. I'll see to it."

At Shepherd's Market, the awnings out against light rain, Daniel and Selim enjoyed a late supper at a restaurant called Al Bustan. It was crowded, a constant buzz of conversation washing over them, but they had a certain privacy in the corner booth where they were sitting.

"Food is poetry to the people who run this restaurant," Selim told him, and sipped his wine. "You are calmer now, I think?"

"Because things are coming together," Daniel said. "But you're right about the food. Though anything would taste good after five years of the cooking in the Lubyanka. It's nice here." He looked around the restaurant. "It reminds me of Algiers."

And that made him think of Shabwa and the desert training camp and all that came since, and his mood darkened.

"What is it, my friend?"

Holley told him. "Nothing was ever the same when they'd finished with me. Algiers and Malik and the business became all I had."

"And now you think you have nothing?"

"In a way. I've been more disappointed than I'd hoped."

"We are all in the hands of Allah. He is responsible for all things."

"Then He willed me to exact a terrible vengeance on those four men who murdered that young woman. That deed changed me entirely. A different man took my place, and still does."

"This is too sad, Daniel, we must think of something better. Have you some time to spare tomorrow or are you trapped by your affairs? I have a small car in a garage I rent not far from here. A Mini Cooper. We could go out for a drive. Have lunch."

Holley thought about it. It wasn't a good idea, but, really, everything was in motion. New York was in play.

The others had their orders. Any remaining communication would be by phone anyway.

"All right, let's do it," Daniel said. "And I'm remembering something about Chekhov. He has a country place called Bolt Hole, located in an interesting part of West Sussex. Salt marshes, lots of sea, a causeway reaching out to a low island with an ancient house. I've seen it on television."

"It sounds fun. Does he go there a lot?"

"I don't think so. He told me he was refused permission for a helicopter pad, so he has to drive."

"So what? We could get to West Sussex in two hours. I have friends nearby." Selim shook his head. "These oligarchs, they are worse than Suleiman the Magnificent. Shall we take that as definite?"

"Absolutely," Holley told him. "We'll leave at ten."

"Then I suggest an early night." Selim raised his hand and called to the waiter for the bill.

Holley undressed and put on a robe, and Caitlin came on the Codex. "I've heard from Barry, and he's heard from Potanin. He said he's going to meet them tomorrow, with a friend of his named Bulganin. He suggested Barry take Miller and Flynn do Blake Johnson."

"Fine. Quogue should be pretty straightforward, but Miller is more difficult," Holley said. "Barry shouldn't underestimate him. Miller's a killer."

"God willing, he prevails," she said.

"Or Allah," he told her. "Same difference."

He poured a nightcap and went and stood at the window, watching the late-night traffic pass. Max Chekhov hadn't got back to him, but he'd clearly kept his promise and passed the details to Potanin. Chekhov probably had a woman or two keeping him busy, not that it mattered. He'd done his job. He wondered how Ivanov was managing to explain his sergeant's unfortunate accident. He'd bet anything Ivanov found a way to absolve himself of any blame. He looked at his watch. He probably should call Lermov himself, but it was too late now, three in the morning in Moscow. It could wait, and he went to bed.

For many years, Holley had had a recurring dream about Rosaleen Coogan and the events of that night. It lasted for a period of three or four weeks, usually during times of great stress and activity. It had not been much of a problem during his years of imprisonment, but now, and for the first time in a while, it surfaced.

It was always the same, a strange black-and-white landscape remarkably similar to film noir, buildings rising into the night streets, and she was there at his side, the only other person in a dark world, and she said she was going and would be back but never did, never came back again, and the streets were like a maze in the darkness as he ran from one place to another and never could find her. The strangest thing of all was trying to wake from that dream. It took an incredible physical struggle, and he would lie there in bed, soaked in sweat and trembling, and feeling a heartbreaking sense of loss for Rosaleen and the fact that she was gone, never to be found.

This time, lying on the bed of his suite in the Albany Regency Hotel, it was different. Somehow, Lady Monica Starling had become part of that dream, she was there with Rosaleen, and it was them both that Daniel was running around seeking, and he suddenly knew, beyond any shadow of a doubt, that no matter what anyone said, or wished or argued, that she'd killed a Provo herself, there was no way he could be a party to killing her, and Rosaleen would have agreed with him.

It somehow gave him a lightness of being, a calm happiness, call it what you like, but it was there for a moment, clear and profound, as if he had been touched by something. He felt a strange sense of peace, a kind of release, as he went to turn on the shower. He could take the men, but not Monica, and Caitlin and all the rest of them would have to accept that.

He started to get dressed but then stopped, and decided it was better to be dressed for action; you never knew what might come up. He put on the nylon-and-titanium bulletproof vest first, which was capable of stopping a .44 round at point-blank range. A white shirt and formal tie covered it, and, once he'd pulled on his trousers, he fastened the holster to his right ankle. When he left the hotel, borrowing one of its umbrellas, in his black suit and black raincoat, he looked like a thoroughly respectable City professional man.

It had rained during the night but stopped by the time Holley went around to Selim's, where he found a simple breakfast of croissants, coffee, and ripe bananas waiting. Selim wore a French beret and a black duster coat as they made their way through several backstreets and came to a mews named Friars Yard. He produced a key and opened the end garage, revealing a black Mini Cooper.

"A factory limited edition, small but deadly. I indulged myself. It will do in excess of a hundred and twenty-five miles an hour."

"And have you?"

"That, Daniel, is my dark secret. Would you care to drive?"

"It's been rather a long time since I did, but Daniel Grimshaw does have a perfectly valid forged license."

"Then put your umbrella in the back with the other one already in there."

"You think it will rain again?"

"Absolutely. This is England, Daniel. Off we go, and if you decide to have a crash, do it with style."

With the driving, it was as if he'd never been away, for the Mini Cooper handled superbly, and they had a good fast run from London to Guildford and all the way to Chichester, where they had a pit stop at the Ship Hotel and more coffee.

After that, they followed the Mini's Sat Nav through a maze of country roads and came to Patch End, and Holley pulled up at the side of the road. There was a salt marsh, an inlet with four houses, three old-fashioned fishing boats beached on the shingle, and a small motorboat.

Selim opened the glove compartment and took out a pair of Zeiss binoculars. He peered down. "There's a woman in the garden of the end house hanging out laundry. Do you want to take a look?"

Holley did and nodded. "I know Chekhov owns a house down there, and I bet that's a lady named Lily White. Her son, Jacob, keeps an eye on things for Chekhov while he's away."

"It wouldn't have much traffic down there. We'll go and see what Bolt Hole has to offer."

A mile farther on, they discovered a pub set back from the road with a sizable garden. The main part of it was undeniably old, but there was a modern extension that suggested a motel. It looked anything but prosperous, and it was just at that moment that the weather broke again.

"Rather sad, when you think of it," Selim said. "Imagine staying at that place in the rain."

"Well, Chekhov fell in love with Bolt Hole, told me so himself," Holley said. "So let's go and see why."

There were no cliffs but a headland of sorts, with a fringe of trees on top, a small car park behind, and the marsh below, with the causeway running out to the island. It was beautiful beyond doubt: the old house, the sea, and, every so often, a strange geyser of foam erupting.

"So that's where the name Bolt Hole comes from," Holley said, raising the binoculars. "Spectacular."

"Very impressive," Selim said. "And so is the motor yacht at the jetty on the seaside."

"It's called the *Mermaid*." Holley focused the binoculars in time to see a thickset, rough-looking man wearing a battered naval cap and an old reefer coat emerge from the wheelhouse.

"Jacob White in the flesh," Holley said. "Talking to someone on his mobile."

"There's a Mercedes coming in from the left down there."

Holley swung around to observe and received a shock, for the Mercedes turned along the causeway, pulled in on the jetty beside the *Mermaid*, and stopped at the gangway, where Jacob White stood waiting. Ivanov got out from behind the wheel, and Chekhov emerged from the passenger side.

"I'd like to say I can't believe it," Holley said. "But I do. Let me fill you in on these two."

He explained, and Selim said, "Well, you could say the plot thickens. But let's move, we may be noticed."

"They weren't supposed to go even near each other. The only communication was supposed to be by Codex. So what are they up to?"

"Ivanov's your biggest problem, the young military action dog who wants to be in charge."

"And Chekhov?"

"My dear Daniel, you took me into your confidence last night. You gave me no specifics, but forgive a man used to subterfuge when he guesses that this all has to do with the Russians. And by the Russians, I assume it leads to Putin."

"The man himself."

"Max Chekhov is an oligarch, and they've fallen increasingly on hard times in the financial mess of the world of today and they need to look to the Kremlin for support. Chekhov has more to contend with than most, since he was chosen to head Belov International when the State took it over again."

"In other words, he's a Putin man." Holley nodded. "Lermov told me that Putin told him Chekhov was the only oligarch he had any time for, and that was only because he had him in his pocket."

"So what would you like to do now?" Selim asked, but didn't get an answer.

A harsh voice called, "Hold on, you two. What are you doing sniffing round here? I saw you looking down at the boat, and you had binoculars."

"I think you're mistaken," Holley called, and hissed at Selim, "Keep going, let's get out of here."

Behind him, Jacob White increased his pace, reached out, grabbed Holley, and swung him around. Selim also turned and saw Chekhov and Ivanov toiling up the path behind.

"My God, it's you," Ivanov called. "Hold him, Jacob."

Holley, on the half turn as Jacob swung him around, delivered a reverse elbow stroke into the mouth, and, as Jacob doubled over, raised a knee in his face that lifted him backwards. The result was quite devastating.

Chekhov and Ivanov paused, Chekhov looking shocked. "Daniel," he said. "What's going on?"

"I might ask you the same thing," Holley answered, and Ivanov pulled a Makarov out of his trench coat pocket.

"My turn, you bastard," he said, and shot him.

It was like a tremendous punch in the chest delivered by a sixteen-stone heavyweight fighter, and Holley staggered, lost his balance, and fell on his back. From the first impact, he had taken one deep breath after another, for sometimes the force of a blow into body armor could induce unconsciousness. All those years ago in the camp, he'd been trained to handle such a situation.

He closed his eyes, heard Chekhov say, "You've killed him, you fool, you've ruined everything."

"The bastard deserved killing." Ivanov dropped to one knee. "I think I'll give him one in the forehead just to make sure."

Holley drew out the Colt .25, opened his eyes, reached up, and shot off half of Ivanov's left ear. Ivanov screamed, dropped the Makarov, and got to his feet, clutching the wound, blood streaming through his fingers.

Holley got up, aware of the pain in his chest and still breathing deeply. "I don't know what's been going on, Max, between you and the boy wonder here. It wasn't supposed to be like this. I've organized everything for Friday, completed my side of the bargain, but what have you and this piece of dung been up to, that's the question. I don't think Lermov will be pleased, and God help you with Putin if he found that everything had been turned into a cock-up because you and Ivanov had a different agenda."

Chekhov was horrified. "I didn't intend anything like this, Daniel, believe me. What am I going to do?"

"There must be a first-aid kit on the *Mermaid*. Strap him up, put him in the backseat, and get back to the Embassy in London. Next time, I really will kill him." He nodded at Jacob White, who had managed to get to his feet. "Maybe the last of the ape-men can give you a helping hand."

"I don't think he can even help himself," Chekhov said, and walked a few yards after them as they went to where the Mini Cooper was parked. He took out his diary and its pencil.

Selim saw what he was doing. "Ah, you are noting the number, hoping to trace me? It is Algerian, my friend, quite untraceable."

Holley turned. "Grow up, Max, or do you want a bullet yourself? Just piss off, and tell anyone who needs to know that everything is organized, or, as I suspect Caitlin Daly would say, on Friday we'll 'astonish' the world."

Selim got behind the wheel. "Get in, and I'll show you what a great driver I am. What would you like to do?"

Holley unbuttoned his shirt, found the Makarov round sticking in his bulletproof vest, and pulled it out. "A well-dressed man shouldn't be without one. As to what I'd like to do. That place, the Ship Hotel in Chichester, where we stopped for coffee, had a decent-looking restaurant. I'd say we could get there in half an hour. Sorry you won't be able to join me in the bottle of champagne I'm going to order."

"Then you'll have to drink it all yourself, dear boy," Selim Malik told him, and they drove away.

The lunch was all that could be expected, and Holley drank far too much champagne, as he admitted, but the real discovery was Selim's driving skill. He was first-rate.

On the way back to London, Holley, half asleep in his seat, said, "I've got to give it to you, Selim. You handle this thing like a racing driver."

"Always my dream," Selim told him. "Many years ago when I was at Oxford University, a policeman who pulled me up for speeding said, 'Who do you think you are, Stirling Moss?'"

"And you were flattered?"

"Who wouldn't be? Britain's all-time favorite star of the racetrack and a true gentleman. Now, of course, I am getting too old."

Holley was aware of nothing more after that because he fell asleep.

He woke with a start to Selim's touch on his shoulder. They were outside the hotel. "Here we are. What now?"

"Have a shower, sort myself out. Check the bruising." Holley managed a laugh.

"So you have nothing particularly important to do?"

"Everything's sorted, Selim, as I told Chekhov. It's all in order. Friday, everything comes together, and we solve the problem for Mister Big at the Kremlin. I've one call to make on my Codex, and then I'm going to turn it off so nobody can get me for the rest of the night."

"I have a suggestion. The Curzon Cinema in Shepherd's Market shows many interesting films. Tonight they show a French film directed by Jean-Pierre Melville in 1956, *Bob le flambeur.* It's a wonderful heist movie—an aging gangster is tempted back into one last fatal throw of the dice."

"That sounds like just my kind of movie," Holley said. "I can't wait. We'll have dinner afterwards. I'll see you in an hour."

When he called Caitlin Daly, he got an instant response. "Where are you?" he asked.

"At my office. Paperwork for the charity, and I've got a forum to attend with Monsignor Murphy."

"Don't you find it difficult to fit everything in?"

"Of course, but it's important, the work we do, and he's used to leaning on me in many ways. He's an important figure in the Catholic Church in London. Even the rich respond to him, and their money is important to us."

"When I read all the files on your people, it fascinated me that the whole Hope of Mary thing came out of Murphy doing a visit to Derry for a few months during the worst of the Troubles and being impressed by the work the Little Sisters of Pity were doing. I never got any idea he was in favor of a violent solution to the Troubles."

"He isn't. To believe in Sinn Fein and a United Ireland was always as natural as breathing for him, and I'm not saying he wouldn't confess an IRA man when the Church said he shouldn't—but not an ounce more than that. He's a great and good man."

"And a bit of a holy fool. I wonder what he'd say about your involvement in the Glorious Cause? You're sure he hasn't got an inkling?"

"Absolutely not. He'd be horrified. Stop this, Daniel, I don't want to hear any more on the subject."

"Have you had any final news from Barry and Flynn?"

"Not yet, but it's only noon over there. Flynn and Bulganin were supposed to go down to this Quogue place."

"You're right. Tomorrow will be soon enough. You'll be having a meeting in the chapel at the refuge, I suppose?"

"You're not going to suggest joining us?"

"There's no need. Everything's worked out. You've done very well. I'm going out to a show, so I'll turn off my mobile. I'll talk to you tomorrow."

He got dressed, thinking about it. She obviously wanted to be in charge, a psychological hang-up, that, because of being leader of the cell for so many years. And that was fine, though he didn't know how she'd react to his insistence that Monica Starling be taken out of the equation. He realized that it'd be better if he told her about it face-to-face, but he would leave that until tomorrow night.

His phone sounded just before he was leaving. It was Chekhov. "Daniel, you've got to understand the pressures I'm under. Ivanov is a madman. I knew he was too good to be true the first time I met him."

"How is the bastard?"

"Never mind that. He shot you in the chest. How did you survive that?"

"I was wearing a bulletproof vest under my shirt. You really should consider it for yourself, Max."

"My God, I'm going to get one straightaway, but about Ivanov. I patched him up on the boat, and drove him back to the Embassy, as you suggested. They had some top surgeon in to stitch him up, but he's going to look very strange."

"What were you doing there in the first place?"

"He was very insistent that I should take him down there and show it to him. He said that perhaps it could be useful sometime."

"In what way?"

"He didn't say. I thought he might want it for weekends. You know, boyfriends and so on."

"I didn't realize his inclinations ran that way. Mind you, that's his business. To each his own. I'm going out, so you needn't try again. If you want to cover your back, phone Lermov and tell him what happened."

"Actually, I already have."

"You're a laugh a minute, Max." Holley switched off and left.

Bob le flambeur was sensationally good and lifted his spirits in spite of the downbeat ending. "Marvelous," he told

Selim as they sat in the booth at Al Busten. "They don't make them like that anymore. I didn't get a chance to tell you, by the way: Chekhov called me."

"What happened?"

Holley told him. "A pity the sod didn't die in the back of the Mercedes."

"You have a point. With such a man, one wonders what he could try next. Your big day, whatever it is, is Friday. I presume that after that your problems will be over?"

"It would be a clean break, let's put it that way."

"So what of tomorrow?"

"I haven't the slightest idea. I have one important phone call to make in the morning. The rest is just time filling."

"Then may I suggest an excellent way to spend the whole day. Twenty miles out of town is a spa and country club of which I happen to be a member. An excellent gymnasium, two swimming pools, more health treatments than you would know what to do with. There is even a golf course."

"I don't play golf."

"You can drive round in a cart with some clubs and try."

"You know something, you're absolutely right," Holley told him, and emptied the champagne bottle into their glasses and toasted him. "And if it's anything like it's been, it'll be a nice day out in the rain."

13

Which it certainly was, but the day was saved by Selim planning ahead and speaking in the intimate way one would to an old friend, to someone called Martha who was, it seemed, director of activities. The result was that when they arrived at ten-thirty and ran from the Mini Cooper through pouring rain to the front entrance, they were met by an attractive fortyish blonde in white slacks and a blue blazer who had a full program organized for them.

Club tracksuits were supplied. Selim went off for a massage, Holley elected to try the gym, where a muscular young man named Harry put him through a series of weight-training classes and, noting his age from the form he'd filled in, observed that he was in remarkable condition and obviously worked out.

Holley didn't tell him he had until recently been a

regular user of the gym facility at the Lubyanka Prison. In any case, when he stripped off his vest, revealing the terrible bruise Ivanov's bullet had made, his explanation—that he'd slipped against the end of a steel bar at a London gym—was received with horror at the lack of professionalism that had allowed such a thing to happen.

He worked his way through a series of weight-lifting exercises and cycles and finally ended up in a sauna for half an hour, then another half hour swimming, and decided he'd had enough. He asked for a fresh tracksuit, went to the lounge bar, ordered a large scotch, and went and lay on a recliner, from which he could look out at the golf course stretching away into an infinity of rain and mist.

He had his Codex in a pocket of the tracksuit, and, when it sounded, he got it out quickly. It was Caitlin Daly. "Where are you?"

"Somewhere in Kent. What have you got for me?"

"The word from Barry is excellent. He tells me that Potanin and the other man, Bulganin, are first-rate. Bulganin and Flynn went to Quogue and sniffed round. There aren't too many people there this time of year, and with the weather, and they located the boat."

"And the Miller hit?"

"Barry said Potanin's provided him with a silenced pistol with hollow-point cartridges. He said Potanin instructed him to wait, identify his target, then shoot him up close, preferably in a crowd situation, and just keep on walking. Nobody sees a thing. Wasn't that the way Mick Collins and his boys operated in Dublin in the old days?"

For the first time, it occurred to Holley that she might

be a raving lunatic. "Well, I suppose there is a certain truth to that, but let's hope for Barry's sake something else turns up. You're seeing the cell again tonight?"

"Yes, everyone's ready for action, it's all systems go."

"There's just one change," Holley said, and when Selim appeared in a robe, a towel around his neck, he put a finger to his lips and motioned him to sit.

"What would that be?"

"The woman, Monica Starling. I've decided against it. You can tell Murray his target is aborted."

Her response was immediate. "You can't do that. It was agreed."

"I've changed my mind. I'm not going to be responsible for the killing of a woman, and, if you've a brain in you at all, you'll know why. That's an end of it. My decision."

"You can't do that. I'm cell leader."

"And I'm the commander of the whole bloody plot," Holley told her. "Without me and the Russians, you wouldn't have an operation. Now you've still got one but without the killing of the woman."

Her reluctance was plain in her voice. "If that's the way it has to be."

"Don't mess with me on this, girl." His voice was hard. "I hold the cards here. I can have word sent to Potanin that it's all off, even order him to dispose of Barry and Flynn."

She was obviously shaken. "No, don't do that."

"I'll call round tonight after your six o'clock meeting and confirm this with you face-to-face. I'll be waiting in the back pew."

"All right. I understand."

He switched off his Codex and turned to Selim, who was looking grave. "Not good, I fear, whatever it is. Who is this woman, have I met her?"

"No, and you wouldn't want to. A deeply disturbed individual, but aren't we all? Now, how about some lunch? After all my exertions, I'm absolutely starving."

After lunch, Selim disappeared to indulge in a final massage of some description and an appointment in the hairdressing salon. Holley felt that enough was enough, although there was no doubt that he felt a lot better than when he'd arrived. He was sitting in the lounge bar, thinking about what had happened with Caitlin Daly, when Martha appeared to inform him that the clothes he'd been wearing when he'd arrived had all been valeted and were waiting for him in the allotted cubicle.

He found perfection. Even his tie had been pressed, the shoes shined. He returned to the bar lounge to find Selim still in a robe but with his hair trimmed and looking suspiciously black.

"You've had a dye job," Holley said.

"And you, my friend, look like a whiskey advert. For a man of forty-nine, you look remarkably fit, Daniel. It's not fair."

"Not much in life is," Holley told him. "Let's have a coffee, then you go and change, and I suggest we make tracks."

Selim waved to the barman as Holley's Codex sounded.

Lermov said, "There you are, Daniel. Time we talked, I think."

"Where are you?"

"Moscow, but soon to leave for the Prime Minister's plane."

"Well, that's nice for you, so close to the seat of power. But remember Icarus. His wings melted and fell off when he flew too close to the sun."

"Ah, you obviously enjoyed the benefits of a classical education."

"Of a grammar school education, Josef, in my case the Leeds variety. What do you want?"

"Daniel, you mustn't go round shooting people, it won't do."

"So you heard about that? From your pet poodle Chekhov, I suppose!"

"Yes, and I know about the incident when Ivanov turned up at the church and tried to force you into the car. He was wrong."

"Glad you agree. But about yesterday's incident, I would point out he shot me first. I'm only speaking to you now thanks to the genius of the Wilkinson Sword Company, which made my bulletproof vest."

"I accept all that, but you've certainly had your revenge. Half an ear gone."

"Well, let's say he's made his mark in the world. I should imagine he'll look satisfactorily grotesque."

"You're a hard man, Daniel, even harder than I'd imagined."

"What you see is *not* what you get with me, Josef. You

should have realized that just as you should have realized what Peter Ivanov is really like under that pretty uniform. He's broken your specific orders in this matter. We were to be voices on the Codex, that's all. He violated that by showing up at the church and yet again by making Chekhov take him to Bolt Hole. What was that all about?"

"I could ask the same of you. Who was your mysterious companion, of the Arabic persuasion?"

"You knew I'd need the services of a banker and weapons supplier, and that was he. I was interested after my discussions with Chekhov about Bolt Hole. It occurred to me that it might offer some sort of temporary sanctuary. He keeps a substantial motor yacht there. In such a vessel, France would be only a short run across the English Channel in time of need, if you follow me. After all, who knows how this thing will end?"

"I see your point. So you and your friend were simply assessing the situation?"

"And completely astonished when Chekhov and Ivanov appeared. The rest, as they say in a mystery novel, you know."

"So to come to what's important, everything is set for tomorrow?"

"Absolutely. You can tell the Prime Minister, if you like."

"I don't think so. I'm a cautious man. I like to be sure. I'd rather wait until it's actually happened and then surprise him."

"Of course, Josef, but do tell Ivanov to do as he's told."

"I already have. I don't suppose there's anything else you need?"

"Not that I can think of. Safe flight, enjoy New York. I trust it will be a memorable visit for you."

"In more ways than one," Lermov told him.

Selim had waved the waiter away and sat there throughout the entire conversation. Now he beckoned the barman back and repeated the order.

"Did you get all that?" Holley asked.

"A trifle one-sided, but what you were saying was interesting. I presume that the person you were talking to is Ivanov's superior?"

"Very much, and just appointed Head of Station for the GRU in London, Colonel Josef Lermov, to be precise. They lost his predecessor in the Thames. Lermov pulled me out of the Lubyanka to try and find a solution to the problem Putin had dropped into his lap. You'll be thrilled to know he's about to leave Moscow as part of Putin's entourage, flying with the great man to New York where he will speak at the United Nations tomorrow night."

"Daniel, I have got beyond being astounded at anything in this business." Selim waved the barman away after he placed the tray on the table. "I suggest we have our coffee and then go back to London, where I presume the final episode will take place. Not long now, I suppose, that's one good thing. The suspense is killing me. What next?"

"I'm expected in Kilburn at round seven o'clock by the lady I was talking to before."

"This is important?"

"Very much so, and also unpleasant, but it has to be done."

"You know, the time I have spent with you has been like a movie," Selim said. "Your story, all the things happening to you, I see only through your eyes and what you choose to tell me, but it's always only part of the story. I don't see what the others in your life do, except in that singular episode involving Chekhov and Ivanov. It's as if you were living life in a film noir seen only from your point of view, inhabited by cinema ghosts, and you are one of them."

"The entire story told in one hour and forty minutes," Holley said. "Just like *Bob le flambeur.*"

"And look what happened to him," Selim replied, and he got up and went off to get dressed.

Selim dropped Holley off at the hotel. "You're sure you don't want to borrow the car?"

"No, I'll be fine with a cab."

"As usual, I don't know what it is you have to do, but I trust it will go well. If you're free later, come and see me. The big day tomorrow may make you restless tonight."

"I know." Holley grinned. "The suspense is killing me now."

Selim drove away, and Holley, discovering it was only

four-thirty, borrowed an umbrella from the doorman and went around Mayfair for forty minutes, rain-walking in a private and enclosed world under the umbrella, but all he was doing was putting off the bad moment, he knew that, and he returned to the hotel and went up to his suite.

He half undressed, taking off his shirt so that he could put on his bulletproof vest again. He strapped on the ankle holster, decided against the Walther PPK for now but slipped the flick-knife into his left trouser pocket. So he was prepared, for it had to be done, though he was not looking forward to it.

He told the cabdriver to drop him at Kilburn High Road and walked through to the park, passing Hope of Mary Hospice and Refuge at half past six. He stood there, umbrella raised against the interminable rain, then walked back to the church through the darkness, left his umbrella in a corner of the porch, and went in.

He stood in the gloom, at first by the door where religious pamphlets of one kind or another were displayed. There was a selection of prayer cards of various kinds, all at a price to help church funding, and there it was, that special "we who are ourselves alone" card. He helped himself, meticulously dropping a couple of pound coins into the box provided. He went and sat on the end of the rear pew and waited.

It was very quiet, the church smell, the guttering candles, but there was no one by the confessional boxes, and the lights had been turned off, probably to save on the electricity bill. There was a gloomy, medieval atmosphere about the place that some might have found menacing, and, in the darkness, things creaked.

A door banged from the direction of the sacristy, and she appeared by the altar and walked towards him, an old khaki trench coat over her shoulders. Her steps echoed hollowly.

He stood to greet her. "So there you are, Caitlin. You've done what I asked?"

She stared at him, proud and bitter. "If it's what you want, then let it be so. I'll not pretend to like it. That she shot dead one of our own while working with Ferguson is a known fact, and I think it's illogical to treat her differently because she's a woman."

"It's what I need, Caitlin, it's as simple as that. So you give me your word that Murray has your orders to abort?"

She crossed herself. "I swear it on my soul, and I'll swear it on anything else you wish—the Bible, if you like."

"I'll be content if you swear it on your own symbol of the prayer most precious in your life above all things." He held up the card. "Swear it on this."

"I swear before God and with all my heart that I have spoken to Patrick Murray in front of his comrades, who can confirm that his mission concerning Monica Starling is aborted."

She held out the card to him, and he said, "No, I'd prefer you to keep it."

"Then if you don't mind, I'll take my leave of you,"

Caitlin Daly said. "A great day tomorrow, God willing. Will we see you in the evening?"

"I think not," Holley said. "I'll leave it to you and the cell. Saturday will be the day to see what's been achieved."

As he turned to go, she caught his arm. "You still don't truly believe in all this, do you?"

His laugh was harsh and genuine. "A bit late in the day to ask me that sort of question. I stopped believing in myself years ago. Once you've made a discovery like that, it's difficult to believe in anything else, but it's your day if it's anybody's. I'll leave it to you and contact you on Saturday morning."

He went out, and she said to herself, "I thought so." There was a slight creak as one of the doors opened in a confessional box, and a man came forward holding a pistol in his right hand. "You heard all that, Patrick?"

"I could have shot him easy."

"Don't be stupid. What would we have done with the body? It would have ruined everything."

"So what happens now? Does what you told me in front of the others still hold?"

"Of course not. Go back to the original instructions and kill the bitch. Now, go on, get out, and keep this to yourself."

He withdrew, the door banged, and it was so quiet, only the Virgin Mary floating in a sea of candlelight, watching her. She looked down at the prayer card. She tore it into little pieces, her face quite calm, then walked back to the sacristy.

Although not of the faith himself, Daniel Holley had seen enough of how important Roman Catholicism was to Irish women to believe that the oath she had given him, sworn on the Virgin herself, would be binding. The memory of his years with his beloved mother was enough to convince him. In the cab during the return journey, he felt considerable relief. He called ahead and told Selim he was on his way. A certain burden had been lifted, and it showed when he got to the shop and rang for entrance.

Selim bustled out wearing his black duster coat. "I could tell by your voice that you are a different man. Am I correct?"

"Yes, I have to admit I'm much relieved."

"Excellent. Five minutes to go for the eight o'clock show at the Curzon. They're showing Alain Delon and Belmondo in *Borsalino*."

"Gangsters again?" Holley said.

"Of course, and why not? Hurry, my boy. We'll just make it."

The film was as stunning as it had been the first time Holley had seen it, decades ago. Later at Al Bustan, they discussed it. "More than any other filmmakers, the French have portrayed the romance of the gangster, have been able to make him a genuine antihero, and there is a certain nobility to such characters," Selim said.

Holley shook his head. "You've been reading too many film magazines, Selim. The one thing that all such films have in common is the ending. Your antihero, usually on his back in some street, a gun in his hand, in the act of dying if not already dead. Where's the nobility in that?"

"But this is not always so, Daniel. You, my boy, are still here despite all the odds, the samurai for real."

"But consider the price, Selim. Has it been worth it? I think not." He got up and reached for his coat. "I'll see you in the morning."

He went out into the narrow street, turning up his collar against the rain, lighter now but still there. He felt a strange content, probably because of the way the problem with Caitlin Daly had resolved itself, and was reasonably satisfied with the way things were going. He assumed that Harry Miller had already departed for New York. What he didn't know was that the Gulfstream carried an additional passenger, one Sean Dillon, who had persuaded Ferguson at the last minute that he should go.

For the moment, all Holley wanted was sleep, for tomorrow would be one of the most important days in his life, and, arriving back at the hotel, he went straight up to his room and turned in.

He had the dream again, if anything more intense than ever, Rosaleen with him an even shorter time, leaving him quite quickly, assuring him that she would return but never doing so. There was the same sense of panic as he ran through those narrow streets and towering buildings in the black-and-white world. This time, it wasn't just the feeling of loss where she was concerned, it was experiencing the sensation that he was the only person in that dark world, and for the first time he struggled and came awake.

He lay there, staring at the ceiling, aware that he was totally alone and always would be. That was his eternal truth and something he'd better face, so he got up, showered and shaved, put on his ankle holster, just in case, and went across to Shepherd's Market.

Selim insisted on making scrambled eggs and toast for them, and Holley sat there in the kitchen watching him cooking. It was absolutely delicious, and he said so, and Selim beamed happily.

"If I learned one great thing from the English when I was at Oxford, it was the art of making perfect scrambled eggs on toast, for it is a great art. Did you know that Ian Fleming is said to have virtually lived on scrambled eggs? He once said in an interview that he could eat them at any time, day or night."

"Selim, you're a good friend, and I know what you're doing. You're trying to take my mind off things, and, yes, I need that. If things go right, they'll start happening in the late afternoon New York time. The other things will happen here late tonight. I am on standby, if you like. It's other people who will actually go to war. The woman that was proving difficult? She is actually in charge of what's happening. I planned things, it's as simple as that. While others go into action, I have to stand back and wait for the result."

"And if it does not produce the expected success, one supposes Mister Big at the Kremlin gets to blame you?"

"So what do I do? The day stretches ahead."

"Care to return to my favorite spa? I could phone Martha and book us in overnight."

Holley was going to say no and then thought, Oh, why not? He could get the verdict there as well as anyplace else. And should the news turn out to be bad—well, he was really going to need that massage.

At the club, things were very much as they had been before, even the weather was the same, late-winter cold and miserable rain. Sitting in the lounge bar at four o'clock in the afternoon on his own after a strenuous round in the gym, Holley received his first voice from the outside world. A call from Chekhov.

"Where are you?" he demanded.

"None of your business," Holley told him. "I'm staying out of the way, that's all you need to know. Everything is in place, so I've stepped back, leaving Caitlin Daly to strut her stuff as cell leader."

"Do you think that's wise?"

"She's earned her spurs, Max. Everyone knows what they've got to do. Ferguson, the Salters, Kurbsky, New York—it's all out of my hands now."

"You seem to have skipped Monica Starling," Chekhov said.

"Because I've taken her off the agenda."

"A sudden attack of conscience?"

"I have no difficulty killing on behalf of a woman, as you well know. But I've never actually killed one, and I don't intend to start now."

"And Caitlin Daly must have hated that."

"How did you know?"

"Think Red Brigade, or go back further, to the French Revolution. She'd have helped female aristocrats up the steps to the guillotine with a smile on her face."

"I think you're being a little hard there, Max. What's the boy wonder up to?"

"They've sewn up his ear. It's covered by a substantial dressing and surgical tape, so you can't see how much damage has been done, but it must be considerable."

"I meant it to be."

"I'm surprised he isn't still in his bed in the sick bay, but he's up and round and glaring at everyone like the Devil himself. I saw him in the canteen with Kerimov, who has dressing taped across his left hand and wears a black sling. It's the only time I've visited the Embassy in the past few days."

"Not that you'd tell me, but has he said anything about me?" Daniel asked.

"As I said, I stick to the plan and stay away from the Embassy as much as possible, which was the order. He hasn't phoned me since the confrontation. But, Daniel, this is why I phoned you—I wanted to let you know that Lermov's been in touch."

"When was this?"

"An hour or so ago. He's arrived in New York. He asked after Ivanov and suggested I should call you."

"Concerned about my welfare, no doubt?" Holley laughed. "Keeping tabs on me, more like. He spoke to me yesterday just before they left Moscow. Asked me to stop shooting people and inquired about how things were going, but I assume he would know anyway because I've kept you informed. It did occur to me that you might have passed it along to him."

"But, my dear Daniel, what is one to do?"

"That's for you to decide. Survival's the name of the game where you're concerned, I can see that, and I don't hold it against you. You can't harm me because I don't trust you for a minute, Max, not even for a little bit."

"Now, that's hard, Daniel," Chekhov told him.

"Yes, isn't it?"

Daniel cut him off, and Selim appeared in a robe. "Just checking. Are you all right?"

"I'm fine. Get back to work," Holley told him. "You've got to think of those pounds."

He waited for the next call, but it was an hour before it came. Lermov said, "I won't ask you where you are. A man of secrets, I think. Is everything still in place?"

"Absolutely. I'm standing back while Caitlin Daly savors her hour of glory."

"No problems, then?"

"One change of plan. I decided to abort the attack on Monica Starling."

"Yes, I heard about that. Did it cause any problem?"

"It wasn't well received, but it's my decision."

"Very noble of you. So now we wait. I wish you luck, Daniel. If you can bring this off, it will be the coup of a lifetime."

Holley sat there, thinking about it. So Chekhov must have been in touch with Lermov the minute he'd put the phone down, which explained Lermov knowing about the Monica Starling business. Well, that was all right. He was reminded of the old Mafia saying: "Keep your friends close but your enemies closer."

He closed his eyes, dozing, and after a while there was a tap on his shoulder, and he opened his eyes and found Harry standing there in his white uniform.

"We're ready for you in the pool now, Mr. Grimshaw, all those special exercises. Lots to do."

Holley got up and followed meekly, for it was filling the time admirably until the final act of the drama.

And so time wore on and the evening came, and then it was time for bed. He slept lightly, too much on his mind, braced for the calls, until finally he was fetched awake by his Codex. He glanced at the bedside clock and saw it was two in the morning. "Daniel," Chekhov said. "I've had a call from Potanin in New York. It's not good."

"Tell me."

"The business at Quogue, Ivan Bulganin was observing from a clump of trees. He saw Flynn shoot Johnson as the boat came in, but Johnson managed to shoot him in return. Flynn went into the water. Bulganin couldn't do anything about it except get the hell out of there, and, as he left, he heard the sound of emergency vehicles arriving."

"And Frank Barry?"

"Miller left the Plaza to go for a walk in Central Park. Barry followed him, and Potanin stalked them. Barry tried to jump Miller, and Miller had what looked like an ankle holster. He shot Barry in the knee and walked away. Potanin couldn't risk any involvement and cleared off."

"Christ, what a bloody cock-up."

"I haven't finished. Barry called in on his mobile from Mercy Hospital. He told Potanin he'd better get him out or else."

"And what did Potanin do?"

"Sent Bulganin round dressed as a doctor and stuck a hypo in him. Some nurse arrived, he punched her and got clean away."

"A total disaster," Holley said.

"It could have been worse. Barry's dead, and Bulganin made sure to pocket his mobile. There's no connection to Belov, or to us."

"Well, that's something, I suppose. Have you informed Lermov?"

"Not yet, but I obviously must. He's at a late dinner at the UN."

"Hardly a good time."

"I understand he's coming back to London tonight."

"Yes. He won't want to confront Putin with this kind of news, but you should tell him, if only to cover yourself," Holley said.

"And Ivanov?"

"He'll find out anyway."

"What about the woman? Has she called? Do you know how things are going here?"

"I told her I'd contact her in the morning, but I meant a more civilized hour than this."

"Well, I think you should tell her about New York as soon as possible."

"You're right, I suppose. I'll call you back. In the old days, they sometimes killed messengers who delivered bad news." Holley's laugh had a certain grimness to it.

"Not nice, Daniel, not nice at all. You'll put me off my breakfast."

Holley got out of bed, put on a robe, then went and sat in an easy chair beside a window that overlooked the terrace and called her. She answered almost instantly.

"Is it you, Daniel?"

"Yes, Caitlin."

She seemed to hesitate, then carried on. "Is there news from New York yet?"

"Where are you?"

"I came over from the presbytery. There's no one round in the church at this time of the morning. I've locked myself in the sacristy."

"Sitting down, I hope, because I've had my friend Chekhov on with news from his security people in New York, and bad news it is."

"Go on," she said in a strangely calm voice.

So he told her.

———————

When he was finished, she said wearily, "Well, God wasn't on our side, that's for sure."

"What happened in London?" Holley said. "Tell me the worst."

"Ferguson and Pool and the limousine. A premature explosion before they got in. Pool had a remote control, so he must have mishandled it, and he was closer to the Amara, so he was killed and Ferguson was simply blown over. Hardly singed, let alone killed."

"And the Salters?"

"I drove Docherty down there myself and hung round to see how he got on. He seemed to get in the pub all right, but after a while there was a disturbance, and he came running out with somebody after him. He got in that old van you mentioned, started up, and drove straight along the jetty into the Thames. I don't know what went wrong. He must have panicked. I got out of there fast and came back here."

"A total failure. Barry and Flynn dead in New York, Pool dead, Docherty very probably. What happened to Cochran?" Holley asked.

"I think we may have struck gold there. He got in the garden and was disturbed by a man who beat him up pretty thoroughly. He said he looked like some ghoul in a horror movie."

"The chemotherapy man," Holley told her. "I walked past the house yesterday, to check it out from the outside, and saw him emerge from a side entrance."

"Another man, Cochran said, came out of the house on the terrace and called: 'Are you all right, Alex?'"

"Alexander Kurbsky, it has to be, and the other guy would be Yuri Bounine. What happened?"

"This Alex relieved Cochran of his wallet. He was distracted by the arrival of his friend, so Cochran managed to run for it, scrambled over the wall, and got away. He also heard women's voices, and one did call out: 'Alexander, are you well?'"

"That's it," Holley said.

"Not quite, Daniel." She was silent for a moment. "We even lost when I lied to you."

In a way, he knew what was coming, and said, "Spit it out."

"Monica Starling." She took a deep breath and told him. "So there you are, and God's curse on me for what I did. She's all right, though."

"And how in the hell would you know?"

"Murray dumped the truck into a tree farther along and went back through the wood along the side of the road. He watched police and ambulance at the scene. There was an old boy with her who'd been bandaged up, but she seemed fine."

"No thanks to you," Holley told her.

"So what happens now?" she asked wearily. "I suppose the Russians will be interested to know that Kurbsky is alive and kicking, if that weird-looking man really is him."

"I'd stake my life on it. I think this strange appearance is just a very clever disguise. If you look at photos of

Alexander Kurbsky, he's a long-haired, bearded cavalier of a man, a swagger to him. It was an absolutely brilliant idea on the part of whoever thought it up to disguise him as the exact opposite."

"So you'll pass the information on to the Russians? What would they do? Kidnap him, I suppose?"

"To do that, they'd have to lay hands on him, and I very much doubt that's going to happen. Charles Ferguson and his friends have just experienced a personal and very organized series of attacks. They're not going to take any chances." Holley shook his head. "Ferguson is going to fear the worst when Kurbsky reports in. He'll make arrangements to get him and the women out of there and pack them off to somewhere safe and secure. Perhaps out of the country."

"Where do you think?"

"Oh, who the hell knows? They're very close with the Americans, they'll probably help. One thing you can be certain about, it will happen today and very quickly."

"So what now?"

"I'll not run out on you."

"I'm glad to hear it. Just before everything hotted up last night, I had a strange call from a man who asked me if I knew where you were. He said he was a Captain Ivanov."

"What did you do?"

"I was up to my eyes with everything. I said I didn't know what he was talking about, and he laughed in a very nasty way and said maybe he should come and see me. I closed down on him. Who is he?"

"I told you I had the Russians behind me in this and asked if it bothered you. You said it didn't and that they were a means to an end. Peter Ivanov is a GRU captain. He's turned out to be a truly bad man. He doesn't like me and thinks he should be the one running things, not that there's much left to run. I'll deal with him."

"Where are you?"

"In the country. I'll be back in town soon. Look for me, girl. Keep the faith."

He sat there, thinking about it. A bloody mess it had turned out to be and still only three o'clock in the morning. Well, no point going back to bed now. He called Selim, who answered groggily.

"Whoever this is, go away."

"It's me, Selim. Stop fooling round. We need to talk. Meet me downstairs in five minutes."

He had actually been sitting in the lounge for fifteen minutes when Selim emerged, looking rumpled.

"So tell me what's so important."

Holley did, from the beginning to the shambles it had now become. Selim listened with a kind of awe. "My dear boy, can this be so? It's better than the midnight movie. What happens now?"

"Charles Ferguson will move quickly to get Kurbsky and those with him to somewhere safe—and that's the end of it."

"The Big Boss in the Kremlin will be disappointed, and I have a feeling Lermov will feel you've let him down."

"Well, that's too bad . . . And if he thinks I'll go back to the Lubyanka, he can think again."

"Fighting talk, that's what I like to hear. Let's see if there's anyone round to give us breakfast, Daniel, and then we'll get back to town and see what's happening."

END GAME

14

Back in London at his hotel, Holley phoned Ivanov in the afternoon. "I presume you've heard the bad news?"

"Chekhov told me as soon as he knew. Not so clever now, Holley, are we? You've failed."

"I suppose you could put it that way," Holley told him. "Has Lermov called?"

"Of course he has and he isn't pleased. I'd say it's back to the Lubyanka for you."

"It's a thought, I suppose. When does he get in?"

"Round midnight, and he's told me to keep a close eye on you. No use in trying to do a runner." He was thoroughly worked up, his voice full of venom.

"Don't be stupid," Holley told him. "How can you keep a close eye on me when you don't even know where I am?"

"I know where the Daly woman is, though."

"That's true, but I warned you about approaching her and I meant what I said. She's had enough on her plate."

"Yes, more bloody failure, as I understand it. Major Chelek has heard what happened to Charles Ferguson last night. Absolutely bloody nothing. A dead chauffeur wasn't the point. I understand the Salters' pub, the Dark Man, is still standing in spite of a suspected arson attack."

"True," Holley said. "And Lady Monica Starling survived the crash with the truck driver who tried to knock her off the road."

"A complete failure, that's the truth of it," Ivanov said. "And what about Kurbsky? Chekhov told me that you had arranged for one of the cell members to break into Kurbsky's aunt's house to find out if he's been hiding there. What happened about that?"

Suddenly, in a moment of revelation, Daniel Holley knew that he'd had enough, and that he didn't really care anymore about Putin being disappointed and Josef Lermov's career prospects facing severe damage. When it came right down to it, even the threat of a return to the Lubyanka didn't worry him, because he was going to run, and keep on running, and they could all go to hell.

What he wasn't going to do was tell Ivanov that Alexander Kurbsky and Yuri Bounine were hiding in his aunt's house, almost certainly awaiting a pickup for pastures new, arranged by Charles Ferguson.

"According to Cochran, the house was empty, everyone gone. That's all I can say."

"Then where are they?"

"I haven't the slightest idea. Maybe Ferguson would know. You could ask him."

"Or that Starling bitch," Ivanov said. "She was more involved with Kurbsky than anyone."

"I don't think you'd get very far asking her, and, as she's Harry Miller's sister and Sean Dillon's lover, I wouldn't advise you to try. Anyway, I'm telling you again. Stay away from Caitlin Daly."

"Go to hell," Ivanov told him, and clicked off.

Holley didn't have to prepare for the possibility of a bad scenario, he knew it was coming. He stripped to the waist and pulled on his bulletproof vest, then dressed again. This time, he backed up the ankle holster and the knife in his left sock with the silenced Walther in the special left-hand breast pocket of his raincoat.

At the shop, Selim let him in, and said, "I see you have your suitcase with you."

"At this stage in the game, a fast exit might be in order. I'm returning your laptop."

"Bring me up-to-date," Selim said.

Holley filled him in. "So there you are, a disaster all round."

"The call from Ivanov doesn't sound good. Do you think he'll go after Daly?"

"I'm sure of it, which is why I'm going there now. Lermov's not due until midnight. Can I borrow the Mini Cooper?"

"Of course you can. I'll get the keys." Selim went out

for a moment, then returned and handed them to Holley. "If you have to park it somewhere, leave the keys inside and lock the door. I have spares if it needs to be picked up. What have you planned?"

"I haven't the slightest idea. I'm at the stage where I'm not playing the game, the game's playing me."

"A most interesting position to be in. I await the outcome with bated breath."

"Then I'll be on my way. Obviously, I'll be in touch."

"Please do, dear friend." Selim embraced him and lightly kissed his cheeks. "Allah protect you."

Holley went out into Shepherd's Market, the door closed behind him. He was alone again.

He'd just started to drive when his Codex sounded, and he pulled over to the side of the road. It was Chekhov, and his first words were, as usual, "Where are you?"

"On the road. What do you want?"

"You spoke to Ivanov, didn't you?"

"Yes."

"You told him that Cochran found the place empty. You were very lucky."

"What do you mean?"

"I mean that Ivanov has some special new electronic gadget from Major Chelek that knocks out security systems. He and Kerimov got inside Chamber Court a short time ago and found it deserted. Not a soul there."

Holley felt immediately cheered. "Ferguson certainly moves fast."

"So where do you think they are?"

"Probably America, Ferguson is owed a lot of favors there, but wherever it is, it will be very, very safe. Ivanov must be going out of his head at that thought."

"What about Caitlin Daly?" Chekhov asked. "She must be devastated at the way things have worked out."

"That's one way of describing it."

"And Lermov gets in at midnight, I hear," Chekhov said. "And won't be pleased."

"You can say that again," Holley told him.

"What are you going to do, get the hell out of there?"

"I'd like to, but there's the woman to consider."

Chekhov laughed incredulously. "Don't be ridiculous, you don't owe her anything."

"Come off it, Max. There she was, living on past glory and her own impossible dream, and she'd still be doing that if I hadn't turned up and made the dream real again."

"Hardly your fault. That was Lermov and Putin at the Kremlin. You didn't have a choice."

"Maybe not, but I can't just run out on her now. I've got to go. I'll speak to you later."

He started to drive but had to pull over to the side as his Codex alerted him again. It was Caitlin Daly in a panic. Sean Dillon had turned up at the church with Billy Salter. Dillon had gone into the confessional box with Monsignor Murphy. It was all there, and Dillon knew everything, and four dead men already—Henry Pool, John Docherty, Frank Barry, and Jack Flynn—all with the card in their wallets. Ferguson and his people were on to them.

Holley agreed with her. At this stage, for Dillon to be

so close was incredible. The prayer cards hadn't helped. Out of the six male cell members, five had carried the card. He certainly hadn't known about that, and he wondered if Caitlin did.

"There's no proof, nothing concrete." He tried to reassure her. "Where are you?"

"At the church. Monsignor Murphy's in his study in the presbytery. I'm in the sacristy. It's the only place where I can be truly alone and lock the door. I'm scared, Daniel, frightened that Ivanov will make an appearance. I dread that he could be here already."

"Are you armed?"

"Yes, I carry a Belgian Leon .25 in my bag."

"That's good, and you know how to use it. I'll see you quite soon. I've got a car. Twenty minutes, with any luck."

He did not see what happened, that was the terrible thing. He drove to Kilburn, parked the Mini Cooper some distance from the church, and could see a small crowd of people standing there in the dusk of early evening, an ambulance and two police cars, policemen taking statements. Monsignor James Murphy was in a dark cloak, talking to one officer, and, from the look of him, greatly distressed. There was a medium-sized truck with one front wheel over a curb, a shaken-looking man in a leather jacket leaning against it, obviously the driver.

Holley stood at the back, and said softly to an old man in a cloth cap standing next to him, "What happened?"

"A terrible business. Monsignor Murphy's housekeeper came running down the path and straight out into the road. I saw the whole thing. Quite a few people did. The driver never stood a chance. I don't know what possessed her."

An older woman in front looked back over her shoulder. "I heard her shouting at somebody. She was saying: 'Get away from me.'"

"And where is she?" Holley asked the man.

"In the ambulance, but she's dead. Like I said, the police are taking a lot of statements. It's a terrible thing, but that poor sod was in no way to blame." He nodded towards the driver.

Holley backed slowly away as more people appeared, drawn to the crowd by the drama of it. He turned and walked back to the Mini Cooper and sat behind the wheel for a while. She had been running from Peter Ivanov. That had to be the explanation.

His anger was very real because he was to blame. He sat there, breathing deeply and gripping the wheel hard, then he called Chekhov. There was no background music, no impression that others were there.

"It's Daniel," he said. "Where are you?"

"At the apartment."

"Do you know what Ivanov's up to?"

Chekhov was obviously reluctant to talk. "He was here a while ago, after he'd discovered that there was no one at Belsize Park. He turned up in a cab, and he had Kerimov with him. The ape-man was wearing big gloves because of his bad hand so he could drive. Ivanov had been drinking."

"What did he want?"

"He said they needed to know where Alexander Kurbsky was, and the obvious person to ask was Monica Starling, because she'd been involved with him from the beginning."

"And that was it?"

"No, he told me he wanted me to lend him one of my Mercedes limousines. I keep three in the underground parking downstairs. He said he didn't want to use an Embassy car."

"To do what?" Holley demanded.

"He was just talking nonsense. He said if he could get his hands on Monica Starling and take her for a ride in the country, he could soon get the truth about Kurbsky out of her." Chekhov laughed uneasily. "Just crazy stuff, Daniel."

"Max, he made threats against Caitlin Daly bad enough to frighten her to death. I've been up to Kilburn, and she was already in a body bag in the ambulance, cops all over the place, the old priest, Murphy, in tears."

"Jesus, Holley, I don't know anything about that. I swear it."

"Okay, then what *do* you know? What did he say about where he would go?"

"That was drunken nonsense. He was rambling on about Bolt Hole, and he said there was a full moon tonight and it would be perfect to go for a sail."

"Which is exactly what the drunken fool intends. Now, this is what you're going to do, and if you let me down, I'll kill you."

"Anything, Daniel, I'll do anything."

"I'm going to ring off. You will call him, assess the situation, and call me. Now, get on with it."

Chekhov was back within five minutes. "He's really tanked up. I asked where he was headed, and he said he already told me. Then he said he had to go now because he had precious cargo in the trunk."

"The stupid bastard, he's actually gone and lifted her," Holley said.

"What are you going to do?" Chekhov asked. "Give Ferguson a call? Miller and Dillon will go crazy when they find out about this."

"No, I've got to think of me here as well as her. I can only bring them into it by delivering myself into their hands, and I'm damned if I'll do that. I've had enough of prison bars to last a lifetime. I'll just have to handle it alone."

"You're crazy, it isn't your business."

"Oh yes it is, Max. I told you before, it's a woman thing with me. I'll go now. I'll have to hurry, but they tell me a Mini Cooper is built for speed, so we'll see."

At least he knew the way, thanks to the day out with Selim, and there was the Sat Nav to follow. He drove fast but stayed alert. The last thing he needed was a police car to stop him for speeding. He had a good fast run to Guildford and all the way to Chichester, had just passed through, when his Codex sounded. He pulled in at a convenient lay-by, turned off his engine, and answered.

"Daniel? Lermov here."

Holley checked his watch and found it was almost ten-thirty. "Where are you? I understood you were getting in at midnight."

"I am," Lermov replied. "I'm calling you from the Falcon. I know everything, including the death of Caitlin Daly."

"You're well informed. Chekhov's been on the phone to you?"

"He knows who his real friends are and not you. You're a loose cannon. I should have realized that."

"The only loose cannon in this whole matter has been your boy wonder, Peter Ivanov. He's responsible for the death of Caitlin Daly because he didn't follow your orders."

"And he'll have to answer for that."

"So what happens to Monica Starling? Obviously, Chekhov must have told you what's going on."

"I've just spoken to Ivanov. It seems they've almost reached their destination. I've ordered him to release her."

"And you think that drunken pig will? He's got to dispose of her, because if she goes free he'll have Charles Ferguson, Miller, and Dillon thirsting for his blood because of what happened to her, and I think you'll find they're not particularly well disposed towards you."

"I'd be very careful where you're taking this, Daniel," Lermov said.

"Ah, Station Gorky awaits, does it? You'll have to catch me first, and I'm still going to Bolt Hole. Peter Ivanov's a dead man."

"Don't be stupid. He knows you're on your way. He'll be expecting you."

"You told him?"

"Chekhov already had."

"I might have known. You're finished, Josef, unless Ivanov puts a bullet in that woman's head and dumps her over the rail of Chekhov's yacht with a few pounds of chains round her ankles. I believe that's what you've told him to do. I, of course, intend to see that he doesn't."

Lermov shouted, "Don't be a fool. He knows you're coming," but Holley cut him off.

He switched off the engine at the narrow approach road leading to the small headland and advanced on foot, keeping to the fringe of trees, taking Selim's Zeiss binoculars with him. There was a single light at the end of the jetty and there was the Mercedes. The canvas stern cover was in place on the yacht, and Monica Starling sat on a folding beach stool, her hands bound behind her. She wore a sweater and slacks, obviously the clothes she'd been wearing when kidnapped, and was facing him so that he could see that her mouth was taped.

He was standing by a small bench seat, there was a footfall behind him, and something nudged him in the back. Kerimov said in Russian, "We've been waiting, me and my friend, the Makarov. It seemed obvious you'd start off here to see what was going on, so I thought I'd greet you. Get your hands behind your neck or I'll blow your spine away." His roaming left hand found the

Walther, which he slipped in his pocket. "Now the ankle holster. Put your foot on the bench." Holley did exactly as he was told, and Kerimov found the Colt and put that in his pocket also.

"Satisfied?" Holley asked, still with his right foot on the bench.

"I will be when you're dead," Kerimov said, and he pushed Holley hard so that he fell over. Kerimov kicked him in the side. "On your feet, you piece of shit, the boss wants a word before I kill you."

Holley found the flick-knife in his left sock, pulled it out as he got up, turned to face Kerimov, pressing the button, and the razor-sharp blade sheared up under the chin into the brain. Kerimov went down hard and kicked for a while, and then was still.

Holley recovered his weapons, wiped the knife, and put the Colt back in the ankle holster. He searched Kerimov briefly and found car keys, which he assumed were for the Mercedes. He started down, the Walther in his left hand. There was no sign of Ivanov. There was a light in the wheelhouse, but it seemed empty. There was soft music playing, a light at the portholes. Perhaps Ivanov was below?

Monica saw him coming and shook her head vigorously, which didn't help at all. He started towards her, a finger to his lips, then took his knife from his right pocket. There was a maniacal laugh behind him, and a bullet caught him squarely in the back and he half turned, and Peter Ivanov was standing up in the wheelhouse.

"Fooled you, you bastard."

Holley dropped the Walther, and Ivanov shot him in the chest, sending him back over the rail into the water. He went down, surfaced, and kicked out into the darkness while Ivanov was still negotiating the companionway to the deck. Holley pulled his way around to the prow, and, at that point, there were a few stone steps up to the jetty. He freed himself from his raincoat and knelt on the bottom step, listening.

"I've killed the bastard, did you see that?" Ivanov was obviously addressing Monica, but then he raised his voice and shouted, "Kerimov, where are you?"

Holley pulled the Colt from the ankle holster, was up the steps in a moment. Monica saw him first and couldn't help reacting. Ivanov swung around in alarm, and Holley said, "This is for Caitlin Daly."

He shot Ivanov between the eyes, the hollow-point cartridge imploding in the brain, instant death, as he went back over the rail.

Holley picked his knife up from the deck and cut Monica's bonds. She tore the tape away and gagged. "God, that hurt. I don't know who the hell you are, but I should warn you there's another one."

"Not anymore. He jumped me up there in the trees. I've taken care of him."

"Permanently?"

"I'd no choice."

"Never mind that. What I'd really like is an explanation. Earlier this evening, I went out to visit a local corner shop in Mayfair when this Mercedes drew up beside me. Before I knew what was happening, they had a bag over my head and forced me into the trunk of the car."

"I should imagine two hours of that must have been hell."

"But who are they, where am I, and who are you? Though thank God for you."

"Your brother is Major Harry Miller, the man in your life is Sean Dillon. Tell them Caitlin Daly is dead, and the man I've just killed was responsible, a GRU captain named Peter Ivanov who worked for Colonel Josef Lermov. They'll know what it's all about, believe me."

"And you?"

"Just call me Daniel." He went to the steps, recovered his raincoat, and found the car keys he'd taken from Keri-mov. "I think you'll find these are for the Mercedes. If you're up to it, I'd drive it back to London if I were you."

"But where am I?"

"In West Sussex, a place called Bolt Hole owned by an oligarch named Max Chekhov. The car's his, too. I think you'll find he's not unknown to your people." He took out his Codex. "A good job these things are water resis-tant. I think you'd better give them a call. They'll be worried. I'm going to get my car."

She was still on the phone when he got back. He took his suitcase with him, went below, dumped his wet clothes, and changed. Both his passports had survived the soak-ing, thanks to their plastic covers, so that was all right.

There was a wardrobe with a wide range of clothes. He helped himself to a fawn trench coat and went back on deck.

She was still on the Codex, paused, and said, "He's here." A moment passed, and she held it out to him. "It's Sean Dillon."

Holley took it from her, and said, "She'll be fine."

Dillon said, "Who the hell are you?"

"There are days when I'm not too sure myself. A cinema ghost, a friend calls me, though you won't know what that means. I don't know where Kurbsky is, but give him my respects. Ivanov and his sergeant actually gained entrance to Chamber Court earlier and found it empty. There's how close it came."

"So there's nothing more I can say or do?" Dillon asked.

"Yes, there is, actually. Alexander Kurbsky's situation is a big problem that would seem beyond solving. I think I've got a solution, and I'd like you to pass it on to Blake Johnson."

"And what would it be?"

The telling only took a couple of minutes, and, when he was finished, Dillon laughed. "Do you know something? I think that could very well be an answer. I'll pass it on."

Holley turned off his Codex. "I'll get moving, and so should you." He passed Monica a plastic bag he'd found in the bedroom below. "One Walther, a Colt .25, and a flick-knife. I'd never get through customs with that lot. Give them to Dillon. He'll know what to do with them."

She accepted the bag and held out her hand. "What can I say?"

"Good-bye would seem to be appropriate." He smiled. "You're one tough lady, Monica Starling." He got in the Mini Cooper and drove away.

She stood there, listening as the noise dwindled. Strange, the sense of loss she felt, and she turned, went to the Mercedes, and drove away herself.

Holley left the Mini Cooper in the long-stay car park at Southampton Airport, booked in a hotel overnight, and flew out on an early flight to Paris. Unable to sleep very well, he'd phoned Selim and told him what had happened.

"A terrible business," Selim said. "What do you think Ferguson will do?"

"He's always had a very efficient disposal system. Rather like undertakers, the people he employs pick up the bodies left over from unfortunate incidents such as this. Ivanov and Kerimov will be reduced to a few pounds of gray ash quicker than you can imagine."

"And Caitlin Daly?"

"Her death means it makes it very easy to treat the whole affair as if it never happened. Blake Johnson, of course, had a bullet in him, but he's on the mend."

"And Josef Lermov?"

"Perhaps it's his turn to do a stint with the GRU at Station Gorky, like Greta. The only certain thing is that Mister Big at the Kremlin is going to feel very let down," Holley said.

"Especially at the continuing lack of information regarding Kurbsky. I would also point out that details about what happened at Bolt Hole will certainly reach the Kremlin and will certainly do your reputation little good there, but, in my opinion, what you did for Lady Monica Starling was magnificent, and I'm sure her friends will share that view."

"Yes, but unfortunately they are all on the wrong side, and don't try to make me out to be some kind of a good guy, not at this stage, Selim. I found out who I truly was all those years ago when I shot dead those four men who'd murdered Rosaleen Coogan. What I am is what I am. It can't be changed now."

"So what next?" Selim said.

"Algiers, I think. I'll see you soon."

Algiers it was, three days later, sitting on the terrace of the old Moorish villa on the hill overlooking the harbor, drinking ice-cold lager.

"So what now?" Malik asked. "Back to business?"

"The death business? God help us, but there's got to be something better. Anyway, the Russians can be very unforgiving. It might be a good idea to vanish into the desert again for a while."

"I don't think you need to worry about any idea of vengeance anymore. There was an interesting story on CNN on the television this morning. I saw it just before you arrived."

"What was it?"

"I'd really prefer you to see for yourself. We'll go in the study. They repeat these things on the hour." So they sat together and waited, and, there it was, an announcement from the White House.

The great Russian novelist, Alexander Kurbsky, suffering from leukemia, had quietly arrived in Florida to seek the finest help available. The President himself welcomed the chance for the United States to offer the very latest in treatment for this truly great man. He was delighted to know how much the government of the Russian Federation had given their support to the move. In the care of his aunt Svetlana and friends, Mr. Kurbsky was recuperating under medical supervision on Heron Island. It had been suggested that he could be a Nobel Prize winner next year, and Prime Minister Vladimir Putin applauded the idea wholeheartedly.

Malik switched off. "How clever. It takes care of so many things, including you. I'll go and open the champagne. Your troubles are over."

"If you believe that, you'll believe anything," Daniel said.

He went out and walked to the balustrade of the terrace overlooking the harbor, and his Codex sounded. He hesitated, for it could be anyone—Lermov, Chekhov, even Putin himself—but there was no point trying to hide.

"Is that you, Mr. Holley? This is Charles Ferguson."

Ah. Charles Ferguson. Daniel took a deep breath. "How did you get my number?"

"Max Chekhov. I had my people lift him once Monica

Starling filled us in on Bolt Hole. He told us all about you."

"The Russians won't like that."

"Then Max will have to keep his door locked," Ferguson said.

"So what do you want with me, now that you know who I am?" Daniel asked.

"I just wanted to thank you for saving Monica's life from that raving lunatic and his sergeant."

"Very civil of you. Any news on Colonel Lermov?"

"Back in Moscow, and, if he's half the man I think he is, he'll have already managed to shift the blame onto the shoulders of the late, unlamented Ivanov." Ferguson paused. "Your plan of attack, Daniel, was really very good. Even Putin will have to admit that. He'll try to pull you back in, you know."

"He can try all he wants. I'm done with him."

"And you think you can survive his displeasure on your own, without friends?"

"Friends like you, General?" Daniel's laugh was short and cold. "You and the Russians—you're two sides of the same coin. There's nothing to choose between you."

"I'm sorry you feel that way. But you know, Daniel, situations have a way of changing. You have my number now. You know where to reach me. Watch your back, Daniel—and, again, many thanks for what you did for Monica."

The line went dead. Daniel checked and, yes, there was Ferguson's number, stored in his phone. Just a click away . . .

He knew there would come a time when he would have to use it, and he knew he would regret it.

He put the phone down on a small table, lay on the cane recliner, looked up at the sun, and closed his eyes.

His troubles had just begun, and there was much to prepare for.